Life Between Seconds

Douglas Weissman

Life Between Seconds

Addison & Highsmith

Addison & Highsmith Publishers

Las Vegas ◊ Chicago ◊ Palm Beach

Published in the United States of America by
Histria Books, a division of Histria LLC
7181 N. Hualapai Way, Ste. 130-86
Las Vegas, NV 89166 USA
HistriaBooks.com

Addison & Highsmith is an imprint of Histria Books. Titles published under the imprints of Histria Books are distributed worldwide.

Library of Congress Control Number: 2022942768

ISBN 978-1-59211-174-9 (hardcover)
ISBN 978-1-59211-244-9 (eBook)

Chapter 1

Peter loved to hear the story of how his father tried to steal the sun.

"It's the reason the poppies exist," his mother said. "Your dad had climbed into the sky and touched the light, actually had his hands gripped around the sun."

"What did it feel like?" Peter asked.

"Have you ever touched a really hot light bulb?" his mom said. "But the sun burned his hands. He pulled away and scattered sunlight over the field, causing all these bright poppies to grow. The sun, angry for having been caught, fell that night."

"It falls every night."

"But that was the first time. It fell and sulked and didn't come back. Your dad gave us these beautiful fields of flowers. But he also brought the darkness."

Peter held tight to his bear in the back seat. The promise of darkness didn't scare him, but the wind always made him nervous. He inhaled the scent of the bear's fur, like wood and soil. The poppies shone orange along the horizon, where flower petals covered the earth like unmelted snowfall. The world pulsed and breathed as it passed through the window into the back seat of the car—the blizzard of orange in the distance cascaded in the breeze. The closer the car came to the poppies, the lower the sun fell. Peter's mom always called it a game, like chicken—they had to make it to the field before the sun set.

The field had become their escape. "Our escape—Sam and Peter's." Peter asked who Sam was. His mom said she was Sam. He didn't stop calling her mom. "This is a place we can run," and they ran there often. Peter would watch his mom paint, more often try to paint, but Peter wanted to run, to shoot through the poppies and feel the brush of the petals on his skin as the wind trailed behind him.

"It wasn't literal," his mom once told him. Peter looked at her, unsure of what she meant. "Forget it," she told him before he asked. She popped a few pills. "Whatever makes you feel better." The pills were sky blue in color. Peter thought of the possibilities of bottling and swallowing the sky; what kind of clouds would drift through his stomach? Would they taste like marshmallows? Then he remembered lightning storms, and the pills made him nervous. His mom could take all the sky pills she wanted, but he wouldn't touch them.

The car jerked to a halt.

"Sorry, darling," his mother said. "We're here."

Peter opened the door. He pushed himself from the seat. He couldn't move. He tugged. He struggled. He stretched. The seatbelt was wrapped around his chest; he unbuckled it.

"Not so fast," his mother said. "Don't forget him." She pointed to the teddy bear in the back seat.

Peter grabbed Claus by the arm and fled the car. He didn't bother to close the door. The tent was in the back seat. His dad had taught his mom how to pitch a tent, but his mom hadn't taught Peter. She was too eager to get the tent set up and paint.

She yelled to Peter; the wind took the words away. But he knew them by heart: *Don't go too far.* He never did. He ran in circles and belly-flopped into the flowers surrounded by orange dots. The soft soil squished under his feet, and the breeze blew at his back while Claus held his hand and urged him forward.

"Look how fast I can run," he called to his mom, but she was setting up the tent and never looked over. Peter breathed in the air, and the field drew into his nose. He huffed, and the soft flowers brushed against the back of his hands, and his heartbeat quickened when the wind blew past him, but he continued forward at the same speed, confident the wind would soon fall behind, and it did fall behind, which made Peter push faster and farther towards the hills where the sun would soon hide. He dug his feet into the earth and jumped into the horizon, to push himself, beat the wind, listen to Claus's advice, touch the sun, and look down from the sky rather than swallow it.

Peter stopped to breathe, and the wind whipped his face. It had caught up to him; it was temperamental—with a faraway source, a sore loser who tended to get physical—always filled with or followed by the faint scent of decayed flesh and rusted metal.

His mom had told him a story about the wind once, with a wolf that breathed in the entire world to blow down anything that stood in his way. It had started with "Once upon a time," and now those words felt pushed as far away as the rest of the story, taken by the wind, like his mom's words, to a place farther than where Peter dared to run.

Peter slid to the ground out of the way of the wind. The smell of fresh dirt filled his nose, and as he pressed his back to the earth, the flowers surrounded his head and covered the partial light of the sky. The poppies cushioned Peter's head. The sky held a blend of sun and stars. Clouds drifted between the light and dark. Peter had no desire to name the cloud animals or count the rings on the clouds to see how old they were.

Peter wrapped his fingers around a poppy. The petals were moist and tender between his fingertips. He half hoped the orange would stain his skin and paint him, hide him in the field, and when his mom called for him, he'd sway in the breeze and blend into the scene he knew she had frozen onto her canvas. But the petals only released water, and Peter left them crumbled in the dirt.

The sky turned dark, and the poppy stems thrashed against his body in the heavy wind. He stood and ran towards the light of the tent.

"Don't even think about diving in here," his mom said as Peter readied for his pounce. "You know the rules." Peter bent down to take off his shoes. The wind pushed at him again. "And don't just slip them off either," she said. "That's how you ruin them."

Peter ducked into the tent. It was large enough for both him and his mom to stand in. It was where she preferred to paint, out of the wind with the flap open to the view. Peter made his way to the cooler and grabbed some grapes. He didn't offer any to Claus. Claus hated red grapes.

His mother had two canvases next to the tent's opening, one on each side. They looked like windows. One was old; it was the first painting Peter had watched her create. She had said she needed release, placed Peter in a high chair, and pressed her brush to canvas. She said this so often when Peter was young; he thought painting was called "release." He would run around the house with paint on his hands, past the kitchen into his parents' room where he would press his wet fingers to empty walls and yell, "Release! Release!" His tiny hands imprinted on the world, his tiny mark made permanent, like his mother's art. Paint was forever, like fun and Claus and his parents, he had thought. Then, in the absence of his father, Peter remembered where the scent of charred flesh and metal came from. Painting wasn't a release, but release, for him, became a prayer.

Peter tossed grapes into his mouth, one by one, and positioned them between his teeth. He wanted to savor the crunch. The squish. The juice. The sweetness. His mouth filled with saliva. He chomped down, chewed the skin. He wiped his mouth with his arm. The tent rustled in the wind but held firm to the ground.

The older painting was of giant hills bordered by Victorian homes and a trolley car. He scanned the painting house-by-house, street-by-street, car-by-car. His mother liked to hide images in her art. She always said the search was half the fun.

"You know where it is," she said. "You've seen it a hundred times."

He scanned the colorful, hilly streets and found the image, his mother's face, painted as the back of the streetcar. Her honey hair ran over the top of the trolley as ribbon, with big clear window eyes and a large advertised smile, not the same smile Peter was used to; it was a smile he had never seen before. More teeth—shiny white—bright, clear eyes.

"That's the only self-portrait I ever painted," she said. Peter bit into another grape. "You ready to see the new one?" she asked. She took the last grape from Peter's hand. He nodded and brought Claus with him. It wasn't a race, but Peter wanted to find the image before Claus. That was their game. The painting didn't have hills; it had mountains—rocky peaks sprouted above the clouds. Birds flew around the base as if they could fly no higher, thwarted by a mountaintop. The clouds, fluffy and mystical, as if they would disappear with one shallow breath, but unable to hide an object any more than Claus could hide his eye patch. The birds' wings flapped and interrupted the silent air that surrounded them. The tiny sky above the mountaintop sat empty.

In the rocks, the small pieces that built the towering summit, he found the secret, on a rock face in the middle—his father, chiseled into the granite, almost invisible. His face full of the wide smile Peter almost couldn't remember, his beard made of granite, his eyes made of soft gray stone that seemed familiar. After his father's death, his mother hid more of him in her paintings—him or the car, sometimes crushed, immortalized in her art.

"You find him?" she asked with a hint of hesitation in her voice. Peter brought his shoulders to his ears and nodded. "Of course you did," she said with a smile, the smile he was used to. She grabbed him and held him between her arms as they faced the paintings split by the tent flap open to the night.

"Do you know where that is?" she asked. Peter shook his head. But he knew. She had told him before, in pictures she had shown in galleries, or thrown in dumpsters, or painted over, or that fell out of her purse in postcards, or that she drew on the walls at home in her sleep, which Peter blamed on Claus. He held Claus closer to him, a sign for Claus not to answer the question.

"That's Peru. Machu Picchu. Your dad loved it there. It was his favorite. I never got to go. Me and your father…." The look Peter had grown used to, where his mother sunk into a far-off stare almost stunned by existence, returned to her face for a brief moment. She returned faster than Peter expected, rubbed her hand through his hair, and said, "You know I'd never leave you, right?"

Peter blinked. He had never thought his mom might leave before. Would she take the sky with her, bottled up in those pills and wiping the world black?

"I promise," she said.

His mom's stomach pushed against his back with every breath.

"Where's that one?" his mom asked. Peter shook his head again. "That's San Francisco. That is my favorite." She was warm around him as if the coldness of her comment had never existed. "What about there?" she pointed to the open tent; a faint orange of the poppies visible in the moonlight; the wind had disappeared with the final trace of the sun. "That's here," Peter giggled.

"Of course it is," his mom said. She ran her fingers down Peter's ribcage. He pressed himself into her, delighted by the attention. Even Claus almost smiled.

"Let's go play," his mom said. Peter giggled again.

"But it's night," he said.

"Is it? Then let's go bounce on the moon!"

The sweetness of Peter's mom's skin replaced the dirt scent of the field, and Peter wanted to melt into her, become the paint she brushed onto her canvas. They pushed open the tent where the night stretched over the quiet poppies and gentle air. Sam held onto Peter, Peter held onto Claus, and together they jumped out of the tent into a dusty hollow that let Peter and Claus dance with his mom one last time.

Chapter 2

The night sky snuck in the window and sparkled on the floor of the nursery. Sofia nudged the mobile out of the way when she leaned over the crib. She felt the wooden stars and planets sway. Valentina's tight scream rose from the crib but didn't pierce or linger; it was more like an intense whisper—sudden and quick. Sofia reached under Valentina's soft body. The brief wisps of sound continued, and Sofia pressed Valentina close to her chest. Can you hear my heartbeat? Quieter with you on my skin.

Valentina continued to cry. Sofia bounced and shushed—danced—shhh. She danced on the night sky that sparkled on the floor, with the sweet sound of her daughter, her creation, her love, her life. And the cry softened and sweetened. And the dance continued. And the night lingered. And they breathed together. And Sofia pressed her cheek to her daughter's cheek. She listened to the delicate breath and felt Valentina's skin plump and cool.

"You are wonderful, my darling. You will be grand. You will grow so beautiful and lovely, with your eyes like emeralds and your skin so soft." They bounced. Valentina hummed. "You will always know that we love you, your papa and I love you, and we always have and always will. You will be so lovely; you will be so tall with legs like your mother's, so slender and graceful, and a mind like your father's, smart and quiet. You will be the object of affection for every man, and women will be jealous but will love you for your kindness. You will be all the things we wish we were and were too stubborn to become, or too weak to try, or too dim-witted to know that that is what we should have been. You will go to university and know the world—see the world. You will be the smartest of us." Sofia rubbed Valentina's hair and smelled passion fruit and chocolate, her own midnight snack mixed with the sweetness of Valentina. Valentina rested her head on Sofia's shoulder. Sofia wanted to melt with her. "How could we have made something so sweet, so precious? So small? But you will grow. And you will meet a man. He will have blonde hair and eyes that can freeze you. He will be tall and understand a hard day's work but will no longer need to work hard days. He will love you for your past and your future, for your smile and your laugh, for your tears and your anger. He will love you for your family, for your hopes and your dreams, for your failures and your idiosyncrasies. He will love you because you are to be loved. But the world can be cruel, my darling. Never let that harm you. Never let that stop you. It will always make you better. You will always be stronger. You will always be sweeter."

"Yes, she will be," Gaston said from the doorway. Sofia stopped bouncing and felt her heart run. Valentina stayed asleep. "I didn't mean to scare you, darling. But she will be—always." He came into the nursery. His robe hung low, almost to his slippers. "She will be more beautiful every day. Maybe as beautiful as you."

"Hush."

"And the world will not be able to harm her." Gaston pressed his lips to Valentina's head.

"Sometimes, I don't want to put her down," Sofia said.

***

The day Sofia learned she was pregnant, she dropped dinner on the kitchen floor. The wood was covered with meat grease and chimichurri sauce. She wanted to surprise Gaston. The splattered food surprised him. So did the news. Gaston twirled Sofia around the kitchen. He didn't care about the meat and the sauce and the mess. She didn't clean up the food for hours. Gaston couldn't stop kissing her stomach.

Sofia loved Gaston's warm lips on her stomach. His hands on her waist. His lips on her mouth. Sofia's belly grew with Valentina, and Gaston grew more excited. Sofia was ready to fill the empty space of their home with a family, with laughter, with memories.

Gaston was at work when Sofia went into labor. She had heard labor horror stories from her mother and her friends. But her feet were swollen, and her hands were swollen, and her body ached, and she was ready to have the baby. Sofia gave birth at home, in her bed, the same bed where Sofia and Gaston had made love for the first time, the same bed where Valentina was conceived, and it was in that room that their family would begin. The doctor instructed Sofia to breathe, and her mother held Sofia's hand.

Sofia screamed. She wanted Gaston. She wanted to squeeze his hand—hard. She wanted to feel his soft lips on her forehead. But she squeezed her mother's hand instead. Sofia pushed. She screamed for Gaston. She sweated through the sheets. She squeezed. She pushed harder.

It's a girl.

The first words Sofia had heard that day. A girl. A beautiful girl. Sofia knew before she saw her baby. Sofia pressed her daughter to her chest and never wanted to let go. She saw Valentina's green eyes—Gaston's eyes. He entered the room.

"It's a girl," Sofia said. Gaston rushed to the bed, sat beside Sofia, and gave her what she wanted—his lips to her forehead. He brushed his hand to their daughter's face.

"What did we say if it was a girl?" he asked.

"She doesn't look like a Maria," Sofia said.

"My grandmother's name was Valeria," he said.

Sofia shook her head. Their baby girl whimpered.

"She is beautiful," Gaston said. "We will love her no matter her name."

"Valentina," Sofia said. "As close to your grandmother's name as we will get."

That night Valentina slept with Sofia and Gaston in the bed where she was born, snuggled to Sofia's chest, Sofia unwilling to put Valentina down in her room, alone. Gaston said he was happy to share the bed that night and forever. Sofia agreed.

***

They slid Valentina into the crib, where the wooden stars and planets hovered and orbited above her while the night sky continued to imitate the mobile on the nursery floor.

"But one day, you won't even be able to pick her up," Gaston said.

"That will be the saddest day of my life," Sofia said.

"If that is the saddest day of your life, you're doing a good job."

"She will be wonderful."

"She is wonderful," he said.

"Yes. She is."

Gaston placed his hand on Sofia's and kissed her cheek. "She will be the best of us both."

Sofia wanted Valentina in her crib—always—frozen in her mind forever, her baby with her thumb in her mouth, swallowed by her pajamas—silent and still—fragile. And theirs.

Chapter 3

Sam had never heard of a bear on a boat, but here she sat, on a boat with a bear. But it wasn't a boat. Not really. She sat in a tub. In the ocean. But if she could sit in it, and it floated, to Sam, it was a boat.

The sun bounced off of the water, and the water bounced off of the tub and made the light unbearable, stuck in Sam's eyes like a stack of needles while she searched for the needle she wanted. The sun never set, not that she remembered, in the daylight hours of an eternal horizon, an eternal sea, an eternal burning sun. The boat rocked or swayed—she drifted from side to side, back and forth, without any reprieve from the light or the rock or the wet and the dry, if she could be wet and dry at the same time.

The bear wore an eye patch and button-down pajamas that mapped the galaxy. He stared over the side of the porcelain and peered into the dark blue water.

It was the bear, the stupid bear that she knew she needed and wanted, that she was happy to have around, for every minute he wouldn't shut up, because she wanted to be around someone, was happy to be around someone when sometimes she thought she saw land on the horizon—a boy standing on the hilltops looking down on them, a familiar shadow she couldn't place in the endless life of hers that may not have been a life at all.

"How'd you get that patch?" Sam asked.

"Fishing," the bear said.

"What kind of fishing?" she asked.

"The kind that gets dangerous when you don't pay attention," he said with a heavy German accent.

A bear and a boat and a mast and the sea.

There was a moment when Sam thought she saw a flash in the distance smash against the already bright sky like a familiar memory of summer lightning, a picture painted of a day when nothing in particular happened, the strangeness of the nothing, the nothing of ordinariness, the extraordinary of the regular, the regularity she found in the extraordinary—except she didn't see the beauty in that eternal sky anymore—if she had ever seen it at all.

The flash she thought she saw turned into a splash that sent water spraying into the tub; it reverberated close to the lip. Sam hoped it was a dolphin or a bird or something that wouldn't tip them over.

Claus stood at the front of the tub with his paw over his eyes, blocking the sun and scanning the distance. Why would he scan the distance when he was the one who had said all they would find was emptiness? She didn't want to believe it, but it was all she had, all she saw within the confines of the porcelain and the itchy wrists that tickled like a fake memory of caterpillars—what she thought a caterpillar would feel like slinking up her wrist.

Another splash broke the silent air. Then another. And another.

"Jesus!" Sam said.

A fish ricocheted off of Sam's head and flailed about the boat. She opened her palm and smacked the fish into the water. She looked at the bear; his ever-grumpy face looked back.

"If you don't like it," she said, "it's all yours next time."

"I planned on eating that," he said.

"Then get your own," she said.

She glared at the bear.

In the fire engine scream of the sunlight—the sound it made in her head—the lack of movement and change began to weigh on her, even if Claus spent the day looking for the nothing spreading out along the sides of the tub while she surfed the calm waters of purgatory.

"I am not looking for anything," Claus said.

"Then why look?" Sam said.

"In case fish come. I like fish."

"We all like fish."

"You do not like fish. You must be careful," the bear said. "You might lose an eye."

"Shut it," Sam said.

"You have not been eating."

"I haven't been hungry. I've been annoyed."

"What does hunger have to do with aggravation and vice versa?" His German accent was thick in the bored air. The sail hung limp and insignificant. The mast swayed.

"It...I just haven't wanted to. I've wanted..." her voice trailed into the stale air and fell into the stagnant water.

"You have wanted too much," Claus said.

"What does that mean?"

"Do you speak English?"

"Obviously."

"Do you know what 'too much' means?"

"Of course," Sam said.

"Then why do I need to explain it to you?"

Sam rubbed her wrist on the porcelain to ease the itch. It didn't. The itch was stuck somewhere between her skin and her tendons, too deep for the porcelain to scratch and too shallow for her thoughts to soothe. The blue sky was bored; a bored blue sky stuck in circular silence until the splashes broke the monotony.

"Would you like to get us more?" Claus asked. Sam didn't trust what she couldn't see, and the water was too dark to see beneath the surface. Claus sighed and unbuttoned his pajama top. The buttons opened, and the planets drifted apart, separated by an abyss of brown fur. Claus had a tattoo, pink, a felt indentation of a heart, adorned by the words, *Try Me*. She wasn't sure if it was rhetorical.

Claus dove into the sea. Hundreds of fish ascended from the water and into the air, pushed themselves from the dark blue depths into the lofty blue light. They fluttered their fins like butterfly wings and flew around the boat in desperation, trying to escape the waterlogged, submerged, and thrashing bear. Claus was a born seaman, complete with eye patch and tattoo. He was the only thing Sam had to connect her to life on land—to connect her to life at all.

Sam rocked in the tub. The tub wallowed in the sea. On the back lip of the tub sat a small motor, rusting. Sam rubbed some of the orange crust away.

"It won't make it work," Claus said as he pulled himself back into the tub. He looked like a wet mop hung upside down, full of sea salt and attitude. He held a fish in his paw.

"Says who?"

"Eat," he said. "You should eat." Claus threw the fish on the floor. "I made a promise. I keep my promises."

"And I don't?" Sam said.

He dropped the fish into the tub and stood in silence. The fish was bigger than Claus. It didn't bother to fight. Claus shook off the water. He ruffled and fluffed in the process. Sam received a shower from Claus's shimmy. He re-dressed himself in his space pajamas, covered his tattooed heart, pulled the planets back together.

"And I don't?" Now she wanted to know, more for herself than for him, because she wasn't sure anymore, but she couldn't imagine a broken promise, the reason she would break one; what was the point of a promise if you broke it?

"No," he said. "You didn't."

She didn't feel hungry. The fish flopped hopelessly on the deck. The tub swayed. She felt sick. The swirl in her stomach felt putrid, but she held on to the change from nothing as if nausea was all it would take to change this world. The angry accent of the bear sounded pitiful, not for him but for her, but it didn't count if she couldn't remember the promises she broke; why couldn't she remember when he could? It didn't seem fair, but this flooded world they floated through allotted for flying fish and talking bears and endless afternoons and eternal horizons. She wanted to puke up something fierce, but nausea left as painfully as it had arrived.

"I wasn't trying to make it work," Sam said, pointing to the motor. Her eyes darted to the fish. She wondered how Claus was capable of catching a fish almost twice his size. "There's got to be something out here. How else could we be here?"

"Because you have wanted too much."

"You can go," she said. She pulled her knees tight to her chest and tucked her chin between. "You don't need to be here."

"Yes, I do," he said. He jumped from the front of the boat. He held another fish in his paw. She hadn't seen one jump out of the water or him reach out to grab one from the fluttering school. The appearance of the fish mattered less than the bright pulse of the sun. "I told you; I keep my promises."

"And I don't." This time Sam stated it, almost believing the words herself, even if she couldn't remember what promise she had broken.

Claus kicked over the fish he had thrown on the floor.

"You should eat."

The powder blue sky faded to burnt orange, bleeding upwards into the red sun. Sam dragged her fingers along the motor, collecting the rust like a second skin. She felt like it should tell her a story, a poem, the time—her life. She hoped it would. If she hoped hard enough, maybe, even after Claus had warned her.

Sam didn't look up from the rust. She knew Claus had made his way to the fish. The crunch of the scales and the crack of the bones rose above Claus's snarls and grunts.

"It's very fresh," he said. He almost smiled. Sam grabbed her fish with both hands, its hopeless eyes almost dense and empty. She was ready to take a bite, the freshest sushi she would ever eat of a kind of fish she didn't know. It didn't bother Claus at all, except for the pity in his voice that had washed over her. She couldn't feel the fish's slippery scales, but it slid through her fingers and fell out of her hands. She grabbed it once more, held on tight, its scales rainbow in the bright day. She dropped it over the side. The fish heaved beneath the surface and into the darkness of the water.

"You can save a life," Claus said. His tone held surprise or mocking with the glare in his good eye burning into her with the same ferocity as the sun.

"Of course," she said. "I'm a lifesaver." She leaned back against the porcelain. Her body bumped against the motor. The motor scraped against the tub.

"Maybe I can find something," Claus said. "Maybe we need to find something." Beneath the silent air, it sounded like Claus mumbled something. The world was bored, she was bored, and it all felt the same. Something about Claus changed, his tone, his fur, his eye—what promise did he keep? In the bright distant horizon, she thought she saw the silhouette of a boy standing on an orange hill that looked like a fake sun. She blinked, and the picture turned back to the bleached empty sky. She rolled her fingers over the motor and breathed, trying to forget the irritation in her wrist that ate at her somewhere beneath her skin, yet remained untouchable. She scratched at the crust. The orange dusted her fingernails. The new ring of her nails on the metal sounded like bells pealing. She scratched harder. The rust flaked, stripped away. She leaned harder against the motor. Her body bumped the metal. The motor lurched—another scrape. The motor inched away. Off the porcelain. Away from the lip. Away from her. Away from Claus. She reached out. The motor dropped. Disappeared. She lunged—

away—too late. Her hands reached out to the water. The scars on her wrists were soft and thin like papier-mâché.

"Broken," Claus said. "Good riddance."

Sam dipped her fingers into the water to wash away the rust; the motor lost to the sea. She twirled her fingers in the ocean. She knew they were wet. But she couldn't feel a thing.

Chapter 4

In the dim light sifting through the cracked door of the building, Peter thought of a world filled with poppy fields, with paintings hung on the horizon as if the sky were a blank wall in need of decoration. Instead of the meadow, the smell of spilt beer smeared with dog shit wafted upwards from the doorstep. Peter stepped through the door—a large block of wood taken straight from a tree, planted in the doorframe, stressed with time—and into clouds of cigarette smoke filling the narrow hallway. The fog of San Francisco was inescapable, he thought, even indoors.

A letter stuck halfway out of mailbox 3A. The writing looked formal, calligraphic. There was no return address. It was a one-way conversation. He searched the stamp for familiar words in case the letter had been intended for him but misplaced. A used imprint punctured the stamp without any familiarity. He reread the calligraphy, the name, the address; it wasn't for him. Peter grabbed the letter and carried it up the stairs. The smell of fried onions and melted butter pushed through the smoke. Music sprang from Sofia's apartment, always loud, full of brass and bass. The door almost beat with the music. The number three had washed away, the letter "A" dangling from a single nail.

"It is open," Sofia said above the blast of sound. Her Spanish accent hung on her as thick as the fog over the city, clung to her no matter how long she had lived in San Francisco. Peter entered. "You are late. Again," she said. "How are you always late when you live across the hall?"

"Pérdon, Sofia. Mea culpa," Peter said; it was about as much Spanish as he remembered because he never really knew Spanish and thought the Latin he knew less of could compensate. Sofia glared at him from the kitchen. He knew she hated when he teased her Catholicism.

"Of course it is your fault," Sofia said. "It is not my fault." She spoke with the same cadence as the radio, rising and falling with each word like a song Peter had grown accustomed to hearing.

He waved the letter in the air. Sofia took a long look at Peter, squinting at the contents of his hand.

"Come," she said. Peter went to the kitchen to greet Sofia with a kiss on each cheek, the way she had always greeted him, but instead, she reached for the bottle of wine, the one he had promised to always bring with him to dinner. She opened the bottle in a fluid motion and poured herself a generous glass, one larger than she had ever taken before.

The faucet dripped into the porcelain sink. He would need to fix that for her. She had never asked for his help, but it didn't stop him from offering. One time he didn't offer at all and just fixed the squeak in the door. Sofia's face had turned red. Tears welled in her eyes.

"It's less noisy this way," Peter had said.

She held her breath until the words slipped out, "I prefer the noise," she whispered. "Please." Peter returned the squeak to the layers of sound in the apartment. It was the least he could do to repay her for all the meals she had fed him.

"Thirsty?" Peter said. Sofia's hand shook around the glass. She took a gulp of wine. The tremor in her body subsided. He couldn't ask what was wrong, not because he didn't want to, but because that wasn't the type of friendship they shared. Peter had introduced Sofia to the funky Red Vic, where they sat on old couches and watched back-to-back Fellini films; she loved *8 ½*, he loved *La Dolce Vita*. They gardened together on the rooftop, where Sofia introduced him to the quality of fresh produce. They promised to trek to Muir woods to see if the redwoods were as magnificent as everyone said. They had a bet: she thought they would be; he thought not. She introduced him to alfajores: creamy dulce de leche sandwiched between buttery cookies. They argued. They shared. They laughed. They drank wine. The conversation always remained superficial, friendly and carefree and caring, but he stayed away from stories about car crashes and floods, and she stayed away from … letters? He wondered.

"Where should I put this?" He held up the envelope. Sofia took another sip of wine and flailed her hand around. Peter took it to mean anywhere. He set it on the radio, the one place he knew she would see it—if not now, eventually.

Sofia put him to work filling filo dough. He folded tiny half-moons in his palms. Sofia had drunk close to half the bottle of wine before dinner was halfway prepared. She placed the half-moons on a buttered pan and put them in the oven.

The room was a delicate balance of voice-over instruments, at times hard to tell what was Sofia's voice versus the brass that flew from the radio.

"We should dance," Sofia said.

"What?" Peter said.

"I used to dance every weekend with my—" she looked towards the radio—the letter. "I loved dancing. In Buenos Aires, people would move until sunrise. I have not danced in years. Dance with me."

"In those shoes?" Peter said.

"Because I am old, I have to wear old woman shoes? These make me feel—"

"Elegant," Peter said.

"Desirable," Sofia said. She clacked her heels against the hardwood floor.

"There's no space to dance in here."

Tonight, Sofia's apartment felt much smaller: the walls thicker. The space stuffier. There was never much to fill the tiny space: chairs to sit on, a table to eat on, plus a throw rug. One magnet miniature of Coit Tower, gray and spherical, hung on the refrigerator door. It didn't hold a recipe, a bill, or a photograph. It almost blended into the empty surface of her kitchen, the same way the tower fused with the fog.

"Slide the table over," Sofia said. She took up the entire kitchen, a thin, rectangular compartment lined with broken appliances.

"We have time before dinner is ready." She took another sip of her wine. "Do not make me ask twice." Peter nudged the table to the wall. Sofia tilted her hand to Peter. He took her fingers and led her to him. She snickered. Peter smiled. She held tight to his hand. Her skin was soft. She closed her eyes and drew a long breath. Even at her age, she flowed gracefully in her heeled shoes, one hand in Peter's the other resting on his chest. The music moved at a fast rhythm, but they swayed at an even pace. Peter didn't want to rush the moment. The locket dangling from Sofia's neck brushed against him as they danced. The cold glinting gold brushed Peter's shirt, making him shiver.

She opened her eyes and looked to the radio again. Her fingers clasped the locket. Her hands shook away any words she tried to form. The song ended. The oven dinged.

"Do I smell smoke?" Peter asked. Sofia gave a stern look, the type his mother would give before saying, "I'm not mad; I'm … disappointed."

"I do not burn empanadas," Sofia said. She shook her head, and the sad smile returned. "You are more graceful than you look. Move the table. Dinner is ready." She returned from the kitchen with the baking sheet filled with browned, savory empanadas. She was right, Peter thought. She hadn't burned a single one.

"These are Argentine empanadas."

"There's a difference?"

Sofia shook her head. The smell of fresh, crisped, buttery dough smeared the apartment walls. It was the first time he had made empanadas; the first time he had eaten empanadas with Sofia; they had a layered flavor, proof she had made them more times than she could count. Then Peter cleaned up. He always helped clean up. He had learned to do the dishes when he lived with his cousin; plates piled up: imitations of skyscrapers until Peter wanted or needed to clean a pot, a pan, a cup, a dish, to make his own dinner. His cousin, if she were home, would yell from the bedroom, "Be a dear and get the rest?" A demand disguised as a favor—if she were home at all. Peter would try to clean away the sour beer stench from her boyfriends or wash away the mold-crusted food from the fridge and the mildew-covered sink. Peter learned how to clean early—it was easy; he had been trying to clean up after himself for years.

"I would help, but I broke a plate last time," Sofia said.

"And two glasses," Peter said. Sofia gave a half-smile.

"And two glasses," Sofia said.

Peter dried the dishes and put them away. He made a cup of coffee, strong, bitter, and black, fresh and hot. He sat on the couch with his arms wrapped around his legs. He rested his back into the cushion and burnt his tongue on the drink, which was how he preferred it. The apartment held the hazy brass from the radio. The letter had jolted when the band boomed at dinner. Now it rested atop the antique speakers. The dim lights of Sofia's apartment allowed the shadows to settle in the open.

Sofia stayed at the table, established in her chair. She turned to Peter. For almost six months, Sofia and Peter had shared dinner. For almost six months, he offered Sofia the couch after they ate. "I prefer to stay at the table," she always said, then they would sip their drinks until the cupboard ran dry, or until Peter had to go to work, or until one of them nodded off. Tonight wasn't much different, except tonight Sofia didn't sip her wine; she swallowed it. Drops spilled down her glass and onto her fingers. She stuck her fingers into her mouth one by one and sucked away the sweet spots of the wine.

"Now, do you know the difference between empanadas from Peru and empanadas from Argentina?"

Smaller, flakier, meatier, without whole olives. Fresh. Buttery. Delicious.

"I hope you make those all the time," Peter said.

"Once a year."

Peter's company didn't last long. He didn't last long, too often ready to jump ship somewhere new, too soon. "A whole year before more empanadas?" He would be gone before then anyway. His ticket to Nepal lay crisp in the tin box beneath his bed where most people kept lint-balls and forgotten monsters.

"No. You have to wait a whole year to eat my empanadas."

"Can I work around that schedule?" Peter said.

"No," Sofia said.

"Oh."

Sofia inhaled her wine. How many glasses had it been? This wasn't like her. Maybe it was the empanadas, a secret sign of escape.

"I don't remember the last time I waited a year for anything."

"You know how they say…." Sofia said. She grabbed her locket once more.

"Patience is a virtue?" Peter said

"No," Sofia said. "Gravity sucks."

"Right," Peter smiled. He had worn the shirt to dinner once, the first time they shared a meal. He had found it in a vintage shop when he first moved to San Francisco. It summed up his life in more ways than anybody who read the shirt could ever imagine. Sofia had stared at the writing for a moment. She tilted her head in confusion and mouthed the words. Peter had stood in the doorframe with the bottle of wine in his hand. The horns from the radio blared next to him before Sofia laughed. "Gravity sucks," she chuckled. "It certainly does." Then she officially invited Peter in to her apartment. The rest of that night, Sofia would randomly laugh out loud, shake her head, and sip her wine. The next day Peter took the shirt, along with a larger load of laundry, to the Laundromat around the corner from his apartment to wash out the grease he had splattered over it at dinner. He turned his back for a minute and returned to find the dryer opened and four pieces of underwear, a pair of pants, three socks, and his *Gravity sucks* shirt missing. He closed the door and finished the cycle. When he sat in the chair, he had to ask himself, why couldn't they at least take that fourth sock?

Peter took a sip of his coffee. The cup no longer warmed his fingers. The heat was gone. Sofia looked at the radio. The letter had stopped dancing on the speaker. It lay docile on the matted surface. It didn't seem important to Sofia, not as important as the wine, not as important as the writing on the envelope made the letter feel.

Peter turned down the brass band. Some nights, like tonight, the music was louder than usual. Lines from the spilled wine stained Sofia's glass. The streaks ran down her bony fingers. She stared into her glass, distracted by the dark red and the light or the fact that the wine was almost gone. The noise of the apartment disappeared. Peter rubbed the broken face of his purple polka dot watch and stepped into a memory; the walls unfolded into an open meadow. Peter sat back on the couch and started to sink.

"It will always hurt," Sofia said. She stood with an unstable sway and moved to the radio, to the letter, tracing her fingers over the ink etched into the envelope. She dipped the corner to her lips and inhaled. She walked back to Peter with the letter in one hand, her locket clasped tightly in her other. "It can get easier."

Sofia sat, dropping the letter in her lap and placing her locket open on the coffee table between them. Tonight, her face was lightly wrinkled. She still had mostly brown hair. Peter could compile each gray hair, like each wrinkle, into the story of Sofia's entire life, wrapped into the details of her face, aged and elegant and poised. The pale light of the room glinted against a photo inside the locket. The photo held Sofia and a girl, twelve maybe, similar smiles, effortless exaggerations, squinted eyes, young—happy. That was Sofia's smile, like her daughter's smile—one before now—where the sadness hadn't yet left the scar tissue of a broken life lingering at the corners of her mouth. Her daughter. Peter assumed Sofia had a family somewhere. He assumed her husband had passed and her children were grown and, like so many children, didn't visit or call or write. I wouldn't be that kind of son, he thought. But he never had the chance to prove it.

***

Sofia lit candles as Peter pretended to study the photo in her locket. Instead, he looked into the flames like a projector playing a movie of his mother or his father, or of the child in Sofia's locket with a motionless smile, a dim light, but bright enough to see in the dark. Peter's mom used to light candles every Friday night. She would wrap him in her sweatered arms, sleeves muddled-black from overuse; she had smelled like honey wine. She'd hover above the flame in silence for ages until she opened her teary eyes, pulled Peter towards her, and said, "Another week done, my darling."

Peter handed the locket back to Sofia and said, "She's beautiful." He looked at the three watches on his wrist, his attempt at a locket like Sofia's, the faces they showed him but no one else—how beautiful those faces would always be—those moments would always be.

"Of course she is. She always will be this beautiful." Sofia finished her glass of wine and held it out to Peter. "I'm old." She slurred. "I can get it myself if you would like, but do not make this old body stand. My knees hurt and my joints ache and—"

"We just danced."

"My head hurts."

"That's from the wine."

"And one more glass will help it go away." Sofia smiled. She tilted her head and her glass towards Peter.

"Just one more." Peter took the glass and headed to the kitchen. "It's because you're old." He poured the wine and took it to Sofia.

"Thank you," she said. "And I'm not that old." She scowled at him, took a gulp of wine, set the glass down.

"It will always hurt," she said.

"It can get easier?"

"We hope."

"Do we?" he asked.

"Sometimes," she said.

Sometimes. It was a hard word to understand how someone could move beyond the forever-pain to a sometimes-pain, how someone could let go of their pain long enough for it to ease, even if just a little.

Sofia leaned into a shadow. The wine weighed heavy on her shoulders. Her body wilted more than usual. "Why would we want it to always be hard? Pain does not always bring redemption. It always hurts—less and less. But always." Sofia swallowed a portion of the wine. She looked at the letter in her lap, folded it in half, and placed the corners over the candle flame. The acrid smell of char flittered from the wisps of smoke. Peter grabbed at the envelope.

"What are you doing?

"I have seen that look before," she said. The notes of sympathy and sadness had fallen away, replaced by rough gravel grating against her words, against Peter's ears.

"What look?" He saw the reflection of himself in her eyes, the specks of fake emotion muddled in his false smile. He looked past Sofia's light brown eyes to where the specks of hazel in his own longing stare looked away, unable to see how she saw him—a scared, long-haired child grasping tight to his teddy bear. The scent of burnt paper clung to the air. Her composed façade had cracked with every sip of wine.

"Your look," she said. "You look to your coffee with sad eyes. Not from now. Not from the conversation. I saw that look the first day we met—that space behind your eyes. I knew better than to ask. Like my smile. I know it is there, but too much time and too many disappointments—I can no longer help it." She looked away from Peter and turned back to the envelope and its crisp, blackened corners. Sofia swayed in her chair—back and forth. She looked around him, not at him, with the tinted glaze of her wino's eyes.

"The letter," he said. "Who is it from?"

"Do not feel bad, cariño. You do not have to say the things you do not want to say." Sofia drew a labored breath. Peter couldn't look at her. His eyes roamed the room to avoid his reflection in her eyes. "Have you ever said them?" she asked.

Have you? He wanted to demand. Instead, Peter sat in the cluttered air of the radio. There was never anyone who he wanted to say the words to. He never wanted to get close enough to the conversation for someone to ask him about the possibility of his parents: what they did, if they were happy, where they were. They were nowhere. And everywhere.

Peter stared at the rug and found faces in the threads: Happy faces, smiles, laughter, blurred faces buried deep in the beige. Sofia's eyes found him through the haze of wine, not like before when her eyes were clouded and lost in the world she drank herself into. He wanted to shout and scream and throw out his hands with how dare you's and with what rights, but instead, he looked at the burnt edges of the letter and thought about all the postcards he never sent, the letters he never received and shook his head.

"Today is the day I celebrate. Celebrate is not the correct word." She scrunched her face and went quiet as she tried to think of the word she wanted, the proper word to express herself in a language that wasn't her own. Each word felt loaded with the weight of the world, the precision of sound and rhythm, and the life of a choice, not because she loved words, but because she needed them to define her past and present. Each word christened with importance because of what she wanted to say in a language that was forced onto her. She couldn't tell Peter about her sadness in Spanish because life had stalled in Spanish—then it was taken away. That's how Peter felt about every word that pushed against the memory of his mother.

"Llorar." Sofia tapped her tongue to the roof of her mouth and clicked.

The room turned cold; the walls tightened around them. The longer he sat there, the more the building sounded ready to crumble, ready to trap him beneath the wreckage, trap them both. Sofia was already there. He could hear it. Buried beneath the rubble, searching for a way out.

Sofia slapped her thigh. "Mourn. I do not like the sound of that word. It sounds too much like a vaca. I am not a cow. I like celebrate better. Yes. I do not mourn today. Let the cows moo-urn. I celebrate. The life that I had and the people I loved. I see those eyes. Just eyes, but sad still. And we have shared. Only dinner. But that is family when people share as often as we do. I do not have much family." The letter pressed firmly against the table, ready to break the legs with its weight.

Sofia tilted her head back and finished the wine. Peter hadn't been a part of a family in a long time. It wasn't just dinner. Peter didn't want to celebrate the family he no longer had. He couldn't understand why she would, why she would celebrate people that chose to be elsewhere. Her husband. Her daughter. They weren't in San Francisco. They were far away from Sofia, and she deserved better than an absent husband and an estranged daughter. Peter deserved better too. He couldn't blame her for wanting to burn the envelope.

Sofia took her locket in her hand and stared at the photo. Her fingers shook. Peter didn't blame her. Now he knew her reason for running.

"My daughter was taken from my husband and me. We never knew what happened. I told Gaston to leave. I could not look at him anymore. His eyes were like hers once."

She rubbed her fingers around the edges of the locket. Peter did the same to his wrist, touched the cool glass of each of the three watches to absorb the memories all at once. The shattered glass of the watch face, its hands on a memory of sweet chai in India, milky thick, and the gap-toothed smile of the woman with silver hair who had given it to him. Another rest stop in his marathon of movement. But he remained silent, unable to find words of comfort, of understanding.

"I left Buenos Aires for here," Sofia said. "San Francisco was my uncle's favorite city. When I was little, he would talk about it."

And my mother would paint it, Peter thought.

"He moved here when I was a teenager but died years before I came to visit—to live."

So did my mother.

"He sent me a postcard once."

She painted herself to look like a streetcar once.

"It had Coit Tower above the city. That is why I came here, close enough to the tower to feel like I have someone watching over me. Even in this, this, fog. I sometimes see the light of the tower shining in that paste."

I came to San Francisco to run into her arms. To see her face one more time. To have her hold me one more time without seeing the blood drip into the ocean and turn the water red. The words were there, in his mind, but stuck somewhere between his head and his heart.

"Where is Gaston?"

"He is still unable to talk. And that is okay." Sofia avoided the letter and looked into her empty glass. She squinted one eye. "One day, he will. One day you will."

Peter put the coffee on the table. It was cold anyway. He rubbed his hands against his thighs. What could Gaston say when he found the words? Words beyond "You were right." Words that would stitch Sofia and Gaston back together, to make each other whole, separate from the other, if not sewn back to one another. What words would Peter find? What words could he use to stitch himself back together when it felt like he had been pulled apart in so many places he couldn't find the pieces of himself with a satellite or a magnifying glass. The lights of the apartment flickered.

"It is fitting," Sofia said. The music stopped. "I suppose."

The lights gave way to darkness; the city went black. The candlelight from the table sputtered up the walls. Sofia still lit a candle after so many years away from Argentina, after so many years waiting for her daughter, as if Valentina would find her way back into Sofia's life by the glimmer of candlelight. The faint glow flickered over the back of her hands—slender, frail, but strong, the hands of an eternal mother, strong enough to hold you, soft enough to love you. He wanted to remember his own mother's hands.

The bells of Saints Peter and Paul church chimed. The candles blinked. The lights returned. The music resumed. Sofia's glass sat empty on the table beside the half-singed letter. Her chin pressed into her chest; her eyes closed. So much weight on her mind, a mountain of memories placed on top of her but her body as light as the bottle she drank as if the enormity of her memories kept her stuck to the earth.

Boats howled in the distance, a reminder of the ghosts Peter wanted to put to rest. Let the fog take the memories as he climbed over the mist, climbed over the world, and looked down on the planes and the birds and the trees and the people.

"It was my mom," he finally said out loud.

Sofia did not stir or turn or wrestle. Peter put the coffee and the wine glass in the sink. He placed the half-charred letter on the fridge beneath the magnet of Coit Tower. He twisted the knob too tight to keep the faucet from dripping. The handwriting continued to stand out against the faded paper, now more prominent against the crispy corners, raised with distinction. He went to the radio and turned off the sound—the apartment filled with the music of the church bells. The door squeaked when he opened it to leave.

"One day," he said. "Maybe one day."

Sofia stirred at the sound.

Chapter 5

Sofia woke to the envelope waiting beneath Coit Tower in the silence of her apartment. Twenty-five years—she would never forget Gaston's handwriting. The radio returned the throngs of horns and bass to the apartment. She went to the kitchen to make herself some maté. She placed the letter next to the sink. Part of her wanted to finish what she started and turn the envelope to ash, wash it down the drain and listen to the stomach-churning roar of the garbage disposal as it tore into the remaining shards, but the embers would probably sink into the carpet and burn the apartment, or the disposal would probably spit up water and soak her clothes leaving the letter intact. When they first met, Gaston had waited outside of her school, calling to her with simple words: "Hello, darling."

"May I walk with you?" he said that first day, and he walked alongside her as if she had accepted his offer. "No," she told him. She remembered the mischievous smile she attempted. "I can hold your books," he said. "Try again tomorrow," she said. How surprised she had been when he showed up the next day.

When the knob turned, the faucet dripped before the water splashed against the porcelain. The water spattered over her shirt. Sofia mindlessly wiped the drops away.

When they had first married, Sofia swirled her new name around her mouth— Sofia Morales—tasted the words—drunk on them—deep in love with the sound of her new name. The first time she lay in bed with Gaston—in their bed—the window had opened to the hot air of a rare quiet night in San Telmo, inside a home ready to be filled with their life. She had drunk a whole bottle of her new name, wore a silent smile when the moonlight peeked through the window and fell on Gaston's face. His face, handsome and mature, unlike the day they met. His cheeks were chiseled, a regal nose, his mustache dark and pencil thin. His scar, a coarse line under his left eye, blacker than the rest of his dark skin. He hated that scar, she knew.

Gaston had stirred at her touch, rubbed his hand over her legs. His hands were more delicate than she had thought they would be, not the hands of the gaucho she had expected, calloused and rough on her skin. But Gaston wasn't a gaucho; he oversaw them, admired them, loved their solitude among one another. He awoke saying those comforting words: "Hello, darling."

She looked to the letter. No return address.

He didn't want a response? How could he not want to hear from her? Had he moved back to San Telmo? Home? A home from which Sofia had separated herself? Even now, she felt Gaston press his lips to her neck. Her body tensed from the tickle of his mustache. She rubbed her hands along his back and traced his muscles. On their first night together, she had been hot and sticky, but for once, she enjoyed it, savored it, the sweat from her body, and from Gaston's. He couldn't have moved home. He had left. He couldn't have gone back. Sofia wouldn't have gone back. But she would have left a return address as well. She would want a response. But that was her. Gaston was not her, not at all. She had made him wait for three months before they went on their first date. Each day he had greeted her, "Hello, darling. May I walk with you?"

Each day Sofia had told him, "Try again tomorrow."

And Gaston did. And Sofia enjoyed it. She liked the attention. She liked the desire. And she liked him. He was the first boy to ever call her beautiful. He was the first boy to ever call her darling; her heart belonged to him, and his heart belonged to her. She adored him for it, even with his chubby cheeks and spotty mustache. She wanted to keep him forever, but she hadn't known how. He never bothered to court her friends who called him handsome. He returned for Sofia, every day for three months, and every day for three months, Sofia sat in class and watched the seconds pass, waiting for the moment she could hear Gaston's voice, the soft sound she wanted to hold onto. She waited for the moments she could tease him because she knew he would come back; he would try again. Until the day he didn't.

Now he didn't want to hear from her, had a hard time writing after so long, didn't want to know if the letter reached her; he wanted to send the letter somewhere, anywhere, and the single thought that it reached her would no more matter to him than if he had sent no letter at all—maybe.

The day he hadn't greeted her at school, Sofia thought Gaston must have been sick. The next day the minutes passed by slower than usual. Sofia knew Gaston would be outside, that she would walk out of the school doors and hear his voice, that her friends would be jealous because he paid them no attention. She had walked from her final class out of school one million times before, but on that day, it was the longest walk of her life. She left the building, closed her eyes, and listened for Gaston. Laughter echoed through the streets. Car horns. Car engines. Bicycle bells. Shoes on cobblestone. A bird. No Gaston. Nor the next day.

One night Sofia's father called her into the parlor. Gaston stood with his hat in his hands. Eleven months had passed. Sofia convinced herself she hadn't been counting. In her father's parlor, she saw a man, and Gaston greeted her as a man.

"Hello, darling," Gaston said.

"Hello—?" she said.

"Sofia," her father said, "this man has asked to take you for a walk."

Gaston offered Sofia his arm. Her father watched. Sofia accepted. Gaston finally took her for a walk.

The streets were filled with music from the cafés that night. Gaston pressed himself close to Sofia, their arms tangled, their shoulders touched. He smelled like grass. She wanted to absorb that smell, to rub it on her skin and never be without it. The letter in her hands held the same scent, of the pampas in Argentina, the horses, the sweet air, air she hadn't smelled in twenty-five years. But she had left

Buenos Aires. She had waited for a letter with hope until the hope turned to fear, the fear turned to stone, and the stone crumbled around her, buried her beneath all the seconds in which he hadn't sent a letter. But he did send a letter—this letter

***

Gaston pressed his lips to Sofia's. She smelled fresh grass, felt the tickle of his mustache on her lip. She wanted the touch of his mustache and the smell of grass when they kissed. She was disappointed when they weren't there.

She remembered their first kiss, lit by gas lamps and starlight. She remembered their first dance on that night in San Telmo. She remembered their first kiss as husband and wife; they stood at the altar before their family and friends, and Gaston wrapped his arms around her tight after they said, "I do." She remembered how, on their first night as husband and wife, the moon cleared from their window, the heavy air disappeared, and the brisk dawn began to creep through the apartment. She remembered when Gaston asked her to marry him, how the guitar purred; the singer's voice hummed and floated through the small room. Gaston offered Sofia a cigarette; she took it; it was her first cigarette. Gaston pulled a lighter from his pocket; he hummed along with the singer. He placed a small box on the table and started to sing the words that the singer must have sung, but Sofia only heard Gaston; "A life with me," he had said. "...Where I only exist for you;" Sofia opened the box, saw the ring—diamond—glistening. She dropped her cigarette, curled up against his body, the comfortable security of her head on his chest, his arms wrapped loosely around her. She had been nineteen but no longer a child.

She remembered their first kiss after Valentina was born: half delirious with exhaustion and pain, covered in sweat and silent, finally, as she held her new love in her arms, her tiny new life. She saw the sparkle in his green eyes when he looked down and touched Valentina, whose eyes were closed. She grabbed his fingertip and held it—and he almost cried. Sofia saw his almost tears, and he leaned in with his smile and kissed her. Those were her favorite kisses. Her first kisses. The ones which she could never, never let go.

***

Sofia poured her tea. She dipped her finger in the water to test the temperature. It burnt her skin. She sucked the heat and the bitterness from her fingertips, a habit she never grew out of, never imagined she would, even though Gaston thought it childish. So had her father.

The long-overdue letter.

Her hands wrapped around the mug. A chill ran down her arms and neck. She did not close her eyes to taste the bittersweet tea, a quick escape from the everyday for all the days she had ever needed an escape. Her heart beat with the clock, counting the seconds with her, for her, since last she had heard from Gaston, and beat for how many times she had thought of him. And how many times she wanted to write or call or trace his memorized face with her fingers into every blank space in her apartment.

She had told him to leave.

Wait until you can speak.

Her words, her wants. But she never stopped wanting.

She reached her fingers under the seal and tore the glue as flecks of blackened paper floated to the floor like burnt snowflakes.

***

This kiss was their first too, their first in months, nothing like the others. Without love. Without care. It was—without. It had been months without a touch, without an embrace. What happened to when a day without each other was torture?

Sofia was here—wrapped in a disenchanted kiss.

She took some of the blame. In her attempt to find Valentina, she had lost their marriage. But so had he. And now she felt alone in a fire, far from safety, locked in a kiss where the truth found her, the truth she didn't want—the truth she wanted to ignore.

He was not the same.

Sofia pulled away.

"Who are you?" she said.

Gaston's eyes: green, vacant, lost.

Silent. She knew he would be. He always was.

She wanted emotion. An answer. Silent and still.

"I can't do this anymore," she said. "I see it in your eyes. You have pulled away from me."

Silent. She heard her heart shatter. Still. Vacant. She wanted none of it.

"You need to leave," she said. "You need to leave now."

She threw herself against him, arms pressed to his chest. She wanted to pound her fists into his heart. Maybe it would beat again. She wanted to slap his face, let her handprint sting. But she pressed her head to his chest like on the night he had proposed and waited for the guitar to purr.

***

She pulled the letter from the envelope. Twenty-five years. No return address. One page. She couldn't feel her heartbeat; it had fallen from her chest. Sofia's hands convulsed. She couldn't focus on the words and instead took in fragments of each sentence.

I will be in San Francisco for business…like to see you…meet you for dinner…La Sirenita…If your answer is yes…delight in the sight of you…

Always yours,

Gaston

Brief: that had always been Gaston. She reread the letter; each time, the same words appeared larger and larger. "Always yours." Had he always been hers? When was the last time she could say he had belonged to her, and her to him?

The letters of his name carried the elegance of his demeanor, the methodical attention to every crossing line and swishing letter turning his name into art, a sketch, a drawing that once belonged to her, an image she would trace with her fingers, her mind, her tongue to taste its sweetness. Until the letters turned into nonsensical scrapes in her head and heart. She should have burnt the letter and watched his name turn to ash. If it hadn't been for Peter, the letter wouldn't be taking up so much space; a letter without a return address, as if he couldn't bear her response, as if she didn't deserve one!

She grabbed the phone from the counter and dialed a number she convinced herself she had forgotten, a number for a home from which she tried desperately to run. A silence ate at her through the earpiece. The receiver stuck to her, froze her in place. She couldn't breathe, waiting for the ring. A voice spoke, but Sofia couldn't understand it over the noise from the radio she refused to turn down. She took a deep breath, gripped the phone tight, and heard the operator's voice, "...not recognized. Please check the number and try again."

Sofia slammed the handset back onto the base. The letter absorbed whatever empty space had been left in the apartment. Seeped into the cracks. Made the air too thick to breathe. Sofia needed space. And air. She pushed through the current of memories and the thick atmosphere littered with words. To the door. Away from the expanding letter.

***

"You need to leave," she said.

He had returned to Buenos Aires once, with a new scar beneath his eye. They had walked through the night—through the music. Sofia brushed her hands over his scar for the first time.

"I was kicked in the face by a stallion they were trying to break," he had said. He hadn't paid attention. "I was thinking of you."

At the time, Sofia didn't care if this was true; she chose to believe it,

"If you ever disappear again, I'll find you and give you a scar that will always make you think of me," she said. But now she was asking him to disappear, all over again, like the life they had lived—the daughter they had lost.

Gaston grabbed her wrists gently and pushed her away from him, from them.

Sofia counted the seconds. A small part of her hoped he would come back and speak, say he was sorry, say he was foolish—say goodbye. He did not even fight to stay. The seconds reached up. Up. Too hard to count. He was the only family she had left. He was—

The door stayed quiet.

***

Leaving the apartment, Sofia took a deep breath. It was her fault. She knew it. She had wanted Valentina to go to university. She told Gaston when Valentina was a baby. Sofia wanted Valentina to be educated, to be worldly, to be smarter than Sofia was. She wanted her daughter to hold the world in her hands.

Sofia had put the thought in Valentina's head, made Valentina want to go. If Valentina hadn't gone to university, she never would have met Philippe. If she had never met Philippe, she never would have gotten involved with politics, known about politics—the shit politics of Argentina. Valentina was too smart for politics. But not after she met Philippe, met Philippe because of Sofia because Sofia wanted Valentina at school. And Sofia's world crumbled in her hands.

The harsh stew of San Francisco weather hung in the sky. It flooded the halls of the building, a mixture of fog and the music Sofia forgot to shut off before she left her apartment. She passed Peter's door and was tempted to knock, pull Peter out of his cardboard box of an apartment, and walk with her. But he would be at work. He wouldn't be around to help her walk or cook through the mess piled in a letter stuffed in her apartment. The gray day absorbed any traces of candlelight. The night had passed her by. The candles had glowed on the table with little life and now sat in a puddle of wax on the tabletop.

The radio shut off. The lights had gone off again. For the moment, she didn't mind the quiet; for the moment, she didn't mind the possibility of darkness. They wrapped around her like old friends.

Twenty-five years. Nowhere near as painful as the first ten. Sofia needed a place to escape the tumult of her thoughts or the possibility that someone heard her thoughts in the silence, in the absence of a horn, a guitar, a squeaky door. But that time had gone. Like Valentina had gone. Like Gaston had gone. But she wasn't ready for him to come back. Sofia stepped from the building and let the cold air fill her lungs. She pulled out the locket and watched the shadows dance on the photo of a happy day, trying to forget the letter for now.

Chapter 6

Peter came to the diner early in the morning, after work, and sunk into a corner table before the crowd crept in. The sun had been up for less than an hour. There wasn't much difference between the gray of the night and the gray of the morning. He wrapped his hands over the mug, and the steam escaped through his fingers. He wanted to hold the steam. The diner was long and thin. The more people came through the door, the smaller the diner felt. The line-cook flipped pancakes; Peter preferred waffles.

"More coffee?" the server asked.

He shook his head, ordered fried eggs and toast. He wanted milk in his coffee but didn't like how it cooled his drink. Sofia always told him to get the milk anyway. Life is too short for no milk in your coffee. Sometimes he agreed. Peter tapped his watch, the broken one, held the green and black face to his ear to hear it tick; but it didn't tick. It wasn't supposed to.

A crowd blocked the glass doors. The diner wasn't set up for crowds, and Peter swam in the thick mix of angry breath and bacon grease. He wanted a cigarette. He wanted to blow smoke into the faces that hovered over him.

He had returned to the cafe near his work every day since he saw her, hoping she would pass by. He tried to convince himself it wasn't as creepy as it sounded. He should have spoken to her—that same thought for a week, when time had stalled for a moment at the museum but started again with the girl moving faster than the seconds, out and away from Peter and into the darkness, before he had a chance to speak—he should have spoken to her at the Exploratorium when he had the chance.

An old man watched Peter, wrinkles around his sunken eyes, a look of entitlement, a promised seat because he was there. By catching Peter's eye, he expected Peter to rush?

Peter leaned into his coffee, closed his eyes, pressed his face into the steam. *I'm not leaving.* He stared into the light eyes and dark wrinkles of the man. Peter sipped his coffee and placed his mug on the table.

The man coughed and looked away. Peter pressed his back against the chair, smiling to himself. The people by the door grumbled. It had been minutes since the crowd came through the doors, their bitter stares forced onto the patrons who already had tables and food in front of them. The crowd had to wait by the entrance with the cold and the fog, or they grumbled about the girl who fought her way to the host stand—her, from the Exploratorium. She was here, alone. Was she here alone? Or with someone in the entitled crowd, the old man maybe? No, alone.

***

Peter pushed his mop through the Exploratorium, the cavernous space filled with hands-on science experiments meant to educate kids on the wonders of science, but just as wondrous to adults who wanted to watch electricity flash in a ball or experience the psychological effect of drinking water from a fountain situated inside of a clean toilet. Peter wiped down the windows, cleaned the tiny and large face-prints from the exhibits, spun metal plates into a sphere to watch different densities spin at different speeds, and returned to his mop until he was sidetracked by a burst of lights. Colors swirled around the floor, lifted to the ceiling, and exploded across the gallery like shattered stained glass—neon green and dark blue, golden yellow, and sun red—scattered across the floor in swirls, accompanied by the faint sound of a piano, the higher keys, tap, tapping, and the lights shifting with the music; the lighter colors flickered to the higher sound, the darker colors to the deeper sound. The bass bounced. Pulsed through Peter. His heart gained an extra beat. The crowd reacted and filled the dance floor and danced in the stained-glass colors of the soundtrack. Peter wanted to leave his mop with the mass of people in the museum, their cameras, and their excessive need to photograph themselves with his mop as if he were a novelty. But he pushed his mop by the exhibits and stopped when the lights flickered into darkness and the music dissolved into silence—then screams and laughter. Small light. Not from museum bulbs, or the backup generator, or a flashlight. A sign lit by battery power: Sunflower Star Fields. Made with Space Dust. The dust made a mosaic on the warehouse floor. The galaxy. Nebulas. Supernovas. Made with dust. Imagined as sunflowers.

Sunflower Star Fields orbited the warehouse floor in the glow-in-the-dark sand universe. Peter wanted to dive into it, his mop in his hands, with the lights of the museum shut off, shut down, shut out. The crowd seeped out of the pitch-black as the neon light crept over their faces, the light of the flowers' fierce orange suns and yellow petals. A girl moved on the far side of the cosmic field, her hair melted into the blackness behind her, and she—paralyzed by the light—and Peter—paralyzed by the light, a child on the first sunny day in decades, afraid of the universe—glowed for a moment in the dark. Faces fell into blackout except for her face, framed by the black and lit by stars and Space Dust in the silent corner of the warehouse; her eyes blue-skied. Peter had the urge to follow her eyes, up and up, next to the sun, and watch the world spin in the spaces between the stars and planets until the warehouse exploded with light. Brightness wiped her framed face away. Peter had to mop up the mess.

***

Peter waved at the hostess. She can sit with me, he tried to say, but only if she's here alone, he said with his hands, because I don't know if she is with someone, but how much could he say with his hands? I don't want to be a third wheel, and he hoped the hostess understood him, but really it's because I don't think I could handle getting in the way of an established relationship, and he hoped he hadn't said anything vulgar. The girl came to the table.

"Have we met before?" she asked.

"Once," he said. "At a thing. Well, we didn't actually meet, but we were there together. Not together, but we were there at the same time. You were there. And I was there too. But we weren't together."

"I think I would have remembered if we had been there together," she said.

Maybe it would be better if he said nothing at all.

He nodded. She stared at him. He had made a mistake. Saying nothing was weird. He should say something.

"Busy day," he said and motioned to the crowd of people at the door. He took a sip of his coffee.

"Apparently," she said. "I guess I'll go wait for a table."

"Wait," he said. "Are you here alone?"

"Why?"

"There's an extra chair. You can avoid the line. I'm Peter."

She looked at the line. He'd lost her. She'd rather wait. He should've skipped the small talk. He could have asked, what's your opinion about the butterfly effect? have you ever played hide and seek in the fog? What's your preference in pizzas? It was too late now. She'd hide herself in the crowd like a pebble in the ocean.

"Carly," she said. She put her coat on the back of the chair and sat down. The old man harrumphed. Peter's smile grew. He knew part of it was because of the old man's annoyance.

"It was at the Exploratorium," Peter said.

"What was?" Carly said.

"That thing that we were at togeth—at the same time."

"What did you think?" she asked.

"I love it. I'm always there. Mostly because I have to be—"

"Have to?"

"I work there. At the museum."

"Me too," she said. "I'm surprised I haven't seen you. I'm the curator for the After Dark exhibits."

"That's incredible!" he said. "I'm the janitor for After Dark. We're practically cousins." Peter took another sip of his coffee. Maybe he shouldn't have told her he was a janitor. He could have made it sound better: Custodial Arts, Sanitation Committee, Mop Squad. No, that wasn't good either. It was too late anyway. He could avoid it if he kept talking.

"There was a piece of art last week," he said. "When the blackout happened, it was the only thing still vibrant. It was made with 'Space Dust.' You know it?"

"'Sunflower Star Fields.' That was mine. It was a shame someone had to clean it up."

"It should have stayed there."

The server refilled Peter's mug. Carly ordered a bacon omelet. Peter asked for milk for his coffee. He tried not to stare at the contrast between her black hair and blue eyes, but it was just as awkward as if he had. He didn't know where to look, at the lemon-print tablecloth, at the faded tile, at the doorway—at her.

"I just meant that it was a great piece," he said.

The server brought some milk for Peter and some coffee for Carly. She told Peter his eggs would be out shortly, and he nodded. He decided to stare at the tablecloth.

"I had trouble with it," she said.

Peter looked at her. He wanted to touch her hair, to brush the dark strands from her eyes, as he had seen his father do for his mother once. He longed for those tender moments between couples that they took for granted, when they could gaze at each other on a park bench and forget the rest of the world existed for breath or two. The world always felt too present, whether in front of him, around him, or pressing down on his shoulders. Carly stared at the table with a look that took her far from the diner, somewhere Peter wanted to follow but couldn't.

"Have you ever drawn a picture," she said, "but when you colored it in, you realized you liked it better in black and white?"

Should he say yes so she wouldn't feel alone? Should he say no because he couldn't really draw in black and white, let alone in color? Even in school, when the other kids drew shoes or their parents or storybooks, Peter wouldn't touch the crayons or markers unless he first shaded his palms with color and tried to press his hands against the paper. But his handprints never stuck.

"That color made the room burst," he said.

"If it weren't for the blackout, no one would have noticed," she said.

"If it weren't for the color, no one would have noticed, even after the blackout."

Peter's eggs arrived. He thanked the server.

"It's hard to put so much time into something and know that it won't be there when you wake up. It makes it harder to organize, create, move forward. Especially if it's so easily washed away. At least Rome still has the Colosseum."

"Yeah, well—Rome wasn't burnt in a day." Peter bit into his toast. He wiped his face with his napkin in case he had jam on his nose.

A boy tapped on the window, then hugged his mother, kissed her cheek, and tapped the glass again. He wore black Velcro shoes. Peter could imagine the rip of the Velcro when the boy took them off. Peter waved, and the boy lunged for his mother and hid under her arm, the safest place in the world.

"I guess he likes you," Carly said.

"The more they like me, the farther they run," said Peter.

Carly's omelet came to the table. Peter smelled the bacon and wished he had ordered some of his own. Was it too soon to ask for some of hers?

"Don't get too concerned," she said. "Someday, they'll get close and stay close."

"Then, hopefully, I won't run—may I have some of your bacon?"

Carly laughed. She cut a piece of her omelet and dropped it on Peter's plate. He picked the bacon out of the eggs with his fork and sipped his coffee. What else could he say? What else should he say? She hadn't run away or thrown her coffee at him; that was good, but she might have been really hungry. But she stayed. He wanted to be with her. He wanted to talk to her. He wanted to be around her. He wanted her.

"I want you—" he said. "I...um...I...wait." Maybe she didn't plan to stay much longer. "I want you to go out with me...I would like to take you out."

He asked. That was the hard part. He told himself it wasn't about her answer, that it's never about the answer. It's always about the question, the anticipation, the anxiety. Most people don't listen for the answer once the question is out. He could relax. But it hadn't been a question; it had been a statement. Who needed a question to sound unsure of themselves when a statement sounded decisive? Did people want decisions? Maybe that made it easier.

"Pay for breakfast, and we'll see," she said.

"If I pay for breakfast, I think we should know," Peter said.

"Okay," she said. She took a pen from her bag, grabbed a napkin from the table, and wrote down her number. "I look forward to it. Thanks for breakfast." She slid the napkin across the table. She stood, grabbed her coat, and walked through the door. The old man was gone. Carly disappeared into the fog.

Chapter 7

Sofia heard the church bells. She had liked the sound of them—once—when they sang like a choir, when the pealing lifted into the air, light and sweet and familiar. Ding, fresh empanadas, melted butter, fried onions, sweet meat. Dong, the market earlier and whether she had bought enough food. Ding, Peter's smile, bright and happy, a smile that lifted the world from his shoulders—a simple smile that made Sofia think the world might turn out all right. Dong, Valentina.

Valentina was gone—had been gone for a long time. The night reminded Sofia of that, as if she needed the reminder. She lit a candle and let the bright light of the apartment absorb the soft flicker from the wick.

She fingered the locket around her neck. She looked at the photo inside. It had become more worn than she ever thought it would, fringed at the edges, colors of sepia memories, of too much time gone by. Valentina's face, happy and naïve, like Sofia's in that moment. The radio had a gentle hum of harps and strings beneath the peal of the bells.

It was ten; the church bells had reminded her of that. When Sofia arrived in San Francisco, she loved this neighborhood because of the bells but avoided the church. The sound brought her comfort; the pews brought her nausea.

In Buenos Aires, she loved to sit in the open space of a church and get lost in the scent of myrrh, the tall spires, the stained glass. She would wait for the sun to strike the glass at such an angle that beams of orange and red and green light would spread over the altar. If Jesus were to come back, he would do so in color, with radiant stained sunshine. But Jesus wasn't returning to her thoughts, hadn't returned to her church, and wouldn't return in her time in San Francisco.

The church made her think of Gaston. The vows Sofia made to him. The vows Gaston made to her. The daughter they had. The daughter they lost. The God he believed in. The daughter he forgot. The vows they lost. The God Sofia ignored. Gaston and the church were almost one and the same; both made her nauseous. How easy the world dropped people into her life and from her life. Valentina and Gaston, but Peter was brought in; Peter who had wrapped extra food on a plate to take home whenever he came for dinner. He spent too much time washing away other people's filth. Sometimes life left too much in its wake to wash away. But Peter said he enjoyed his work. He got free access to a science museum. Sofia had never been. It was a children's museum, and she didn't have any children. Not anymore.

Sofia closed the locket, grabbed the lonely plate of food, and headed to the sink. The faucet dripped beneath the vacant window. The cigarette haze from the hallway seeped beneath the door into her apartment. The air felt thick. She had rarely heard more than three words from her neighbors, but she had never wanted to. Peter had popped out of her garden like the tomatoes she grew, the roses she cared for.

A loud knock on the door poured through the apartment. It pounded over the music from the radio. Sofia dropped her dish, startled by the knock. The glass plate hit the porcelain and shattered. The noise teased her.

For almost fifteen years she had lived on the third floor without knowing anyone in her building. When she left Argentina, she was glad to have solitude, reassured by her distance from nosy neighbors. She let the door squeak in case someone entered the apartment in the middle of the night. One night, it was July, with dinner in the oven, music loud in the empty apartment, when Sofia heard a knock at the door. She couldn't pretend she wasn't home. She was ready to wait a few minutes for the knock to quiet. For the person to leave. For herself to run. But her life in San Francisco was free of fear or was supposed to be—free of the fear that her neighbors would overhear her, would inform on her, that the government would knock down her door and drag her out by her hair. That she would disappear—like her daughter.

Sofia went to the door and looked through the peephole. At first, she swore she saw green eyes staring back at her, eyes filled with panic. Sofia scrambled to open the door, sure Valentina had returned and somehow found Sofia amidst the melee of their lives. When Sofia flung open the door, brown eyes stared back at her. Big and brown. Brown and red. Red and young. Sofia turned down the music.

"Hi," the girl said. "I'm Linda. I live downstairs. Do you have a phone I can use? It's a bit of an emergency." Linda held a piece of paper in her hand. Colors showed through, but Sofia couldn't guess what the paper contained.

Sofia escorted Linda to the kitchen counter and handed her the phone. "Could they make these apartments any smaller?" Linda asked. Her English was proper and polite. Not like the people Sofia had met in the city, not often polite and most often hurried. Sofia returned to the stove and tried not to eavesdrop on Linda's conversation, another habit. If you listen, you might hear. If you hear, you might know. Part of the reason Sofia kept the music loud, alone or with company—the sound hid her voice, or the voices in the room, from the outside world, the world that pressed its ears to the walls of Buenos Aires and had pulled voices away by their vocal cords, silenced, unable to scream for help. Sofia tried not to listen, but certain words like love and mom and please were hard to ignore. It reminded her too much of a conversation Valentina might have had once.

Linda hung up the phone. She held back tears. She opened the paper and traced her fingers over the picture. Sofia could make out an image through the opposite side of the paper. It showed three people under an umbrella in a rainstorm. Sofia couldn't let the girl leave in such a state. She invited her to stay for dinner.

"I should be getting back," Linda said. "And I would hate to intrude."

"Por favor," Sofia said. "Do not let an old woman dine alone. For an Argentine, it is like limbo on a unicycle."

"That does sound unpleasant," said Linda.

Sofia divided up the cannelloni she had made.

"And take some bread," Sofia said.

Linda pushed the cannelloni around her plate. She took small bites. The girl was thin; had she been sick?

"Can I get you something else?" Sofia asked.

Linda pushed her hair up with both hands. "You're probably wondering about the phone call. Why it was such an emergency."

"That is your business. Just because it is my phone does not mean it is my business."

"How can someone take something away when they know it's the only thing you have?"

Sofia didn't know how to respond. There was a spot behind the eyes where desperation sat and pulsed. Sofia knew it well, how it felt, how it looked, red and blurry tears that dammed up and never broke down, and the higher it dammed, the more release was needed. She saw it in Linda when she had opened the door. Sofia wasn't sure she wanted to help or if she could help, beyond food and a phone. She wasn't sure she wanted to hear more. Linda was a stranger, a young stranger. But Sofia knew what those eyes meant. She felt the desperation pulse behind her own eyes. Not as often as years ago.

"What did they take away, sweet girl?"

The girl didn't seem to hear. A girl. That was all she was. Just a girl. She hugged the drawing to her chest. Rocked back and forth. Beneath the music, her voice was quiet; the old chair creaked.

Was she on drugs? Was that the problem? This was San Francisco. Drugs were everywhere. So Sofia had heard. She didn't need that kind of trouble in her home. She shouldn't have invited her in.

Linda pulled her hair back again. The tears slid down her cheeks, dripping from one eye at a time. "Have you ever been to Idaho?"

Sofia had not.

"Don't ever go," Linda said. "There's nothing there. That's why I left Caldwell. I always wanted to live in San Francisco, or at least I thought I did. I don't know. I don't remember who I was before."

Before what? Was it drugs? It must have been drugs.

"And there was a boy," Linda laughed. "There's always a boy, right? I thought he was such a great musician. I was convinced he would play in all the famous places, and he would become famous, and we'd tour the country together. But once I got pregnant—" The girl's voice broke. "I'm sorry, this is too much. I should go."

Sofia placed her hand over the girl's. It was too much, but she wanted to know. "Continue, please."

Linda slid the paper towards Sofia. It showed a little girl underneath the umbrella between a woman and a person in a red hoodie, but the person in the hoodie was turned around. The drawing was of the back of the person's head. "You do everything you can to protect someone, but other people don't see it that way because all they care about are arrangements and provisions and…but what about love? Shouldn't that count?"

"Where is your baby?"

"Lucille is almost six now. She's with my mother." Linda rubbed her face with the palms of her hands. "And all she remembers of me is the back of my head."

This girl had lost a child. And not much more than a child herself.

Sofia offered to make alfajores, the crumble of the cookie and the sweet dulce de leche always helped her on hard days. Linda declined but thanked her for the meal and the phone call.

"Perhaps we can dine again," said Sofia,

"Perhaps," said Linda with a soft, grateful smile.

The next day Sofia took a box of alfajores to the first floor.

"I wanted to give you some," Sofia said. "And to thank you for the company."

The air felt empty without the music to surround them—to surround the conversation—even if out of habit. Sofia kept her voice low.

"I should be thanking you," Linda said. "You helped me more than you know."

"Are you not happy with the alfajores?" Sofia asked.

"Of course I am. Why?"

"Because you are not eating one," Sofia said. "And why are you wearing a robe in this weather? You will get sick."

Linda laughed.

"How rude of me," Linda said. "I didn't even invite you in." She took a bite of the cookie. "The alfajores are delicious."

The apartment smelled of vanilla from a candle on the table. A candle, a table, and a couch filled the room. There were no other rooms.

"What do you need?" Sofia asked.

"Nothing," said Linda. "Nothing that I can't do for myself."

The choices this girl made. The apartment shrank, the vanilla disappeared, and the stench of stale Chinese noodles and curry sprang from the walls, the smells the candle tried to hide.

Sofia loved to cook, loved the company, loved feeling wanted, feeling needed. She had missed the sound of a girl's laughter, the shriek of joy, the heavy gasp that came from uncontrollable giggles. Their conversations were not filled with uncontrollable joy, but they weren't filled with sadness.

One day Linda had vanished, another disappeared person in the pile of people missing from Sofia's life. Sofia had tried to tell herself it hadn't hurt, that she barely knew the girl. But underneath the pulse of drums beating from the radio, Sofia reminded herself, *this is why you don't open the door for strangers. One way or the other, you end up alone.*

Tonight, the peal of the bells had faded, and the dim light in her apartment made Sofia's head ache. She checked the door. No one stood in the hall. She turned up the radio with the hope that whoever stood on the opposite side of the door wouldn't hear the latch unlock, wouldn't notice, wouldn't care about the nosy habits of an old woman, one they could assume was part deaf, possibly blind, and of no threat to their antics. Her heart ached in her chest, ready to burst from its speed, her fear.

It had all felt too long. The nights, the days, the weeks, the years—and now the silence between knocks. She could feel each and every second pull at her skin—gray her hair. Each and every second passed in slow motion, extended her life beyond eternity—ever since Valentina disappeared. Her child that had no choice. Not like Linda, who had had a choice, who could have and may have returned home to be a daughter, to be a mother. Sofia couldn't choose to do either.

The night had passed her by. The candle glowed on the table with little life wafting in the breeze of Sofia's breath. Sofia opened the door to an empty hallway. An envelope was taped to her door. At first, she looked both ways in the heavy smoke of the passage

"Gaston?" she whispered. Then she let out a deep sigh in the hollowed-out tunnel of the building. With each breath, she let go of the fear that a cloaked figure had waited in the shadows, eager to reap the rewards after half a lifetime of stalking her. The envelope, she realized, came from the landlord. It held a receipt of the month's rent. When she shut the door, the lights shut off. The radio quieted. Candlelight lit the room. The weight of the envelope, all words, everywhere, became too much to look at.

She pulled at the locket and tried to absorb the faces she had memorized in the shadows of her life, the nightmares that danced in the silence of the city, filled with the echoes of empty knocking, with Sofia still waiting for answers.

Chapter 8

The roof had been empty at first, full of gravel and a view of the ocean on a clear day if Sofia could only see past the church spires; and if a clear day happened more often in San Francisco. She dug her hands into a pot and let the wet soil fold around her fingers. Some days she could imagine the hush of the ocean through the quiet of the city morning until the bells rang right through her. On the roof, surrounded by the comforts of her whispering plants, the need for the city's noise waned but returned once she closed the door to the roof, when she returned to life, or the absence of it.

No one knew how to get on the roof. That's what the landlord had told her when Sofia moved in. She was sure no one would miss the emptiness. No one cared about the roof—its openness. Her life in San Francisco was an endless empty space. She needed to fill it. On the nights Sofia walked the streets to watch the city calm itself, she couldn't see past the trees or the buildings. The streets constricted, people surrounded her, fog surrounded her; she was stuck in a city full of life, but not her own. The trees above her shoved their leaves into the tiny open spaces of the skyline to keep Sofia grounded, to where the only things she saw were branches and birds and their nests. Some days she thought of the eggs in the birds' nests and how she could take them, crack them, fry them up with some butter and toast. She was never sure how the tree grew through the concrete and blocked a sky already covered in clouds. She wanted to climb the highest hill and, with her fingers, pull apart the dark gray clouds that sank into the streets and made the world darker.

A leaf twirled through the damp hallway and fluttered back and forth from wall to wall, floor to ceiling. It stopped in mid-air, under the dim light, until a breeze from nowhere blew in the seawater from the ocean that Sofia couldn't see but knew swelled beyond the trees and the homes. For too long, she felt herself a volcano ready to erupt. She constantly swallowed the explosion, felt it burn down her throat and into her stomach, where it stayed and churned. She was tired. Tired of it all. Tired of waiting for the cataclysm of her anger to tear her apart, outside and in. She wanted to close her eyes and bathe herself in the scent of the sea in the hope that it would settle the volcano. But fire still makes water boil.

A leaf crunched when it slid to the far end of the hallway, caught between the breeze and the wall. Red and full of veins, the type of red that showed the leaf was ready to be raked into a pile and crunched by children, each child comforted by the sound, like hugs from their mothers, she thought. The leaf struggled against the breeze. Tilted. Danced. A fragile ballerina. The leaf pressed into the corner where Sofia saw the crease of a door panel, hidden by paint and seclusion.

She stepped to investigate the panel, searched for a handle, pressed her hands against the crease to feel the ragged face, found putty caked on the surface. She pressed the panel harder and heard a small pop. The panel pushed out, the size of a cupboard; Sofia had lived in a cupboard ever since she moved to the city, a cupboard that she could never have survived when she was younger.

A narrow staircase made of cobwebs and mold was hidden in the cupboard. Sofia climbed the cobwebs through the dim light, the dank stairwell almost closing in. She climbed to the top of the stairs, through the door and into the open sky, over the trees, onto the gray of the gravel roof, where the emptiness enveloped her. Where the empty space of the city was almost as suffocating as the crowded streets and the lives that weren't her life, the full life she thought she would have had, should have had but didn't, where she could have been a woman in a café, with a large hat to keep the sun out of her eyes while she watched the world slowly pass by, with her coffee and cigarettes, with Gaston and his silver lighter, the flame never dying.

She enjoyed the roof, how it stood above the treetops that blocked her view of everything. The city looked smaller when on top of it. When she looked over the ledge to see the water, a flower floated down from the sky. She tried to find where the flower could have come from, where the world could have dropped flower petals when the trees were below and the sky rained water not roses.

And the streets of San Francisco shifted from trash and asphalt to the gas lamps and cobblestones of Buenos Aires. And the petals floated through the air like a paintbrush ready to twist the gray sky to red and drip down the excess moisture.

"I want a garden," Valentina said. Her curls bounced up and down with her. The image of Valentina felt real. It had to be her standing at the edge of the roof, looking back at Sofia.

"What would you do with a garden?" Sofia said.

"I would grow things." Valentina wore her white hat. The brim covered her face from the sun. Made her eyes glow emerald. She wore her white dress with a black belt. White shoes with black socks. Black hair with fake curls. And a bright smile. Valentina, the one thing large enough to fill the emptiness, here, just as Sofia remembered her.

"What kinds of things?" Sofia asked. "Sheep and dogs and large cats?"

They sat on the roof of their building, with space enough for a garden or a small forest.

"That's silly. Animals do not grow."

"Your father grows animals."

Valentina puffed out her lips, looked at the brim of her hat. "No. He feeds horses and cows. He...he...um—"

"Raises?"

"Raises! Cows and horses...I want a garden."

"Where would we put a garden? In our kitchen?"

"Can we put a garden in the kitchen?"

"I don't think our kitchen is big enough, darling."

Sofia took a sip of her maté. The sun was hot. The tea was hotter. But it cooled her down. The world from her roof, she could see it all from the center of her universe and wanted the planets to revolve fast enough for her to change the future or fix the past. She could hear the clack of passers-by, the hum of cars, the strum of guitars, the vibrations of bass, the bang of drums, the levity of laughter, and she never had to leave the roof. At night the stars flickered; in the day, the sun shined. Some days it felt like all the best sounds in the world happened all at once.

"Here?" Valentina said.

"But you're standing there." Valentina giggled.

"I would like a garden on the roof. I can grow anything. Everything! Um…um…carrots?" Valentina looked for approval. "And basil? And passion fruit?"

"But passion fruit grows on trees."

"I cannot have trees in my garden?" Valentina pouted. She grabbed the hem of her dress and crunched the fabric in her tiny fist.

"Roses?" asked Sofia.

A slight breeze eased the heat. Valentina ran to the side of the roof and looked over.

"A tree can grow this high. I will plant it on the street. I will water it every day."

"Only the tree, darling? What about the rest of the garden and all the space here on the roof?"

"What about the passion fruit?"

"What about the carrots? What about the roses?"

"I do not want roses. Red is for boys."

"Not always." Sofia licked her lips. She didn't wear lipstick on Sundays. Gaston had said those lips were for him, not for God.

"Yes. Always." Valentina made up her mind, and she was too young to have the world explained otherwise. There'd be plenty of time for her to learn about red and lips and—

"Roses don't always have to be red." Sofia moved to the edge of the roof where Valentina looked over the ledge for a spot to plant a seed that would grow as high as the building where she could water each leaf, each piece of fruit, drop the water down onto the roots to make sure the tree had enough life to flourish in the cobblestone forest they lived in, the cobblestones that Sofia loved, even in heels, even when the gas lamps spilled onto the stones and the smell in the summer heat reeked like a barstool, because when Sofia stood on the street and looked down the road, every cobbled stone echoed peoples' rhythms, fast or slow, hard or soft, rushed or controlled, and a passion fruit tree would only add shade and the crinkle of leaves, in the wind or underfoot, to the sounds of her life. But a tree could never grow here, on the roof or down below, but how could she tell Valentina, who had made up her mind? Valentina, who didn't want roses? Who dripped passion fruit juice down her chin whenever she ate a slice? Who, when Sofia would try to clean off her messy chin, would squirm and scream, "I'm saving it for later!"

"We could plant white roses. Like you. My beautiful rose petal."

Valentina scrunched her nose. "Rose petal?"

"Soft and sweet." Sofia picked her white rose and breathed her in. Soft and sweet. She preferred white roses to red ones. The breeze shook her petal away. "A tree will not work here, darling."

"There cannot be a garden without trees. Eden had trees."

"Eden had snakes too. Do you want snakes in your garden?"

Valentina only used what she learned in Sunday school classes to get what she wanted. If God gave it to someone else, why couldn't Valentina's parents give it to her? Mother is the name of God in the hearts of children, and it was hard not to tell Valentina that there was a difference between God and her parents. She was almost old enough to know.

"I want to dig my hands into dirt and grow life. Like papa grows life."

"Not in your new dress."

Valentina took off her hat and looked at it. Lips puffed. Fingers stroked the ridge. "I will need a new hat."

"You want to grow cattle on the roof?"

"I do not want cows. I want a garden. Like Eden."

"You want a world, like Eden."

"The world is not a garden."

Sofia put Valentina's hat back on her head, brought her close to her.

"Darling, wait, and I promise the world will one day be small enough to hold in your hands. Garden or not."

The bells of Saints Peter and Paul chimed. Sofia crunched gravel beneath her feet, the empty space too much. The sky blocked the view of the sea. The city kept moving, all without her.

She felt the volcano ready to burst from deep inside her.

She had screamed one million times before, to let out the past, to see if the sky would open up and accept her voice as a sacrifice, as she burned her throat with fire. As she burned her eyes with tears. As her voice burned her ears until they blistered. Sofia felt her world bubble from her toes, the pressure almost ripping her from the roof, tearing her life from her body piece by piece until her skin ripped from her bones. The world will be easier to hold in my hands when it's turned to dust.

The scream caught in her throat. The sound turned to ash. Ash fell from her mouth and covered her feet. It fell all around her, ready to turn her into a mountaintop, the volcano inside her dried up, ready for extinction. The world felt extinct beyond the bay she couldn't see, a world she hadn't felt a part of since the plane descended into the clouds of San Francisco. And she was ready for the world to turn to ash and blow away. The petals fell to the gravel, and Sofia wanted to dig into the roof and let a flower bloom.

The church bells covered the sky. The petals tumbled across the roof and off the side.

It took Sofia a few days to find the proper pots, long and narrow, which could line the empty spaces and bloom Eden. It took her a few days more to figure out how to get the pots up the stairs and onto the roof. She tried to carry the first pot herself, but it was easier to pay a few men with some pizza and beer, some men she knew she had never seen before. Men she would never see again. She wanted to escape the cupboard she was in, where she could watch new life blossom. And the men brought up the pots that filled the empty spaces with a life Sofia wanted to cultivate; the pots extended across the rooftop like a forest without foliage, full of dirt, ready to thrive.

Sofia dug her hands into a pot and let the wet soil fold around her fingers. She filled the dirt with tomatoes and radishes, mint and basil, carrots and beets. But in one pot, close to the edge—where the petals had tumbled over—Sofia planted a rosebush, a white one, and waited for the blossoms and the thorns.

Chapter 9

Peter had the tin box open in his cardboard box of an apartment. The wind blew hard against the window. The frame rattled in the tight space. Stamps covered the box from around the world: Pisa, Barcelona, New York, Krakow, Delhi, Sydney, parading across the lid, carried by the strength of the tin and the weight of the box's contents. The Golden Gate Bridge didn't decorate the lid. The fog always muddled the red of the structure anyway, Peter thought.

Peter's father had given him the box when it was filled with love letters and a pocket watch for his mother, sent from Peru—with love. The letters always said with love, not just in the text, but written over the stamps, in bold. It was so she knew I kissed the note before I sent it, his father had said.

Peter unlatched his watches. His mother had bought them all for him when he was young. Your dad bought you a bear, she had told him, he is for protection, but I bought you something better, and she opened the tin box she had lined with SWATCH watches, enough to last two lifetimes. She rubbed her hands through his hair, I bought you time, all the time you could ever need, and she closed the box and placed it under Peter's bed, where the monsters hid. It was the first time he ever thought to put the box somewhere hidden, and when the monsters were gone, the ghosts moved in.

Peter guided his fingers through the box. The texture of each watch differed in the way the bands felt, how the glass had broken or splintered, whether the hands had fallen off over time or stayed on the face to act as decoration only. The years were painted on the watchstraps. The memories built into their notches. Peter mistook a knock on the door for the rattling window. The knock came harder and harder, verging on frantic.

"Peter?" Sofia's voice was soft, as if she feared someone else might hear. He opened the door.

"I thought it was the wind," Peter said.

"I know that problem too," Sofia said. Sofia stood in the doorway. She looked afraid to enter Peter's apartment. He had always gone to her place. She had never seen his, even though it was across the hall. Sometimes the shortest distances can feel the farthest away; the Redwoods were only an hour from the city, yet Peter still hadn't gone to see them, neither had Sofia, he knew.

"Come in," Peter said. He stepped closer to his bed and attempted to clear away the watches. He bunched them into a pile and placed them back in the box underneath the stamps written with love that he hadn't the heart to read again. How often had he thought of leaving the box by the trash, ready to be rid of the stamps, the letters, the watches, or doing as Sofia had tried with letters and burning them one-by-one. He had even tried to bury the box in the sand on the narrow shore of North Beach; he had convinced himself his mom would have wanted it that way, to have a part of her blend into a part of the city—but he couldn't do it.

"I feel a storm is coming," Sofia said.

"Sorry it's such a mess in here," Peter said.

"The wind is strong. I worry it will get stronger."

"And tear down the house made of sticks," Peter mumbled.

"Pardon me?" Sofia said. She sat down on the chair by Peter's desk. He was suddenly aware of the lack of seats in his apartment. Peter offered Sofia the bed.

"A lady does not sit on a gentleman's bed."

"Is that what I am?" Peter said.

"It wouldn't change if you were a scoundrel," she said. "Maybe I should not have come in at all." Sofia glanced at the box. "So many places. Have you called them all home?"

"I don't think I've called any of them home. At least not for long."

"Home has a special feeling," Sofia said. "There are not many places that have that feeling for everyone."

Peter sat on the bed and guarded the box. "Some people feel that way about everywhere they go."

"Is that how you feel?" Sofia said.

At the bottom of the box sat Peter's ticket to Nepal. He would have to redeem it soon if he would redeem it at all. His bed sank beneath the weight of the ticket, the watches, himself, the home he tried to recreate. The last time Peter felt at home, he had stood on the hillside overlooking the poppy field overrun with mud. The rains had swept in from the sea and flooded the remains of his childhood, the home that his mother had brought him to, where the horizon was a forever to which he could touch his painted hands and almost reach the sun.

The water rose in the valley below, in the tumult of rain, when water bombed from the sky and rose from the dirt, when water swallowed the stems and the petals until the orange turned black and smothered the golden glow, and the water buried the dying earth. Peter couldn't save the poppies two-by-two, pack them into his tin-box and save his world; each splash of rain was one step closer to the flood. He had no petals to drain the color from and no way to paint his hands, press them against the wall of the horizon and freeze the field forever. The field became another supposed forever gone forever. The dark sky shouted over Peter's head with thunder and lightning bolts, as the sea captured the memories of his childhood and drowned them.

The wind pounded against the walls of his apartment. Sofia drifted away in her far-off stare. For the moment, Peter knew, she floated far beyond the borders of San Francisco. Peter wondered where her mind took her. He rubbed his wrist, the watches, and tried not to fall back into the poppy field. Sofia's eyes focused, and she looked back at Peter.

"Is everything okay?" Peter said.

"Of course," she said. "Sometimes the wind…" her voice trailed off, overtaken by the rattle of the windows. She took a deep breath and exhaled.

"I'll huff, and I'll puff," Peter said. He rubbed his fingers over the stamps on his box.

"The wolf?" Sofia said.

"You know the story?" Peter said.

"Los Tres Cerditos," Sofia said. She twirled the chain of her locket around her fingers. "I would tell the story to my daughter. She always laughed when the wolf tried to blow down the house made of bricks." The wind howled, and the building rumbled.

"Sometimes, I think this building is made of twigs," Peter said.

"What is in the box?" Sofia said. "Other than your homes."

Sofia's gaze was forgiving and curious. He had wanted to know where her thoughts took her, but now her curiosity brought her to his memories, his past, and he wanted to share. He needed to explain. He felt ready to let Sofia into the world living inside the box he carried around with him. He wanted to paint a picture of his father from the letters his father had sent: a man with a backpack and torn shoes, waves of brown in his hair and mud stains on his shins, with his thumb out and a world to explore. Peter could almost remember a time when he sat on his father's lap in a dune buggy and flew over sand dunes, raced along the shoreline, and ate sandwiches that had sand in them. Peter wanted to tell Sofia about his mother and the watches and how when he looked over the bay, he swore he saw a shadow of his mother and his teddy bear in a tub, her fingers trailing in the water, splitting the sea.

But he instead said, "Nothing. Garbage, really." He looked to the shabby carpet, ashamed of the ghosts he couldn't hide from, ashamed of the woman he couldn't tell the truth to.

"You can fit a lot of nothing in a box like that. But not much garbage."

"I used to have dreams about the wolf," Peter said. "He always seemed to be around."

"Maybe it is the wind," Sofia said. "It is hard to make it go away. For me, I—I think it is time to go. Thank you for letting me...sit." Sofia took another look around the room. "Next time, we will have a drink in my home."

"I look forward to it."

"Perhaps there will be empanadas," she said. She gave a gentle smile as she walked to the door.

When Peter stood from the bed, the box tipped over and fell open. The watches spilled over his bed once more. If Sofia noticed, she didn't say a word. The ashen watch with flecks of mud sat atop the pile of broken timepieces. When Sofia closed the door, the room shook.

And Peter was sucked back to the rooftop of the house in the suburbs at the moment he thought he could fly. Brown tilted tiles framed the home with blue skies and brown grass, black asphalt with few cars, gray sidewalks with few users. When his mother lay on the couch full of booze and cigarettes, Claus told Peter to fly, and Peter thought he could. With feathers wrapped around his arms and wrists, because feathers made birds fly, where the wind would bounce off the feathers' ridges and push him into the air. Claus was there to tell Peter the truth of the wind, the truth they both knew, that it was against them—tried to hold them down, press them deeper into the earth or push them farther from the huff and puff of the source. Because the Wolf made the wind.

The three pigs were too little and too stupid to build their homes out of anything better than twigs. The Wolf knew that Claus and Peter were too smart to build their home of twigs and too stubborn to let the wind push them back into the ground where the worms hid and the rocks grew because Peter and Claus were not worms and were tougher than rocks, and would push beyond the wind if that's what it took to show the Wolf that there was more to the world than fallen homes and decomposing bodies.

The sloping roof was perfect, allowing for a quicker start. Peter could swoop towards the brown grass and arch his body up, the same as the birds do every day when they see the worms loose in the mud and helpless.

Because Peter and Claus were the birds. The Wolf was the worm.

The quill of the feathers dug into Peter's skin. The Wolf tormented Peter's mother and Peter and Claus, with the constant breeze that rushed through their yard and the street and the town, that pushed over telephone poles, that broke light posts and street lights, that pulled off roof shingles and uprooted trees, but not for much longer.

The sun was cold and distant. Peter stood ready to push the wind away and have it brush past his wings and over his feathers, away from the Wolf forever. The only way out was to push through, to reach down into the Wolf's throat and pull out his lungs. That's what Claus said. That's what Peter agreed to.

Peter jumped, and the wind lifted him into the sky towards the sun. Peter feared flying too close to the sun where the heat could force its way into his wings and melt the glue, but his wings would not melt on a cold day with the sun present but far away. The walls of the sky vibrated around him in the open air as he drifted up and flapped his arms.

Claus's instructions: dip down before the wind picks you back up, angle into the sun to keep hidden from the Wolf, or our plan will fail. The wind would push harder until the windows cracked and pulsed and broke and shattered. A shattered window was a nightmare that could cut Peter a million ways into a million pieces.

The clouds rolled into the sky and covered the heat and the shine. The world went gray. Peter never made it to the sun. The wind swelled shut when it began to rain, and Peter's wings went thick with wet, dripped over his arms, and forced him onto the ground, under the leaves and into the roots and the mud. It could have been worse, Claus had said, no broken bones or ripped-out stuffing. But Peter wasn't made of stuffing.

The wet wings bound Peter's body. The cocoon sheltered him from the rain as he walked back to the house where he knew his mother—inside of the tattered walls and the fragile windows—waited asleep. Not asleep but unconscious. Not unconscious but unknowing.

Peter picked up Claus and wrapped him inside the cocoon where they could stay warm as they dried. Claus wrapped his paws around Peter's neck, and Peter wrapped his wings around them both, the cut on his cheek fresh and not yet ready to scab over. He opened the door and felt the house asleep.

The lights flickered in his apartment. The hands of the watches slept for good on the cracked faces, dried up and empty except for the remnants of Claus and the house asleep inside the cracked windows of the city where the sun never shined. Peter ran his fingers over the glass and felt the bumps of the broken—from the inside.

Peter imagined the ports and landmarks his father had seen. He wondered where his mother and Claus floated to now. What far-off places did they visit—a far-off place they called home, a place Peter did not know of anywhere or was aware of anywhere—which had postcards that could appear at his door or under the door. Postcards that seeped through the cracks of Peter's life and into his apartment at a time when the world was small enough to wrap in wet wings and cover the pain with love.

The cold rushed in through the cracks in the window and spread to the far corners of the room. Peter threw the watch on the bed. It bounced. And he wrapped himself in his arms and wished he had wings. And wished he had fur. And wished he could charge after Sofia and ask her to read him the story of the *Three Little Pigs*. And he could laugh at the Wolf when he tried to blow down the house made of bricks. But instead, he listened to the wind and wished for his bed to open like the door had, where he once felt his house asleep.

Chapter 10

The slab of VB hit the table with a crash. Tony's kitchen was the smallest room in his flat.

Slab. Peter liked how the word sounded, the seduction of the "sl," the length of the "a," when all it meant was a twenty-four pack of beer. His friends opened the box and grabbed the bottles.

"Long day, mate?" Tony said. Tony ran a hand through his hair. Blonde and shredded; it covered his eyes, the iconic surfer whether he surfed or not. He handed Peter a beer.

"No longer than usual," Peter said. He opened the beer. Peter had never much cared for American beer. Every Australian he met talked about how horrid it was. But Peter would sing the praises of American beer over the tart piss-water that was Victoria Bitter. It was palatable because he drank it cold enough to nearly freeze. Hard to have any flavor when the beer was so cold, the sun was so hot, and the people were so friendly.

"What you get on to?" Tony asked.

"Went on a walkabout," Peter said. Walkabout. Two words he learned to string into one in Australia; a word with movement, a word with weight. I have nowhere to go. Nowhere to be. I can walk about town, walk about the street. I can walkabout the world. He didn't stay put for very long, and he was almost at the point that he couldn't remember how long he had stayed, if soon he would leave, if the world felt lighter Down Under. He couldn't touch down further away from the cities his mom froze in her art than when he reached Sydney. It was far away from the sky-top mountains, cloud-covered cities, and a sea of unpromising poppies. It was more than a walkabout. Peter was on a walkabout, a walk about his life and the life he wanted to live, the life he wanted to leave behind, the search for somewhere smaller than himself that he could fit into because he wanted to be larger than he felt. But all he found was himself—the same.

How long had it been? When the generic air of the airport swam around him, wrapped him in stale, toilet-paper-thin comfort? He had pressed his face to the window and watched the airplanes lift and land, made of metal, full of people, and graceless; the closest he had ever been to a plane, the first time he'd ever been in an airport. Snot ran down the glass in streaks, remnants of a cold, not from him but that nonetheless affected everyone, almost made him want to sneeze, like a contagious yawn. England before here and Spain before England, all mapped out in his head, the before and the after: Australia, South East Asia, India. He would stay for as long as he could. Nowhere else to be. Nowhere he wanted to be. Nowhere except for gone. When the plane lifted into the air, Peter unbuckled his belt early and watched through the window as he got the closest he had ever been to touching the sun. The sky wasn't blue but was beautiful. If he had known the sky was this endless when he was younger, he might have tried to swallow it after all.

"You take a look at the Opera House then?" Mads asked. Always with a smile. Never aggressive. Peter enjoyed her smile. It welcomed him. He liked her haircut, long bangs, but short like a pixie, like Tony's, but better.

One word. Yes. He wanted to say it. Yes. No need to elaborate. Say yes. The Opera House. Answer. One word.

"Yeah," he said.

"Isn't it amazing?" Mads asked. Tony took a sip of beer. He rolled his eyes. Had he heard this conversation before? Tony leaned against the cupboard. Mads looked at him, slapped his chest. He almost spit out his beer but kept most of it back into his mouth with his hand. She looked back to Peter, her smile sharp. It made her beautiful instead of pretty.

"Of course," he said. "As long as you don't hit me."

"Shut up," she said. "You know it's beautiful. That's why people want to see it; who doesn't want to see the Opera House?"

Peter didn't. He could have done without the sails. He could have done without the beige brick esplanade beneath them. He could have done without the arch of the Harbor Bridge in the background. It wasn't the brick or the bridge. The Opera House, its drawn sails eternal on the waterfront, one atop the other, ready to drift into the open and empty sea, the sun hot and heavy on the rest of the world. Peter had seen one too many sails caught in the sun, too many sails caught in the wind, too many sails with too much salt in his nose, too many sails cast towards the horizon with his bear, with his mom—one too many sails set and left, without him.

"You're right," he said to Mads. "Who doesn't." Peter opened another beer.

"Why Sydney?" Mads asked.

The question people asked no matter where he went, no matter how long he stayed. It came with an easy answer. Why not? Most people enjoyed the answer because, after all, why not?

"But really," Mads asked.

"I could ask you the same," he said. "Or Tony."

"Melbourne got too cold and too wet," Tony said. "I needed more swimmers, fewer penguins."

"I grew up here," Mads said.

"Doesn't mean you had to stay," Peter said. "Lots of people don't stay."

"And lots do," she said. Peter nodded, took a sip of his beer. His nose scrunched when the beer warmed and staled in his mouth.

"Why didn't you stay?" Mads asked. "Wasn't fast enough?" Too close. It felt too close. Go a different direction.

"I didn't want to get caught," he said.

Tony laughed. "Been there," he said.

Mads continued to smile. Peter reached up to the counter, didn't need to stand, grabbed the bag of crisps, and opened them. Crisps, another word he enjoyed—softer, nicer than chips. Mads and Tony reached for the crisps.

The conversation was similar to the one in London. Why London, why not? Where else have you been? Drink? Have you seen the sights? Drink? Where you off to next? Drink? It was easy enough to repeat. His whole time in London: with Hannah: To the pub? Why not. With Lora: To the club? Why not. With James: Ibiza? Why not. It was the same in Spain. Why Madrid, why not? Drink? Why Seville, why not? Drink? All the same. Easy enough to dodge. Easy enough to drink. Repeat what people were interested in. Take a drink. They didn't care about his past. Peter's time in London felt like it scrambled into one long day. He saw the Crown Jewels, the Tower of London, Big Ben, the London Eye, Piccadilly Circus, but on the map of his mind, they were placed right next to one another, lined a single street in London surrounded by the pubs and the clubs he remembered better. Another drink. London was the first city he had seen outside of the States, and it was the first city that opened Peter up to forgetting or the hope of forgetting. Another drink. London, with heavy rain and dark clouds, black umbrellas, jolly accents, and starchy food that formed a brick in his stomach but tasted better than what his cousin had fed him. London started Peter's walkabout when he realized what the world could be, how far the world could take him, how far the horizon ran. Another drink. He could hide as someone new in each city because people cared about the things he had seen that they hadn't, the things he had done that they hadn't. They wanted to know about the world around them through his eyes and envy his decisions, not pity his past. And he didn't want their pity or their understanding; he wanted their company and their laughter. No sailboats. No shame. Another drink. His watches, when they asked, an American trend. But one's broke. Another story. Always another story.

"How'd you get the name Mads?" Peter asked.

"It's 'cause she's bat shit crazy," Tony said. Mads slapped his chest again.

"It's short for Madeline. Not too interesting."

"It's all interesting," Peter said. "Besides, with the way you hit Tony, maybe bat shit crazy isn't too far off." She laughed and pushed the hair from her eyes. It was always a delicate moment, a simple gesture, a sweet gesture, even when it didn't mean a thing. The sun had set over Sydney years before Peter ever arrived and now the slab was half gone. Peter, Tony, and Mads left for the bars and the cheap pizza. Mads smiled and hung onto Peter's arm. She smelled of caramel. He tasted the sour beer. He let her in just enough. Told her just enough. Asked about her. They walked away from the sails of Sydney, which drifted into the distance, where tomorrow Peter hoped the sun would rise and where his mind forgot to remember what he wanted to forget. He liked her smile. He liked her laugh. It was enough for him—for now.

Chapter 11

Sam wrapped her fingers around the metal prongs that stuck out from the mast, expecting her skin to burn, but her skin didn't burn. The sun pulsed while Sam climbed the unsteady mast.

The sails had not been set, and if she set them, perhaps they would catch a trace of a breeze, a push in some direction. While she climbed, the boat rocked back and forth.

"Where are you going?" Claus yelled.

"Up," she said.

"I can see that."

"I wasn't sure with your eye."

"I am not blind," he said.

She expected the climb to be harder. She wasn't sure why. She knew each pull strained her muscles, but she couldn't feel the pain. Her fingernails scratched against her palms, but she couldn't feel the irritation. Her wrists were weak, but she only felt them itch.

"What do you want from up there?"

"The crow's nest."

"There are no birds here."

"I want the view."

"Of what?"

Of land, or waves, or a clearer view of the silhouette she sometimes saw in the distance, or the place beyond the horizon. Sam didn't care, as long as it was somewhere other than here, a place beyond the nothing she was stuck in—inside and out. She continued her climb.

"Careful of the fish," Claus said.

"What fish?" A large carp flew by Sam's head. It fell into the water without a splash. Claus held his paws to his stomach. Laughed. He made the same snarls and grunts when he ate, a violent chortle short of breath.

"Why are you throwing fish?" Sam said.

"Why are you climbing the mast?"

"To cast the sails."

"To keep you from touching anything," Claus said.

"To get anywhere."

"We are somewhere."

"Anywhere else," Sam said.

"That takes time."

How long could a second take when seconds didn't exist, not to Sam, not in this place where nothing existed, and if nothing existed, how could time exist? Seconds couldn't pass in a place where birds didn't fly by and a breeze didn't blow past, and the sun never set, and Sam couldn't feel—

"I'm sick of Time!"

"You are sick?" Claus said.

"I am tired."

"You are sick, or you are tired?"

"I am sick and tired."

"A breeze will not make you better."

"Then I'll jump," Sam said.

"No, you will not."

She wanted to spread her arms and fly to the horizon where the sun was supposed to set, maybe she could make the sun fall, crash even, behind the wall of sky—for as long as she could remember, the sun stood still, frozen even, but she couldn't remember much.

"I won't?"

"I do not know."

"I will," she said.

"Not again."

"Again?"

"At all," Claus said.

"Again?"

"You will not."

Sam reached the top of the mast, halfway between the water and the sun. She sat on the crossbar and pulled herself close to the tip of the mast. The sun was a light bulb; she searched for the switch in the sky but found nothing. There was no reprieve from the light, from the water. There was no horizon. There was an ocean for infinity—beyond where the eye could see because as far as Sam could tell, she saw it all. The water surrounded the tub, and the vast emptiness absorbed her. She had nowhere to go. Nowhere but down. The light spread over the dark water, covered the surface rather than piercing deeper and illuminating the darkness below, the lone darkness, beneath the tub, in a different world she couldn't see.

The sky was blank. The water was forever. She heard silence. The tub went nowhere.

"There is not much you can do from up there," Claus said.

"It's about the same as I can do from down there," she said.

The water was dark and perfect. On another day, maybe, that wasn't here, maybe, she would have appreciated the view, maybe, with someone else, someone not Claus—maybe.

Sam stared into the sky, deeper into the sun, ready to challenge the light to a staring contest, a game of iridescent chicken. She hoped the sun would blink first. At least it would be a change. The closer she came to the sun's eye, the better the chance she had of winning.

A string dangled near the end of the crossbar, hanging from the sky. Sam couldn't understand how she hadn't seen it before.

"I found it!" she called to Claus.

"Nein, you did not," he said.

"You don't even know what I found."

"I know you did not find anything, so you could not have found it."

Sam got to her knees and wrapped her hands around the crossbar, ready to crawl to the edge.

"The light switch." She pointed to the sky. "Trust me."

"You should come back down."

"I will when I shut off the sun."

"It will not work. The sun. It cannot be shut off."

Sam crawled towards the edge of the crossbar. She felt every sway of the tub. Her heart should have been on fire, her veins full of blood, but she felt neither and thought she must be calm. She reached the end and stretched her arm to the string.

"I almost have it."

"There is nothing to have."

The string brushed against Sam's fingertips, almost—out of reach. She could reach if she stood, the water calm below. She could do it; she wanted to; she needed a change, the hope of a future, the memories of a past. The boat swayed, and her hands shook as she got to her feet, continuing to hold the crossbar. Her body should have ached. She should have been tired. Her wrists itched—that was all.

The sun stared down at her; ready to lose, she thought. She released the crossbar. The boat swayed. The water still. Claus watched. Sam reached. Outstretched. The string in her palm. The rough string. The bright sun. Sam pulled. The string broke. The sun shined. The boat swayed. Sam balanced. Claus yelled. Sam unbalanced, arms out, string in hand, water still. She smiled when she fell, felt the breeze, falling. Falling. And hit the water with no splash.

Chapter 12

The door closed and echoed through the Saints Peter and Paul church, a sound from which Sofia wished she could escape, but surrounded her instead, enclosed in a box and uncomfortable, ready to be buried in darkness. Still, sunlight shined through the stained glass, sequential stories that lined the wall, began at the door, right of the entrance with the last story at the altar: Jesus and the Apostles, Jesus with a fish, Jesus with a leper, Jesus in heaven. The glass reached into the sky of the church and opened the dark box Sofia couldn't move in. Each window radiated color like a glass painting on a billboard, shouting, *Look at the Great Christ!*

She expected the aroma of frankincense, the delicate black licorice of myrrh that once emanated from the burning incense, coupled with the smell of wax from the flickering candles. Instead, she couldn't escape the scent of dough clinging to her fingers, her clothes, and the soft specks of flour she wiped away from her upper lip. She had spent the early hours of the morning preparing dough for empanadas. It needed time to rest. The radio couldn't muffle the sound of the expanding dough. Sofia spent minutes staring at the letter stuffed beneath the matted gray surface of Coit Tower on her refrigerator. The vibration of the dough grew deafening beneath Sofia's ignorance of who these empanadas would feed. Sofia couldn't count the years since she last stepped into a church. Her mother took her often when Sofia was young. Her mother always stared at the glass stories—and Sofia always stared at the stories too, which were drawn by windows and told by sunlight. When Sofia's mother had died, Sofia left Valentina with a nanny the day of the funeral. She didn't want her child to be around death and sadness; Valentina had only been a baby. Now churches reminded Sofia too much of what life had taken away, and the prayers never answered. All the churches looked the same, all the colors muddled, all the ethereal air smothered. When Valentina disappeared, Sofia walked into a church once more, for the first time since her mother had died. Sofia couldn't have counted the days since last she attended mass, but she couldn't escape the climbing number of days since she had last seen her daughter.

Fifty-seven days, twelve hours, thirteen minutes since Philippe told her about Valentina.

The church was empty except for Sofia—for her and God, above the altar, a constant reminder He died for our sins—her sins, the sins she didn't know about, wasn't sure about, the sins she searched her life to remember so she could repent for them, find the redemption she needed or wanted so she could look God in the eye and not feel so useless.

His eyes, blue like the sky but deeper than the sky, as if the entire sky were made of His eyes so that when she looked up, it wasn't space she saw between earth and the moon but God. The harder she looked, the further she could see into His past to where the darkness took over, where only shreds of light filled the void of the lives He had taken, whether through flood or famine or that one time it rained sulfur. Now night had gotten darker with fewer stars to see, less light from God in the deep black, more light from buildings and streets, cars and homes—her home, where Valentina should have been, not sucked into the depth of God's merciless eyes because Sofia couldn't find the awful sin she had committed that took her baby away. All signs of life faded into the dark of the night sky. The answerless question ate at her lips like decay: Why am I being punished? No answers came from the light or the dark, no reassurance of hope to hold onto.

When she was young, people stood in line at mass to drink the blood of Christ, invoke the Father: in nomine Patris—absorb His body: et Filii—and sit down forgiven, justified: et Spiritus Sancti—because He was infallible, all-knowing, in the crowd's eyes, had all the answers, in the crowd's eyes—the unshaken church-goers that looked into God's eyes and didn't see darkness, didn't see a flood or pillars of salt; they saw sorrowful eyes, imploring eyes, come sit, hopeful eyes, pray, repent, I forgive eyes. In Those eyes, Sofia saw how deep emptiness could go.

Fifty-seven days, thirty-one hours and six minutes...since she heard Valentina's laugh. How Sofia wished she had made Valentina laugh then. How she still wished it now.

The stained glass flickered in the sun. The warmth didn't reach Sofia, only the fading light. She was forced to come to church as a child; she had no choice. The same obligation she placed on Valentina. This was more Gaston's wish. There was a part of Sofia that wanted what she and her mother had, a moment alone with each other. Now Sofia was back in the absence of her mother—her daughter, with the same Christ from childhood above the altar, the eternal Christ that her mother used to ignore as she watched the stories on the wall and the lines of the penitent loomed long.

Sofia would run up and down the aisles, again and again, while her mother was lost in the light of the glass. The light would shine through the colors and move the stories like a flipbook when Sofia ran to the altar from the doorway. One day the squeak in her shoes softened, the wind in her hair stopped. The glass flipped through biblical history where Sofia watched the geometric shapes of the cross while the sun pierced the glass clouds and projected the crucifixion onto the floor, where Sofia no longer watched the glass but the ground.

Glass people flickered blood-orange like a kaleidoscope. With every flick of light, the people rose from the tiles, twisted to a deeper glow that filled the depths of the church. Her mother didn't notice. With disjointed movements, the crystal crowd stood before the cross and reached to touch Jesus' feet, catch the glass blood that dripped for them as if He were the source of warmth in the cold, their cheeks flushed, glass tears, stained hands, without sound, myrrh in Sofia's nose, cartoon's running through her head.

A voice murmured softly in her ear, a voice she assumed would be powerful, thunderous, but instead was a meek whisper.

Through the quiet call of an awkward angelic sound, she thought, *I am what I am, or heard*, or hummed in her head. She wanted to laugh. She wanted to skip up and down the aisle, repeating the words she heard in the church.

Kaleidoscope Jesus stood in front of her with a glass of wine. He reached out to her, ignored the glass crowd around Him that wanted to touch Him, praise Him; He offered Sofia wine, the blood of Christ for her in the twisted light of the stained-glass story, her hair in curls, barely tall enough to reach his waist, too short to reach the glass if she wanted to. Still, she looked into His eternal eyes and refused the wine, tormented by the darkness beyond the light in His eyes, as if she could have seen the absence of stars in her future.

"Time to go," her mother said.

The glass flipped into the walls. The sunshine lessened, and the darkness crept back into the hall. Her mother grabbed her hand; it was colder than the church. Sofia felt His eyes follow her—from the storybook windows, from the altar cross, from the darkness, from the sky.

Now, without her mother, Sofia stood at the glass, full of the same stories but with less light shining through. Laughing again to herself as the janitor whistled the Popeye theme song. *I am what I am.*

It was the first smile she had felt since Valentina—how part of her wanted to fight it, how it crept onto her lips like a burglar in an attempt to steal her grief. How would her mother have handled the fifty-seven days? With tears? With prayers? With fists and screams? With forgetting? It wasn't easy to forget. Sofia wouldn't want to forget, even if it were easy. She once had hope. Is that what her mother would have had—hope? Her mother hadn't prayed often, not that Sofia could remember. She couldn't remember any of her mother's prayers or if she had any at all. Her mother always seemed happy; the arguments between Sofia's parents were silent or behind closed doors. If she hadn't been happy, she was content, except when she came to church to look at the glass, lost in a world of stained stories, praying for a different life or hoping for a better one, for the son her parents never had, or for the sister Sofia never had. But when her mother wrapped Sofia in her arms, Sofia felt the same as when she wrapped Valentina in her arms—complete.

Sofia rubbed her arms: empty. The glass began to flicker, and Crystal Jesus came down and put His hand out to touch her, to comfort her. She refused Him. She didn't want Him. He shimmered and twitched in the dull light. Even God needs the light. Then a face, Valentina's face, stained with a careless smile, with a silent laugh, rosy glass and sparkling. Sofia tried to touch Valentina, to hold Valentina, join her with the stained glass. The sound of the door echoed through the church, scared away the Son, disappeared Valentina's face, left Sofia alone.

Fifty-seven days, twenty-one hours, nine minutes. How long since she had seen Valentina? In person—able to touch her, to see how the corners of her eyes creased when she screamed, how she squinted slightly, how Sofia could smell her daughter on her skin still—sweet like a white rose—in this church where her mother once was, where Valentina's face just was, where the glass history is, where the janitor's whistle faded.

Twenty-five years since Valentina disappeared, and Sofia hadn't brought herself to enter a church since Buenos Aires. The glass that encased hope had shattered long ago. The bells chimed with the time. The dough would have risen by now. She could practically hear the echo of the bubbling yeast underneath the harsh crash of her footsteps in the church. The dough could have expanded to fill her entire apartment and creep through the cracks beneath her door to spread across the building, feeding on the city like an insatiable blob—a story absent from the bright glow of the windows, like the story of her and Gaston, their failed life together, or the missing life of Valentina.

Sofia practically ran from the nave of Saints Peter and Paul Church. The steps didn't bother her. She didn't notice the cold afternoon or the rambling crowds of North Beach. Steam drifted out of Mario's Bohemian Cigar Café across the square. Sofia ran through the shadows cast by the steeple. The bells had stopped pealing. The light started to die.

Chapter 13

The strong wind pushed the fog into the city but not out. Trees shook from their branches, empty of leaves, and swung their trunks; the leaves jerked into the air until taken by the fog.

Peter sat in a nearly empty café close to work but felt cramped as he stared out the window holding a cup of crappy coffee. An old man coughed. The gravelly mucus broke in his lungs. He wore plaid and read the paper with a magnifying glass. What kept him from glasses? Pride, stubbornness, health insurance? The man calculated the spread of his cream cheese on his bagel. Tongue thoughtful between his lips. His hands shook, but not when he held the knife. The scrape of the bagel sounded like the man's cough. The man took a bite. The crunch resounded over the low hum of classical music. He chewed slow—the way Peter's father might have chewed. He had cream cheese on his upper lip. It stayed there. He took another bite. He looked happy in his plaid shirt and tennis shoes. He was alone. Peter could be happy like that, situated, seasoned, practiced, comfortable—alone.

There was a knock at the window; Carly waved. He waved back. She pointed inside. He said, "Come in." She wore a beanie, black like her hair. She lit up the fog. The wind didn't bother her. He stood to greet her. He smelled plums in her hair. They sat.

"Why haven't you called?" she asked. She kept her beanie on, along with her coat, faded and rosy.

"I did," Peter said. He looked at her like he could see inside of her because that was what he wanted, to be able to look into her eyes and see all the details of her life, her dreams—past and present—to run away with the circus as a tightrope walker, to holiday in sunk beneath the sand in the clear blue water, resting near the trees with the monkey's howling in the background. Her secrets—big and small—deep and superficial—her family's war criminal past, or that she bites her toenails and saves them in a glass next to her cookie jar. He wanted to look at her the way he thought she looked at him, but eyes were a window to nothing. But her eyes were the color of the sky, and he hoped he hadn't missed his chance to swallow the sky.

"Why didn't you leave a message?" she asked. She didn't look away, not like on their date. If it could be called a date. Did breakfast count? She stayed and ate. He had paid. He got her number. That counted. To Peter, at least. If that didn't count, then he had never been on a date. He never took a girl bowling, or to a skating rink, a movie, or on vacation. Breakfast was the closest he had come to a date. It counted.

"I did," he said. The old man ate the second half of his bagel, the cream cheese still on his face.

"Why didn't I get it?" she asked. She had seemed happy when she came into the café; now, confusion replaced joy.

"I called the number you gave me." He had called; he had left a message.

"You couldn't have," she said. "I would have gotten something. Wouldn't I?" She creased her eyebrows. He told her the number. He had memorized it by accident in the time he had sat with the napkin in his hands full of the doubts of whether or not he should call. The doubts filled his head and his apartment until he waded through the doubts and picked up the phone. She blushed.

"I'm going to get a coffee. Would you like one?" she said.

Peter shook his head. He sipped his coffee. There was some heat left. He didn't like when she walked away, the distance, for a brief minute that stretched too long.

He had seen too many backs in his life or imagined the backs that he hadn't seen of the people who were now gone and the people he had shown his back to. He was tired of everyone leaving. Himself included.

The bagel crunched. The man chewed. His throat twitched when he swallowed. He raised a napkin to his face and wiped the cream cheese from his mouth.

Carly sat back down. "I'm sorry," she said. "I can't believe I gave you the wrong number." She looked at her coffee cup.

"Someone's going to be creeped out," he said. "Wonder how I got their number. And why I left a message."

"You leave creepy messages?" she asked.

"No more creepy than me, so, yes?"

Carly's palms wrapped around her cup, fingers intertwined. She stared at the steam as it escaped from the hole in the lid. He wanted to wrap his hands around hers. He wanted to lean in and kiss her—her cheek, her lips, her neck, press his lips to her ear and whisper sweet words like his father had done to his mother, like his father must have done, while his mom laughed because his dad's beard tickled her neck, soft breath on her skin, lips almost dipped into her ear, and whispered nothing sweetly.

"I'm glad I ran into you," she said. "Maybe I'm stalking you." She smiled and looked up from her coffee. It was a delicate balance, how much of her stare he could take without blushing, how long he could stare at her without the need to look away, because some part of him wanted to stare at her until he went blind, like the sun, too bright to look at forever, but he couldn't stop, didn't want to stop; Peter wanted to memorize every eyelash and spark in Carly's eyes, every strand of hair that fell over her face, like Sofia said she had done with Gaston, not on purpose, she said, it happened over time. Peter could spend his life waking up with Carly next to him, or spend his life with his eyes closed, painting Carly on the back of his eyelids, as his mother had painted his father—into forever—except Peter didn't want forever to come so fast this time.

"A good stalker always gets there first," he said.

"So you're stalking me?" she asked. Peter liked the way she tilted her head when she asked.

"Of course not," he said. "But purple and brown wallpaper? Risky." She slapped his hand and laughed. He laughed too. He wanted her to touch his hand again, to touch his hand and hold onto it.

The old man stood up and dropped his magnifying glass. Peter waited to hear it shatter. Nothing. The man picked up his things as slowly as he had chewed his bagel, stuffed them into his brown satchel, and shuffled out the door. The old man was almost lifted by the wind and dragged out to sea. But the wind stopped, and the man was taken by the fog.

"Let's go for a walk," she said. "It's stuffy in here."

"You'd be more comfortable without the coat," Peter said.

"I'll get you filled up, and we can walk about," she said. "My way of apologizing for giving you the wrong number."

Did she know what walkabout meant, the journey, the search, the rite of passage? How often they came for him, these ceremonies, and how he made them as often as possible, staying one step ahead of the flood that never stopped coming, always one step ahead, always moving. This could be the start of a different journey, their journey together, the first step—together, where they could find each other. Peter sipped his coffee; it had gotten cold.

"Let's go for a walk," he said. "But first, I get my coffee." She took his cup to the counter, and they left the café.

The fog hung over the streets like concrete. Peter was happy to have a hot cup of coffee and to be with Carly. Fairy lights decorated the streets, strung over buildings, hung across streets, which helped brighten the gray afternoon.

Carly stopped at a corner to admire a pile of broken tables. Tabletops cracked like jagged rocks, legs split in half or crumpled, black and white and blue tables with the paint scratched and scraped away, piled on top of one another, hanging onto one another, off of one another, a house of cards on a windy fault line, piled up and falling over, under the tiny, twinkling lights that made the fog glow.

"Do you have a pen?" she said. She scanned the pile of tables. "It looks like a volcano. Or a butterfly."

Peter searched his body. He knew he didn't have a pen.

"A butterfly volcano," he said. "I don't have a pen. Broken tables?"

"Of course," she said. "They're beautiful. Look at them from another direction. They transform." Carly circled the tables, looked at the fractured shadows, stepped into the street to see the pile from a distance.

Eternal tables, stacked up and around one another. A family dinner, Peter thought. A feast, the type of feast he never had, that his father may have had on one of his adventures, or that his parents would have had to celebrate each other or to pretend they had the lives they wanted, tables topped with food from everywhere. Every time you turned around, a new table, a new culture, burgers to tacos, Indian to Moroccan. Peter stepped up to the seafood table in his mind, and the fairy lights burst and shattered and rained around him.

Carly's body slowed, her finger raised to touch a broken leg, her body leaned close to the tables, the viscera of the broken art and the shower of light trickled over them frozen in mid-air. Peter wanted to step in close to her, frozen in time, lean into her thoughts, to wrap her arms around his and guide his fingers to paint the tables, to see how she saw these cornered broken tables as an erupting butterfly, to show her he saw butterflies in the sky of her eyes, which burst in the light, while black strands of hair dangled around her eyes and looked like night sneaking in over the blue. Peter could count the freckles on her cheeks on one hand—and he did, four—and this was how he wanted to see her, always, a statue with sky in her eyes, and him, closer to heaven now than when on a mountaintop. He wanted to open a window into her mind and freeze an image of himself there, where she would always see him, want him, remember him.

Her finger began to wiggle, and her body began to move, and the lights receded into their bulbs. Carly moved around the tables until she had exhausted every angle. The hand on one of Peter's watches stopped still, the glass disintegrated.

"You're not going to take anything with you?" Peter said. He thought she'd at least take a photo or part of the volcano. They walked. "You don't want me to take them for you?" It was hard to look at a person when walking. Carly watched the sidewalk.

"It wouldn't be the same elsewhere," she said. "I try not to touch broken things." Peter wanted to take her hand, but she shoved it into her pocket, safe from the outside world as if she knew how broken he was. If she only knew.

"What would you rather do?" Peter said, "break or fix. For your art, I mean." They continued to walk. Peter thought his words had been left behind and hoped she caught them before they were too far away.

"Create," she said.

"So, fix," he said. "That's the same thing, isn't it?" She stopped. Looked at Peter. There was no way to lose words if you weren't walking away from them.

"Not always," she said. She started to walk, didn't wait for Peter. People crowded the sidewalk until compacted, ants shoving in all directions while wearing suits and trench coats, parkas, and tweeds, all trying to get away. And him. He wanted to catch Carly, not watch the distance grow between them.

"I didn't realize you fell behind."

"I didn't realize we were in a race," he said. "We don't have anywhere to go."

"It's a fast road to nowhere," she said. "I always try to get there first."

"I've been to nowhere," he said. "I'd rather stay here."

"And what was nowhere like?"

"Wasn't much to see, really. But I don't remember getting there this fast."

"Maybe we can go together sometime." Carly grabbed his hand. "If I slow down some."

Her hand was warm on his hand. Her skin was soft on his skin. He felt like he could smell her sweetness through her touch. As if a familiar tattoo had formed over his heart, and she took its advice—try me. He walked a little slower. He wanted the road to nowhere to be the slowest road in history, for each step to take years, as long as she held his hand, because somehow, in her hands, he felt a little less broken, and it was the most complete he had felt in a long time.

"The company's not the greatest there. Why go at all?"

"You had company last time?" she said.

"My dad." He rubbed his cheek. His coffee got colder.

"He wasn't good company?"

"Not after he died." Peter tried to make it sound like a joke. As if it could make them laugh. Nobody laughed. Even Peter didn't find it funny. It felt better to talk about his father when he moved, when he left the words behind him. Carly squeezed Peter's hand tighter. A little less broken.

"I'm sorry," she said. She looked at him while they walked and somehow avoided the traffic.

"You didn't hit him with the car," he said. A quiet second—through the people, car horns, trolley cars. "Sorry." Peter couldn't avoid the crowd.

"I like it," she said.

He wanted to tell her about his past; he wanted to tell her about what really brought him to San Francisco. He wanted so much.

"And your mom?"

"At sea." He lied. To her, or to himself? He knew where his mom was and where she wasn't. Too hard to explain. Too much to explain. About her wrists. About her boat. About the chase. About his walkabout. About how Carly's eyes reminded him of his mother—of the sky, the sky he wanted to run to, or from; the sky he wanted to jump into and touch the sun. Maybe Carly could help him reach, through her eyes, through the space she created with stardust and sunflowers. Close enough.

"Must be hard to have your family so far away," she said.

He should tell her the truth. He should tell her what he meant. He wanted to blurt it out. I'm alone. They left me. It's a fucked-up chase, and I'm losing.

"Oceans can be temperamental," he said. Sometimes they knock on your door.

"I'm going to head home," she said.

"I can walk you."

"You're sweet. This is my real number."

"I thought you didn't have a pen," he said.

"I never said that. I asked if you had one. I don't touch broken things. Not unless I'm going to fix them." She kissed the crease of Peter's mouth, that quiet place where his lips met his cheek. Almost whole.

"Goodnight," she said. "And this time, leave a message." She walked away.

"I did leave a message."

He traced his fingers over where her lips had been. The swarm of pedestrians had calmed. Someone had left a small couch on the sidewalk corner. Peter wondered how Carly would look at this type of furniture, whether she would want to sketch it, fix it, or wonder about why the couch had been abandoned. It waited under the street sign for someone who wanted to take it home. The streets emptied, and the bars filled up. The rowdy cries of Happy Hour vibrated the city more than the foghorns blowing against the shoreline. Peter saw Sofia throwing bread to the ground in the park, with the noise of the city no longer a blanket for Peter to hide in, his lips no longer humming from Carly's kiss.

Chapter 14

The raw dough continued to stick to Sofia's fingers, with the flour working its way into the tiny creases in the wrinkles of her hands, tracing her years like a map leading to a place from which she had fought so hard to escape. She kneaded the dough hard on the counter, pressing her knuckles into the malleable texture that ebbed, flowed, dented, and never fought back. The scent of raw egg had faded beneath the earthy musk of the flour. She inhaled the deep aroma that reminded her of dying grass on the pampas in autumn, even after decades away from the open golden fields. The grass had a different scent in San Francisco, absent the herbs, spices, and life of Argentina. The grass in the city looked like weeds, sprung up between the cracks in the sidewalk or spread across the park in haphazard mounds that smelled more of rubbish than the countryside.

The radio hung thick in the haze of powder flying through the room, a fog imitating the stew of San Francisco. Every tap, pat, and slap of the dough caused another eruption of flour to burst through the kitchen, spit white dust onto Sofia's cheeks, turn the sweat into a paste on her forehead, cling to her hair, twisting the brown strands gray, teasing what time hadn't done but still could, taking away her last connection to youth. Her bones cracked as she rolled the dough onto the counter. She rolled in a rocking motion, not back and forth like a child, but with the smooth, slight bend to the left, back to the center, and over to the right. She swayed with her hips to the beat of the drums reverberating against the tin in the kitchen and the magnet of Coit Tower that bounced on the refrigerator. The letter decorated the doorway beneath the tower that had always seemed safe to her, a beacon of distant freedom and security because no one had known where to find her. Until the letter arrived at her door.

Sofia took the moisturized edge of her right hand and brushed it against the soft, flattened dough, checking for lumps or air pockets. She then coated the dough with butter on both sides. The melted butter added a fatty, delicious scent to the kitchen amidst the unending earthy fragrance of flour. The letter, the boy, the music, the candles; it had taken one night with Peter to remind her of her love of cooking after how many years searching for ways to purge her body. She had convinced herself the empanadas were never hers to share, hers to give away; she made them to nourish her soul and those of her loved ones.

But wouldn't that be selfish? She thought. Hadn't she spent too many years hiding away her love of baking from the world, and therefore keeping another labor of love from their enjoyment? Like the world deserved another tribute of love, like the world deserved another piece of Sofia as tribute.

The dough took on tiny half-moon shapes filled with sautéed mushrooms and cheese, or minced meat and olives, or sautéed apples with cinnamon and sugar, chicken and onions, steak and garlic soaked in achiote.

"I understand how you feel," Sofia said to the half-moons. "You are half-formed. Something is missing from you. And you only grow smaller with every bite. You give, and you give all of yourself to another until you are gone. Then whoever eats you moves to another empanada."

She placed the raw batch on a baking sheet and popped it in the oven. The fog of flour continued to hover over the kitchen. The perfume of browning dough from the empanadas drifted through the white cloud in the kitchen. The color of the crisp dough reminded her of Gaston's skin, the way it browned in the summer sun when he worked with the horses in the fields. He could ride for hours across the pampas and return with sun-kissed cheeks and the scent of fresh grass drizzled with dew. The browning dough aroma turned acrid. Smoke poured from the oven. The scent, the smoke, the billowing clouds of burnt air would contaminate the cookies she wanted to bake, the dulce de leche she needed to stir; the acrid reek would stick to her skin. It would take days to get rid of the burnt stink as if it seeped into her wrinkles and found a home in her bones. She had scorched the empanadas. The outer skin blackened to charcoal. Smoke continued to mix with the dense veil of flour. The letter trembled against the refrigerator as if taunting her, loud against the noise from the radio and the roar of the oven as she aired out the smoke through the window facing a brick wall. She had never burnt her empanadas before and found it a sign from a deity she no longer believed in or one of the ghosts who followed her around the city: that recipe wasn't for her to share with the greater world.

Even after twenty-five years, the smell of empanadas still bothered Sofia. And the stench of burnt dough followed her from the apartment. The cold afternoon left the grass in Washington Square wet and the soil damp. It wasn't a park but a mud pit. Her breath smoked in quick, forceful puffs. Sofia bought a focaccia from the Italian bakery and sat in Washington Square, in the shadows of the steeple.

Sofia sat on the bench and tore absently from the loaf. The bread piled at her feet, the day absent of birds, empty of dogs, but filled with enough fog for Sofia to hope it would cloud her memories because the light she had once clung to was finally gone.

Chapter 15

Peter coughed in the fog of the city. He placed his hand on Sofia's shoulder. It was the frailest she had ever felt in his hands.

"I had made a lot of meat," Sofia said. She stared down at the pile of bread near her shoes with a sliver of a focaccia loaf remaining in her hands. Moisture from the air made the pieces soggy. They could have disintegrated with a single touch of Peter's shoe.

"It looks delicious," Peter said.

"It is at home," Sofia said. "I was planning a dinner." Sofia took pride in her cooking, in the ingredients she used. Sofia didn't often stay in quiet places. And Peter had never seen her let food turn soggy.

"Earlier, I had knocked, but no one—" she shook away the statement with her hand and threw another piece of bread to the floor. Sofia had left her life in Buenos Aires behind, the life where time spent unseen could mean someone was arrested, detained, locked up—lost. That was what she once told Peter. Sofia had explained her reservations about opening her door to strangers, to anyone at all, except for him—now—and that single girl Sofia had once let use her phone. "Mail can be a very big burden." Sofia toed a piece of bread. The wet dough flattened under her foot.

Peter nodded his head. He took a seat next to Sofia.

She held the round loaf in her hands, and her arms shook. "I bought it for the birds. Sometimes they are depressed. It is very cold. Those that do not migrate can become very sad in this gray weather."

"What about the meat?" Peter said.

"That was for us," Sofia said. "You looked like you needed a meal. You are so thin, and it is very cold here."

Peter had never heard such concern from Sofia before. More often than not, she would use guilt to feed him. "It is okay if you are not hungry," she would say. "I have made this wonderful food and spent so much of the day trying to cook a meal you will enjoy. If you are not hungry, though, it will have to go to waste." Peter would then clear his plate and often go for seconds. He had never heard Sofia so candid.

"I was coming home from work," Peter said.

"Yes," Sofia said. "We have to work. We have to feed these birds." The pile of breadcrumbs grew.

It was hard to make the birds happy when Peter held onto his own happiness with his teeth. Sooner or later, his teeth would tear from his gums, and happiness would fall away.

"When you did not answer your door, I worried—" the bells returned and rattled around the fog. "I did not think you worked today."

"You made a lot of meat?" Peter said. "That is hard to pass up."

Sofia had torn and thrown half the loaf to the ground.

The fog muddled the city lights.

"We could head inside," Peter said. Sofia didn't look ready to move. Her body stuck to the park bench beneath the weight of the half-loaf of bread. The church eclipsed the dim lights. The shadow of the spires moved closer.

"Peter," Sofia said. She smiled, not the smile Peter was used to. It was forced and unnatural. "I don't know if I'm ready."

"We can stay here," Peter said. "I can grab the meat, and we can picnic on the grass. It'll be like camping. Have you ever been camping? I once hiked up Macchu Picchu. I camped the entire way. It will be fun."

Sofia tore another piece of bread and threw it to the ground. "I do not want to catch anything," she said.

"You caught me," Peter said. "And I am not easily caught." Peter tapped Sofia's knee. "What made you want to feed the birds? It couldn't have been the weather."

"Birds love to play in las nubes. We can't see them, but they play."

"You tried to lure them from the fog with breadcrumbs?"

"No seas ridiculo." Sofia spoke Spanish when she was upset. "If storks carry babies, then pigeons carry the post, and I have never liked pigeons."

"I thought that it was the guy in the short-shorts and the safari hat."

"Him too."

"Did you poison the bread?"

Sofia opened her hand and looked at Peter. "No seas ridiculo."

"I'm not sure what that means," Peter said.

"Don't be silly," Sofia said.

"Good." He reached for the breadcrumbs and stuffed them in his mouth. "I needed a bite." Sofia laughed, light and airy. She hadn't laughed like that in days. Peter had watched the shift from hidden to exposed when Sofia had felt safe enough from her past not to feel threatened by it.

"My father had carrier pigeons," she said. "He would send mail back and forth to his friends around Argentina. He said it was a habit from the war. He enjoyed it. Once to punish me, he made me clean the cages. I have hated pigeons ever since. But I always imagine them in the clouds, at play, surrounded by many other birds, all with a mission, storks with babies, magpies for play—"

"And pigeons with the post."

"Yes. Pigeons with the post."

Peter thought of a heavy wind blown through an exaltation of larks on their way to "Don Giovanni," or a dog that pounced on a murder of crows en route to a gang fight. Or pigeons in helmets and goggles flying through explosions and foxholes to deliver the mail; always an adventure.

"Do I scare the birds?"

"You couldn't scare a fly."

Sofia clenched the edges of the bread in her fists.

"I know," she said. Peter took his hand away from Sofia's shoulder; the touch of Carly's lips had faded, but he knew he wanted to feel them brush his cheek again, his lips. "I know there are no birds today. I know the crumbs are at my feet." She stared at the grass, or the crumbs, or both. Her eyes were empty, the city almost silent.

Peter had heard true silence once: when words failed, when sound failed, deep silences that swept away the entire world, when nothing, nowhere, could make a sound. He had stood on the dock and waved goodbye to his mother and Claus as they floated into nowhere or everywhere when the bright light of the sun first faded behind the fog. Peter heard that same silence now, surrounded by the endless movement of the city he once thought he could hide in. Except, in the constant bombardment of noise, Peter found a circle of silence that surrounded him and Sofia like the eye of a storm.

"You have to go to work," Sofia said. "You should go."

"I don't today. I have time off." He could put work off for a few days if he needed to, if she needed him to.

Sofia's eyes looked empty. Peter barely noticed the lights of the city flicker and shut off. Dusk settled somewhere behind the clouds.

"She left," Sofia said. "She's gone. She did not say goodbye. She disappeared. And when you did not answer your door—"

She disappeared. It was never about Peter. Or maybe it had been once. Maybe it still was, somewhere deep down, but Peter hadn't disappeared. Valentina had gone without a trace. A face on Sofia's list of disappeared—faces taken away from her—by choice, their own choice, or by the choice of God. The same God that

Peter's mother prayed to? That took his mother. The same God that Sofia prayed to? That took Sofia's child. That created the world? That took the world away. That rested on the seventh day. How could God take so many and still have time to rest? Peter hadn't had a chance to rest since he watched his mother sail away. He had been running ever since.

Peter sat on the bench with Sofia; the park was empty of people, empty of life, empty of sound. He pulled Sofia into his arms. He could never leave her like that. He could never leave her. Not now, not after this.

"I'll never do that to you," he said. It was a promise he had never made before. It was a promise he wanted to keep.

Sofia pressed her head to his chest. She smelled like sweet wine. Peter held her close. She didn't make a sound. He didn't make a sound. He couldn't.

The streetlamps stood around the park useless. The birds stayed away from the breadcrumbs. He remembered the letter he had placed on the radio.

"Did you read the…" Peter's voice trailed off into the odd quiet of the city. He didn't repeat the word but instead drew a box with his fingers.

"The past never dies," she said. Peter felt a chill. The shadows almost engulfed the park as the gray fell beyond the water, leaving dark mist in its wake. Peter buttoned his coat and flipped his collar, but the chill remained. It wasn't from the cold. "It catches up."

"What if you just keep running?"

"You get tired." Sofia shivered. Peter caught her staring at the night like a collected shadow.

"The sun's gone. We should get inside."

"Have you ever watched a sunrise?" Sofia said.

"Once or twice," Peter said. He couldn't count how many times he had watched the sunrise, waited for the light to push away the fog and the mist, with Claus in his arms, try and see if his dad would be outside his window when the mist lifted and the world cleared, or to make sure the wind was calm because the

Wolf was gone. The world never cleared. Too many sunrises to count. Always colorful. Always disappointing. "We should go inside. It's cold."

"I have never seen a sunrise on purpose."

"Can you watch a sunrise by accident?"

"A sunset is a blessing, and a sunrise is a maldición. A curse, you know."

"I always loved sunrise." He put his hands in his pockets to warm himself. "I thought it was the most peaceful part of the day. It was the world and me. When the sunlight could make the world new."

"That is the curse," she said. "The day is over. It is a reminder that you can never have it back again. Too many days I want back that the sunrise took away."

"You get a new day." He shrugged. "Some days, I don't want back."

"What if the last day was perfect? Smart people sleep through the sunrise." She reached into her pocket, retrieved the letter, and handed it to Peter. He remembered the writing, how the envelope danced with the radio. In the weight of the night, the letter didn't feel as light as it had when he first found it in Sofia's mailbox. It was short. She sighed. "I don't think I am ready to see him."

"Ready?" And Peter understood. Sofia looked molded to the uncomfortable solitude of the bench. Like the man from the café, but instead of contentment, she held the opposite. Routine leads to complacency, to resentment, to fragility, to senility, to stuck. That was the man at the café, the face of Peter's father at an age he never knew. An age Peter was afraid to know. Not the age, the familiarity with the place. Or the person, and how haunting it was and would be—to be tender to a thing after so long.

"Yes," she said. "Ready. To know if after all this time. Of her. If Gaston and I lost each other because we lost Valentina."

"We should get out of here," Peter said. Sofia kept still. "I mean, for the day." Peter looked into her glassy stare. "The redwoods. We should see the redwoods."

"You have to go," Sofia said. "You cannot miss work." She pressed her soft hands against Peter's cheek.

"I don't have to," he repeated. "I'll call in for tomorrow too. A family emergency." Sofia smiled a smile he had seen once before, in the locket she had opened for him, but it looked new to her face, like a new light had come on in a corner of a room he had never seen. She patted his hand with a soft strength.

"It is cold, and I am ready to go inside. Come. I have made a lot of meat."

Sofia slipped her arm through Peter's. The breadcrumbs compacted beneath their feet. Sofia trembled. Peter wondered if it was from the cold. The light was gone. Peter once loved the new day, the new sunrise. Catch the ray of light, and the past will never catch you. The sun looked different every morning, from every angle, like Carly's broken tables. The sun looked different from every city. Except the sun had never shined in San Francisco.

"What are you going to do with the letter?" Peter said. "Hang it up on the fridge?"

"Maybe I'll bury it," Sofia said with a tired smile.

When Peter opened the door to the apartment, the murky light returned to the hall. The smell of char hung on the walls, different from the stench of cigarettes he had become accustomed to. The streetlamps shined once more. It didn't look like the sun, but it was bright enough to guide Peter and Sofia up the stairs for the moment.

Chapter 16

The rain bucketed down, and the stone steps turned into a river. Peter continued to breathe deep, to bring as much air to his lungs as possible. Each gasp burned. Ached.

He had walked for five days, followed Miguel, the man he had paid to get him from Cuzco to Machu Picchu. No cars. No motors. Two porters: Juanito and his older brother Chino. They both wore red and white fútbal jerseys, fans of Club Cienciano. Juanito, squat with a bowl haircut, walked the trail in sandals, his thick feet covered in mud as the water washed over them. Chino was taller, not by much, darker, and wrinkled. He wore torn-up tennis shoes and looked Chinese. That's why he was called Chino, Miguel had said. Miguel spoke bad English. Peter spoke bad Spanish. Together they spoke bad conversation. The porters spoke Quechua. Miguel didn't offer to teach Peter, and Peter didn't mind not knowing. They got along fine.

But Peter did learn new words and phrases in Spanish; he traded his English as currency to Miguel. Peter knew how valuable English could be for a tour guide, and he lacked the cash to pay Miguel to bring him up the mountain. Peter offered to teach Juanito and Chino too, in exchange for carrying his bags. He hadn't been sure how the altitude would affect him when he started the trek: 2,720-meters above sea level made it hard to think, let alone truck a bag. The porters didn't want to learn English.

Peter was stuck with his backpack. He was lucky he had packed light. Two pairs of jeans. Six pairs of socks. Three t-shirts. One sweater. One jacket. The shoes on his feet. The pack on his back. A Nalgene bottle. A poncho that covered his head and backpack. A water-resistant sleeping bag. The hat on his head. Three SWATCH watches strapped to his wrist; one was broken. A tin box.

It was all Peter had packed since he bought his one-way ticket away from the cities and people that his mom had painted into forever. He had stamped the box with the cities he had seen. The clothes had changed, but not the amount of clothing. Peter hadn't planned to come to Machu Picchu, but the more time he spent running from his mom's paintings, the more he was drawn to the cities inside them. One day he might go to San Francisco—one day. When he was ready. If he would ever be ready.

Peter didn't have water-resistant shoes or hiking boots; he trudged through the mud-covered jungle and high altitudes in his blue Converse, ready for the rain. The green world absorbed him. The coca leaves were bitter—in his teeth when he chewed, in his tea when he drank, in his nose when he huffed. It helped against altitude sickness, kept his head straight, his guts in his stomach. At least that's what Miguel told him.

When they had pressed through Dead Woman's Pass, the porters blew past Peter and Miguel. Juanito and Chino could finish the trek in a day. There was an annual race.

"The fast time is twelve hours," Miguel said.

"And it's only taken us five days," Peter said. He tried to even out his breath to push himself up the 4,215-meter peak, the highest of the trek. He wanted to bribe a porter. To jump on their back and fly up the mountain. To swallow all the air on earth because it was somehow somewhere else. Four nights of camping. Five days of endless rain. Jungle puddles. Forever clouds and mudslides. And Peter never stopped smiling, even through borderline hyperventilation. The jungle was merciless, but he drank water from the leaves, as Miguel showed him. Juanito and Chino cooked rice, beans, and alpaca, made tea, and laughed. On the second night, Juanito had laid out the tarp. Peter asked if he could help erect the tent. Chino shook his head.

"That is work for porters," Miguel said. "Calmado."

"I never knew how to make a tent," Peter said. Peter imagined his dad on the same mountain with a tent strapped to his back, able to remove the tent from his back with a flick of his wrist and have the tent pitch itself. Peter never learned the wrist flick or where to place the tent pegs and the poles. He wanted to learn now.

Miguel whispered to Chino. Peter held the metal pegs. Juanito smiled and waved Peter to him. He pointed to the pegs, held up a finger, and pointed to the four corners of the tarp. Peter set the pegs, hammered them into the ground, and was finally taught how to set a tent. They huddled on the tarp and under the tent together. Peter sat with Miguel. Both used small words.

"And tu familia?"

"Gone. Yours?"

"Very much están vivos. Vienes conmigo. After we finish. You come to me for to stay."

Peter agreed. He wanted to see Peru, a country his mom had never experienced. The country his dad had wandered and wondered through. His father's postcards left trails, with love, words Peter had already given up on.

Juanito and Chino had finished their duties. Peter had eaten with them, slept near them, shared the tight spaces in the vast forest. Never said a word to them other than thank you. But they always smiled at him. And Peter smiled back, the silent smile of an adventure, of a journey made—even if just for Peter, his struggle up a mountain that Juanito and Chino could do barefoot and blindfolded. For Peter, it was a push. For his legs. For his lungs. For his ghosts. Juanito, Chino, and Miguel helped Peter push through the trek. Helped push Peter up the mountain. They had made the journey together, beyond the meters and the brush and the cold and the rain. Somewhere in the days—in the quiet, where their smiles were all they needed. When breakfast ended and the tents were packed, everyone felt the unbearable lightness of the air, and the nausea wasn't from the altitude or a cold from the constant rain. They hugged. Soft smiles. Juanito and Chino left for the train. Peter and Miguel left to reach Huayna Picchu before sunrise. Tourists on the trail would want to see the sun at the Sun Gate. It would be overcrowded and loud if anyone could see through the clouds and heavy rain.

In the darkness before dawn, they pushed by stone walls and decrepit stairs that Miguel knew by heart, that Peter couldn't see until they came to the base of a mountain where a closet guarded the entrance. A guard had them write their names in a book. Miguel and Peter were the first two to check into Huayna Picchu that morning. Now Peter trudged through the river of mud as the purple light of dawn crept through the rain and the cold water rushed over his toes. Miguel was once again in front, holding a steel cable someone had bolted to the mountain with good sense.

"Is it always like this?" Peter asked.

"No," said Miguel, "hace buen tiempo." Was he serious? Was now nicer than usual?

The water rushed. Peter slipped. Caught himself on the cable. The stone stairs were thinner than paper. The rain made the walls of the mountain pack up and fall downhill. Miguel helped Peter and his waterlogged Converse from the rush of the river. Peter carried half the mountain in his shoes. He wanted to sink deeper into the mud but pushed through and up the steep slope, tugged himself through the narrower passages. Miguel moved behind Peter and caught him when he fell. Helped support his ascent until there were no more stairs to climb.

"Bienvenido to the cielo," Miguel said.

Peter stood on top of a sharp granite ledge and, for a second, saw the blank space where the mountain's edge met the open sky. He stepped onto the thin layer of grass. He stepped closer to the edge. The rain stopped. Or maybe they were above the rain. The dim light of the sun bled over the mountains. Machu Picchu, the powerful city beneath him. Scattered temples of solid rock high on the mountaintop that mingled with the clouds, and Peter above it all. Above the river that carved the mountains. Above the valley. Above the farms. Above the ruins. Above history. Above the mountain where his mom hid his dad's face. High in the sky above the clouds, where he could whisper his hopes to the sun.

Short of breath, his sneakers soggy, Peter took off his backpack and danced. He kicked up water from the grass. He kicked water from his shoes. He hunched over, out of breath. Gasped for air. No regrets. Not from the urge to kick up puddles. Or from the weight of his pack. He pulled a black pouch from the tin box. The rain a distant memory. The dark purple of the morning crept away. Miguel led Peter to softer grass and a better view where the stones of the ancient city rested on the clouds instead of granite, where Peter found a pocket of air to breathe deep.

Miguel dug a hole in the soft earth and offered Peter a coca leaf. Peter took the leaf and followed Miguel. They lifted their leaves, bowed to the north, the south, the east, and the west; they placed the leaves in the hole with a rock they had brought from the bottom of the trail.

"For Pacha Mama," Miguel said. "Arrive safe. Go safe."

Peter removed his father's pocket watch from the bag, silver plated with crooked Roman numerals. Always late, his mother had said. A curse. Peter traced his fingers over the watch. He couldn't remember much of his father. A beard and a bear. Both brown. Both smelled like mothballs. The watch's hands hadn't moved in years. He had been late to his own funeral, Peter thought. Another dream of Peter's father's could-have-beens that made Peter's memories of his father real in that part of his life he couldn't remember. Not his father's life. Not his father's funeral—except here, on a mountain Peter knew his father had climbed, Peter could bury the memory.

Peter placed the watch in the hole. Miguel and Peter both put in Jolly Ranchers, two each—one cherry, one grape—and covered the sacrifice with mud and grass. Miguel said a prayer to seal their gifts to Pacha Mama, a mother Peter didn't believe in at home but could love in Peru. A quiet he could love in Peru. A quiet he hoped he could take with him down the mountain, but where he knew the ghosts would follow.

The rain stopped. Peter sat at the top of the world, above the birds—above the clouds, and looked down on the dots that wandered lost and confused. They had no idea how small they were. The white clouds floated under Huayna Picchu. Under Peter's feet. The birds flew quietly below. Peter stood higher than the birds dared to fly. The clouds shifted; some looked like trains, some rabbits. The swirls of orange and blue swallowed the sky. No clouds overhead. No clouds over the top of the world.

Peter un-strapped another watch; it was red and looked like a chili pepper. He smashed the watch on the rock they sat on. He felt the world stop when he heard the river below him, not rushing, the water waiting to move again, while the birds held onto the air, and the dots in the ancient city froze on the plateau forever. If Peter wanted it to last forever.

Peter could see the scratches in the sky; the stretch marks the world created when it grew, faded red across the sky where the sun once rose and fell, but here on the mountain, Peter could almost touch the sun if he reached deeper into where the blue met the purple in the distance, but the quiet of the birds was lost from beneath him, and the clouds below began to shift once more, shaped into a bathtub with a sail, or a crushed van, gliding across the sky. Peter looked at the hands of the watch, stopped still and broken, and placed it in the tin box.

"Por qué has hecho eso?" asked Miguel.

"Some people have photos," Peter said. "I have watches."

Chapter 17

Sofia walked through the streets of the Mission and hid in its Spanish, written on storefronts, written on signs, floating in the air. She was glad of the anonymity. This was another day she would have preferred to be deaf rather than speak English. Sometimes she wanted to forget there was a life before now, that she could have come to San Francisco for other reasons, better reasons, to be a model or a painter, or a poet, a poet that wrote about the beauty of the fog, how it swallowed the bridge almost whole sometimes, with bits of red and cable poking out from the top as if to show the world it struggled but survived. Instead, she always felt the fog close, wrap around her body like an iron maiden, and waited for the spikes to dig in deep and bleed her dry.

The fog hung on her clothes, and she felt wet. How many years and the fog only gets thicker. Her shirt felt heavy on her shoulders. The language around her familiar but different. She walked past the grocers; heavy fruit displayed on the streets. The bakeries with pastries for Semana Santa year-round. An alley: the graffiti: art she couldn't understand written in letters that didn't look like letters or frayed words that assured her FERNANDO WAS HERE! Maybe he had been there, but he sure wasn't there now, and by the time he was dead, who was going to care that he had been there at all? Her fingers traced the alley wall, over the colors of the art she couldn't understand. Above her fingers, bright colors over dark, she found the words written like a kite, Ya Veremos. She wanted to hide from them in the fog. Away from the alley and the familiar sounds, away from the houses and the broken furniture on the corners, toward the park where she could hide in a crowd or watch the children. Where she hoped the words wouldn't find her but she was unable to forget them because she had agreed—we will see.

"I thought you would bring one dozen," a short man with a full black mustache said behind the counter of the corner tienda.

"Pablito," Sofia said. She kissed his cheeks and handed over two large boxes of alfajores and a single empanada, one she had salvaged from the smoke in her kitchen.

"This does not look like a dozen empanadas," Pablito said.

"You have one hundred alfajores, as per usual," Sofia said.

"But not one dozen—"

"Enough with the empanadas, Pablito. You sound too much like Chichi." A frail Chihuahua lay on a small, pink pillow bed behind the tienda counter. She lifted her head at the sound of her name but lost interest when no one acknowledged her further. "You think I should put that much effort into making a whole dozen when you are only sampling them? You tell me you will buy them, and I will make you enough to feed an army, just like the alfajores."

Pablito rested his elbows on the counter and placed his chin in his hands. He pursed his lips and blew through his mouth, making his lips rumble. "You said you would give me—"

"I said you would want a dozen at least," Sofia said. "I never said I would give you one dozen." The quick fluidity of Spanish rolled off her tongue. She embraced the returning musicality of the language, the way it danced around her to a familiar rhythm she missed when absent. She spent so much time between words when the music from the radio acted as the only language to which she could force herself to listen. But the subtle differences between Sofia's Spanish and Pablito's Spanish wedged them apart, keeping Sofia at a distance from the comforts of the Mission with disparities in dialect rearing its head in unexpected places, from the speed with which Sofia spoke to how she pronounced the double "ll," which sounded more like the way English speakers said the word jar. She said alverja; Pablito said chícharo. Both meant pea. They both spoke Spanish, supposedly, she thought. The fog already clinging to her coat felt heavier.

Pablito took a bite of the empanada, closed his eyes, and exhaled through his nose. He spoke before he swallowed the mouthful.

"These don't taste like Salvadorian empanadas," he said.

"That is because I am not from El Salvador," Sofia said.

"But I am," he said. "And this is a Salvadorian market."

"I had no idea," Sofia said. "In that case, I can take back my alfajores, which you had once said were a best seller. After all, like my empanadas, they are from Argentina. I also expect your supply of Salsa Lizano from Costa Rica and those bottles of Mescal from Mexico to be gone the next time I walk by." She smiled. Pablito sighed again.

"Can you make one hundred of these?"

Sofia nodded. Pablito smiled before stuffing more empanada into his mouth. Sofia turned away from the tienda, and the fog swarmed around her. It filled the air with a sour scent, reminiscent of rotting fruit, dousing the spark of her little victory. She followed the cracks in the sidewalk. The fog reminded her of the smoke from her kitchen, from the burnt empanadas, outlining empty silhouettes.

Church bells rang around the Mission. Sofia found herself at the base of the church steps and spat. At the church. On the church. The fog hid her from possible foul stares. The Spanish façade, the remnants of history in the shadow of the more recent and gaudy cathedral; she didn't care for either. Sofia saw the gate at the side of the mission. She wanted to sit. She went to the gate and cursed when she stepped in the spit she had left for the church, each step pressed hard into the concrete to try and rid her shoe of her own filth. But she wanted a garden—a bench, a rest.

The gate was cold and creaked when she opened it, corroded hinges. The cobblestones of the walkway had smoothed from time and visitors. Branches hid the mission. Fog hid the steeples. Sofia felt hidden and, for the moment, breathed in her refuge.

Sofia could feel where the stones separated as she moved towards a bench. A gardener on his hands and knees in front of the tombstones cut the grass with miniature scissors. His mustache hung lightly over his lips. He nodded to her when she sat. The cold steel passed through her skirt, through her stockings, through her skin. She looked into the garden, and the headstones, the markers, the trees trimmed back, the lack of flowers, the grass perfect, made her shiver.

"Házte cómodo," he said. He leaned over the grass and clipped the blades. It was an odd thing to say to a person he didn't know. She did as he suggested, happy for some form of familiarity, and attempted to get comfortable any way she could, for a minute, until her feet were ready to move again. She nodded.

Sofia wasn't sure where to look, where to stare. Away was not an option. She looked at the walkway, how the stones smoothed and merged together from time, how stones grew smooth when walked on, how hearts grew rigid when walked over, and bodies grew wrinkled. Eventually, everything crumbled and faded.

"You want one?" He held out a pack of Marlboros.

"Will someone mind?" she said.

"Like who?" he motioned to the yard. "I don't think we'll have an issue."

Sofia went to him and took a cigarette from his pack. He lit his first and offered her the lighter.

"Why are you here?" he asked. "No one is here to visit. Not that kind of place."

He had a silver mustache that flashed full and bright like a torch. Marlboros and the mustache, the attention to detail in the grass he cut—for a second, maybe, he could have been Gaston, strained and changed through loss, so much that he followed Sofia to San Francisco, and after years of solitude, revealed himself here, in a place their daughter could have been, or they could have been, one day, together. He could have been Gaston, maybe, on another day, in another life. But it wasn't. Not here. Not today.

"You ever visit an antique? No one visits antiques."

Sofia puffed the cigarette. She looked into the yard, at the headstones decrepit and wet, though some still held pebbles, signs of remembrance.

"Some people remember antiques." She pointed the cigarette at the yard.

"Field trips don't count. Kids put pebbles on the oldest person here."

"Why are you here?"

"I'm old," he said. "There should be pebbles at my feet."

Sofia coughed and fixed her scarf. The smoke was acrid. Not all pebbles are for the old. She read the names and dates on the nearest row. Some dated back to the 19th century, all Spanish names, some without births, only expirations, some spotted with graffiti, random histories defaced, without anyone to remember them. Except for the irregular tourist.

"I wanted a sit," she said. "I thought this was a garden."

"It is," he said. "It's a fucked-up garden." He laughed. She didn't. "You want to lay a pebble for me?"

"I don't know you," she said.

"That makes two of us."

"I don't know your name."

"My wife chooses to forget it too."

"What is your name?"

"My name? My name. It's not important." He took a long drag from his cigarette and stared into the yard. "None of these names are important. Except for maybe that guy's." He pointed at one of the headstones; frayed words scrawled in blue marker, familiar, Fernando Was Here! "People remember winners," he said. He pointed at the stones. "They've lost."

"Why haven't you cleaned it?"

He stood, brushed his knees, patted his stomach. "Not yet."

"We will see."

He ran tobacco-stained fingers over his mustache. It settled over his lip. He said goodbye to Sofia and walked to the headstone Fernando had claimed.

"Goodbye to the bear," he said. He left a pebble on the ledge, went into the church, and Sofia could almost see the tip of a blue marker in his back pocket before he disappeared.

Sofia dropped her cigarette on the grass and walked to the headstone, the one he had touched; the one Fernando had claimed, taken as his own, stolen from the person underneath, a person laid down to be remembered, her place to be marked where she rested forever.

Sofia slumped, her clothes suddenly too heavy, her body tired, drained of existence. The sweet smell of a white rose.

"Mamma?" Valentina's voice said, echoing against the headstones.

"Mamma?"

The voice crept through the city on the back of the fog. It soaked into the grass and pounded Fernando's paint. Fernando, who wanted to be remembered for where he had been, but he was not here. She was here—Sofia. With Fernando's remains, his words written on stone. Unfair for Fernando to be here. For his name to be painted on the grocery wall. For him to be in this city. And Sofia listened again—to Valentina. To the body she could not mark. The words written in her memory.

"I have been waiting for you." Sofia felt Valentina's hand on her cheek—soft skin. Warm touch. "I am here, my darling. Where are you?"

"I am close. Always close," Valentina said.

"But where are you?" The warm touch gone. A chill down Sofia's spine. "I have lost you. You aren't here. With me. I never should have let you go. With Philippe. To that meeting. I could have kept you close, with me, and you would be here, with me, with your father, and we would be together, happy, in Buenos Aires, together, and you would be married, and happy, with children—happy."

"You didn't have a choice," Valentina said. "I would have gone anyway."

"I should have said no. You shouldn't have been taken away. Where did they take you? What did they do to you? I could have stopped you from leaving. Leaving me. Leaving home. When are you coming home? We can go home."

"You are home," Valentina said. "I am home."

"I can't see you," Sofia said. "Do you look the same? A child? Beautiful."

"They beat me," Valentina said. "With fists. With metal. They shaved my head. Rubbed salt in my blood. But they sent me home. You were gone. I am still beautiful. I am still a child. I am home. With you."

"I am so far from home. Far from you. Worlds apart." No wind. No words. Quiet. No breath. Silence.

Sofia's hands shook. She grabbed the rock the man left, larger than a pebble—jagged. She slammed it into Fernando's name. She listened for her daughter. Another hit. She smelled the rose. The stone unhurt. Fernando stuck. Sofia stabbed at it. Threw the rock. She willed the headstone to break. Pushed it. Her hands dry and cracked. The stone cold and wet. Fernando's name etched across the face. Over the single date. Over the name. Intact. She wished for his name to disappear—for Valentina's name to take its place, her body to be marked or spared or known. And Sofia felt the fog creep into her lungs, stuffing them with wet rags. She leaned against the stone—decrepit. She tried to catch a breath, her hands on her knees, her body pushing the stone.

She found a breath, the only one she could catch, and she held onto it. She pushed against Fernando for balance, to help herself back to stability. She pushed. She breathed. She pushed. The stone cracked—Fernando's name split. Chunks of stone crumbled into the grass. Sofia took another breath and heard herself exhale. We will see.

Chapter 18

Sofia's skin didn't fit, too tight like the apartment she now called home in a new city with dirty streets paved with asphalt and the music emotionless, without rhythm. The man's hands wrapped around her shoulders, cold, his lips against her neck. She didn't want to look at him.

She had felt Gaston leave long before he left. Forever had passed. He was gone, and she followed him out. Out of the apartment, out of the city, and broke—broke down, broke away. He had left, and she was alone. For years in Buenos Aires, she had felt alone. For two years in San Francisco, she had been alone. She didn't have to be. Not tonight.

The man's hands reached for her hips and pulled her closer to him. She felt him hard and in control, in the unfamiliar: the apartment, the city, the fog, his hands, his face, when he kissed her roughly.

She was at a bar she had been to before, the one with dark lighting, torn upholstery, and air that smelled of piss. The man bought her a drink. He called her beautiful. Touched her shoulder. Asked what songs she liked. None. Touched her knee. He bought her a drink. The air was rancid. He grabbed her hand. She bought a drink. She led him out. He kissed her. She turned away. Playful? He kissed her neck. She let him. He grabbed her ass. He kissed her lips. She turned away. They went to her apartment. He kissed her neck. She let him. The music off. He rubbed her breasts over her dress. She looked away. Out the window—at the streetlights, glowing.

His fingers gripped her zipper. She waited for him to tick each tooth, slow—anticipate the body beneath. Each click another second he waited. She somehow more powerful than before, but the power never came. She jerked, unsure if the zipper made it all the way down. She wanted him to continue. Unzip her skin and let her breathe.

Her dress dropped. She fought the urge to cover herself, as she had with Gaston the first time, unsure of her body. The man's lips uncomfortable on her back. His fingers too fat. His hands too dry. His skin too pale. Her skin too tight. But she wanted it in the darkness of her apartment; she rolled the word over her tongue in English, uncertain and uncomfortable. Home is where she stood naked with this man with stale beer breath that she could smell when he kissed her back, and the stubble of his chin scraped her.

Home, in English, a hum that she wanted to continue, rock herself to sleep on the couch with no visitors because she still couldn't fathom the idea of friendly neighbors and felt more comfortable with a stranger from a bar that smelled of piss where she could creep into the shadows and not worry that someone who wasn't looking for her might have found her. This man turned her around and tried to kiss her lips, but she turned away, again, not playful. He kept kissing her and unlatched her bra, pressed himself against her, and her nipples were hard against him but from the chill of his body and the air, and she wanted to combust and burn but couldn't and felt dry, in her mouth, on her skin too tight. Would he care with his body close to her, but she didn't care if he would, or he did because she didn't care about him or who he was because of who he wasn't.

She led him to the bed, empty, made each morning, a habit of which she never rid herself. She fell into the sheets, wanted to wrap herself in them, fuse the cotton to her body—warm and clear. He fell heavily onto her. Heavier breath. Dry chalk-voiced from cigarettes. She could use a cigarette.

Gaston always carried Marlboros; he didn't smoke. They'd be at a café; she'd finish her cappuccino and bat her eyelashes. He'd reach into his coat pocket and offer. She'd take. He'd light. She'd inhale. He'd smile. Now, no breath and no air, smothered by spilt bottles of beer on skin and the will to catch on fire, in her eyes or head or anywhere. Her insides corroding with a chance to disappear altogether, as a child disappears into dreams or games or politics.

It wasn't Valentina's fault for Gaston and Sofia's separation, but Sofia sometimes blamed her, blamed the memory of her, blamed the absence of her, without which Gaston would have stayed, Valentina would have been married, Sofia wouldn't be alone. The selfish acts of invincible children.

Sofia dug her nails into the man's flesh. She wanted to feel hot blood drip down her body, then punish herself for her defamation. She wrapped her legs around him and wanted him to thrust harder, wanted him to tear her inside and out, to tatter her body so her thoughts would follow, to show the scars people couldn't see. He had to tame her, show her civilization, but she didn't want to be civilized, had seen the price of civilization and would rather stay feral, and wanted him to smack her across the face, hard enough to leave his hand, to slam his fist into her jaw, hard enough to knock her out, wrap his fingers around her throat and grip tight—no thoughts while unconscious; no sounds of music. He did nothing.

She was bored. Not bored but tired. Tired of his grunts, of his face, his lips, her thoughts. She rolled him over with the will to take charge. She pressed her hands to his chest and thrust her hips. He was rigid and burned inside her, but it was better than the nothing she felt from him before. She was ready for him to leave, get out and never see him again.

She had never wanted to hurt Gaston. He was gentle and considerate. He knew her and her body. He would tease himself, roll down her dress until he touched each inch of her with his fingertips or his tongue until she dripped. She'd tease herself with soft lips to his thighs, to feel him hard. They'd roll into each other. She didn't want him to leave. She couldn't believe that he did. How could he leave her without an explanation? But she knew how. She knew why. It was what made her so angry. It was what made her so lonely. It was what made it her fault.

She pulsed on top of the man, faster. Harder. The sour beer filled the room. Her skin ached with irritation. She pulsed harder and balled her fists, pounded his chest, held her breath. It was her fault she was alone. It was her fault Gaston had left. She had pushed him away. If Valentina had been around, none of this ever would have happened.

She pounded the man's chest. He brushed the hair from her cheek—too familiar.

Her fist hit his face—heavy.

He screamed and grabbed his eye. He wanted to continue, she knew, but she didn't. It was her excuse to stop. She offered him an ice pack. He said no. She offered him a drink. He said he should leave. She didn't stop him—the apartment quiet. She put on a robe. He barely put on his clothes.

She never apologized.

Chapter 19

The restaurant was twilight without color, candles, or wine in the darkness. If the lights went out, no one would have known. Peter sat across from Carly. A simple conversation played in his mind, a conversation he's had hundreds of times before. About Australia and the Red Desert, or Thailand and elephants and waterfalls. The hardest part was to initiate the conversation, but she was here, and that was a start.

Carly took a sip of wine. Peter had ordered a bottle of Cabernet—foreign, to see if she was a California wine snob, to see if she liked the taste: dark fruit, chocolate velvet in his mouth, textures to savor, and tonight he wanted to indulge. She said nothing.

"Long day?" he asked. Jump right in; pretend the conversation had already started.

"Lately," she said, "it's hard to imagine what people want to know and how they are willing to learn it. It's a day. Sometimes lousy ones happen."

"That's the job of a teacher," he said. "Hardest job in the world."

"You're a teacher? Because I thought you were a janitor."

"I am a janitor," he said, "but a teacher, in a way. I can teach you how to wipe away a handprint. Or about the places I've seen, the things I've seen."

"You've seen a lot, have you?" she asked. She seemed more bored than interested. Peter had never imagined someone bored with him, with his stories. "What makes what you've seen better?"

"Who said better?" he said. "Just different. It's all different."

Carly half-smiled. "It's been a very long day." She moved dark strands of hair from her eyes and tucked them behind her ear. Her dress was black. It was hard to know where her hair stopped and her dress began. Peter sipped his wine.

The waiter came to the table. Carly ordered prawns and linguini, Peter pumpkin ravioli. It came in a duck sauce. He loved sweet pasta and savory sauce. He was as excited for the meal as he had been for the date. The phone call, the message. This is Peter. I hope it's the right number this time. I bought you breakfast once. You gave me the wrong number. You bought me a coffee. We went on a walk. Can I take you out again? Or for the first time? Did breakfast count? Did the coffee count? Or the walk? Can I take you on a third date, if all those others counted? Would it be a second date? How long is this message? Do you listen to your messages? We'll find out together. The codeword is Dinner-date. When Carly called back, Peter said hello. Carly said, Dinner-date.

Peter didn't know if he should wear a tie, how fancy he thought the meal should be. She knew he was a janitor. He wanted to impress her. That's why he chose the tie, orange, his shirt white. He wanted to stand out in the darkness. The hardest decision was whether to roll up his sleeves or keep his watches covered. He had rolled up his sleeves, more out of habit than a desire to show off his watches. He could talk about his watches if she asked. He had told people about them before, in a way, in a way he thought would interest them, in a way he thought wouldn't say too much about the life he didn't want to say much about. The watches climbed his arm. Carly didn't mention them.

"Tell me something about you," she said.

"I move around a lot, and now I'm in San Francisco. You know the rest."

"Family, work, school?"

"I chose adventure." He thought it was a good way to bring the conversation to his travels, the conversation he knew.

"Parents?" she said. "Too soon to talk about family?" The start of a conversation he wasn't ready to have. Peter shrugged and took a gulp of water. "I grew up in San Francisco," she said. "My mother passed away about five years ago. I haven't seen my father in a long time." Her answer was abrasive, a dodge with quick honesty, the opposite of Peter's deception, a dodge through change. There was so much missing. He could see it in her eyes, the sadness that peeked through the darkness of the restaurant. He knew that sadness.

"What's missing?" he said. "You need to answer the question or ask a different one." He hoped she would ask a different question or be the type of person who became so wrapped up in her own story she would forget to ask about his, at least for now.

Carly looked at the table. Her finger traced the red reflection of the wine. "My father drank—a lot. He'd come home from work, and my mother would send me to the store, to a friend's, to the park, anywhere to get away for a while. Sometimes I came home too early. Sometimes I didn't come home at all.

"One day, she got the courage to leave, took me right out the door with her. But we never left the city, and it was always a worry that we would run into him."

"Did you?" Peter asked.

"I thought I saw him once. In Union Square a few years ago. But it was a homeless guy. I didn't look too hard." Carly took a piece of bread and dipped it in olive oil. It dripped on the table and was absorbed by the tablecloth. "Your turn. How long has your mom been at sea?"

He had played her game and lost, lost his comfort and his control over the conversation. He liked her smile. He didn't want it to end.

"Almost as long as my dad's been away," he said.

"How long ago was that?"

"A while ago. This watch?" He pointed.

"It's broken," Carly said.

"It happened when I was in Egypt," Peter said. He stood on the shore of the Red Sea with the warm water at his toes, thoughts of the life in the water at his feet and not the life in the water that followed him, the sun bright behind the gray

clouds but still bronzed his skin and burned the metal on the watch. He stood at
the water's edge with his arms spread wide like he thought Moses had done. Peter
wondered if the sea would part for him if he stood there long enough.

"My mom told me a story about Moses, once." Peter took another sip of wine.
"It wasn't really about Moses but the march across the Red Sea." He looked at
Carly to see if she paid attention. She did. She didn't look bored. He wanted to
watch her in silence, to let the candlelight be stars in her hair.

"And this watch reminds you of that?"

"Moses parts the sea and the waves tower over the people. They follow Moses
into the mud, but they don't see the mud; they don't pay attention to the mud.
They see the parted sea, the sky molded to the waves. They watch the fish through
the water. They see sunken ships and buried treasures. They're in awe of this moment and will remember it forever."

"How could they not?"

"At the back of the line was an old man. He was so far back he didn't see the
waves part. His head was down the whole time. All he noticed was the mud between his toes, the heat in the air. His sweaty body. His thirst. He walked through
the mud and complained about Moses and never even realized what he'd done.
What Moses had done. He just wanted to wash off his feet."

Carly laughed. She looked down when she laughed.

"Sometimes, you have to look up to make sure you're not missing something.
My mom told me that story sometime after my dad died."

"She seems like a smart lady," Carly said.

"That depends," Peter said. Carly raised her eyebrows. "It depends on who in
the story you think she is."

The waiter came to the table and set the plates down.

"Want some?" Peter asked before she could ask another question about his
mother.

"Please." She offered him a plate.

Peter heard the scrape of Carly's fork as it pushed the pasta. The room became quiet. The flame of the candle ballooned and drifted above the table so Peter could memorize her face, with her hair fallen over her eyes that burst blue in the darkness, her figure glowing from the flame of the candle. He wanted to run his hands through her hair and push back the strands that fell over her eyes so he could fall through the sky or float above the clouds where the mountains met the top of the world, with her—together. But for now, she had a smile without sadness, and her eyes were large and bright. To be able to touch her skin and have her sink into him where she could see his world, and he wouldn't have to say out loud the words he had not said and never wanted to say, and she would know what at sea meant, and she would know that he didn't lie because he never wanted to lie to her.

The waiter moved. The candles blinked. Carly's plate banged against the table.

"This looks so wonderful," she said.

"Yes," Peter said. "It does."

Chapter 20

The heat covered the city, a layered grid that roasted the neighborhood and forced people to run through the sprinklers to cool off, or maybe it was raining. Peter wouldn't be in the front yard if there were rain. It couldn't have been rain; it must have been the heat and the sprinklers.

Peter sat on the grass and enjoyed the damp ground. He ran his fingers over the blades and they tickled his palms when he brushed them back and forth. He could feel the grass but couldn't see it; the blades blended into a block of muddled green, of which he sat in the middle, watching the brown deep in the corner creep centerward.

The asphalt waved in the heat, too hot to touch and too far for Peter to reach. He tugged at the green block beneath him. He filled his hands with grass and dirt and wanted to stuff the ground into his mouth, chew on the grit, but found the concrete more appealing.

Peter hadn't made it halfway to the road before the screech trailed by a thump broke him down, broke the heat and the yelp that followed. He fell back and stared at the street. A dog—it must have been a dog, with gold fur and a pink tongue and eyes fading black—beneath the car, but the sound of the screech and the thump and the yelp were as far as the memory. The car was red, a blurry red that blended with golden fur, and the smell of hot metal drifted from the growing puddle that crawled from the dog and sizzled on the asphalt.

Peter felt the pressure of giant hands wrap around his ribs and lift him. His father's voice: It's ok, you're all right. The sun was blocked by the oval shadow of his father's face and his squared shoulders, but Peter couldn't see his father's mouth or his father's eyes, only the shape that should have held those details. You're fine, everything is fine. His father whispered between the sounds of shhh. Peter wanted to stop crying before he knew he had started. The soft shhh helped him breathe deep when he pressed his head into his father, and he thought if he could stay in his father's arms long enough, he could erase the thought that came with the dog. He pressed his hands onto his father's chest as if he painted him, while he whispered release through his tears, to paint his father into forever.

His father knew, somehow, or maybe didn't, but he whispered more, the words close to Peter's ear: I'll always be here.

The sun disappeared, and the cool air moved through the house; his dad held Peter against his body, the hiss and whimper of the car and fur far enough away to be forgotten. His dad danced with a bear, which was fuzzy and in pajamas, graceful in his dance and intent on rubbing his nose against Peter's, a bear smelling of cotton and mothballs.

He'll always be here to protect you.

Peter held onto the bear and pressed his hand against his chest, *Release*, he thought, a forever he promised himself, and squeezed it close to him. The itchy fleece pajamas scratched his neck, his dad kissed his forehead, and he fell asleep on his dad's chest. He woke later with Claus in his arms: on the side of the half-paved road where the wind blew hard with the Wolf nearby. The Wolf must have been nearby because of the hard wind, the first wind Peter could remember, or thought he remembered after connecting the stories from storybooks and his cousin, about that night when his dad disappeared. Peter jammed together the stories whether the information fit or not and wound up with holes in the puzzle large enough to drive a broken and battered van through, but it was the story he believed because it was the story he grew up with. The story he created that no one could take away.

He watched the van get hit and fold in half, dad behind the wheel, behind the cracked windshield with a lost smile. Tires folded sideways. Car parts in the air, splintered and scattered around the road. The thick crunch of metal. The red traffic light blinked on and off, or the red ambulance lights blinked on and off, or the street lights blinked on and off in the red pool that crawled through the broken glass, and Peter waited for the world to go black and return to color with the van put back together, with his father put back together. Where his father still held him in his arms. The world remade, reshaped, redrawn. But the wind faded—forever faded. His father was gone, and the car was crushed. The blue sky went dark because all the blue was sucked into the tiny pill that Peter's mom swallowed, the entire sky swallowed and gone, and the hot yelp of the dog stayed with Peter longer than the memory of his father's smile.

Chapter 21

Sam held Claus close to her chest. She had tried to sleep but couldn't. The more she tried, the tighter she held Claus. The tighter she held Claus, the more she couldn't sleep. His fur itched her nose. He smelled too much like fish. He twitched in his sleep. He wasn't the reason she couldn't rest, but it didn't stop her from blaming him.

They lay in the tub. Sam's knees pressed to her chest. Claus nuzzled into her arms. Even bears liked to cuddle. The sun hovered over the horizon. Daylight and darker daylight. It wasn't really dark when she closed her eyes. The sun shined through.

"Where are we going?" Sam said.

Claus pointed to the sail. "At this rate, nowhere."

Sam sighed and tried again to sleep. She wanted out of the tub. Surrounded by water, she would have nowhere to go but down. Maybe sinking would bring more…anything. She could use Claus as a paddle or wet his pajamas and use those as a paddle. She could try to huff and puff and blow the sail out. Or she could continue to do nothing. Her wrists itched. The only feeling she remembered—itchy wrists.

Claus jumped from Sam's arms and ran to the other end of the tub. He sniffed the air.

"Wind," he said. "We haven't had wind in a long time."

"That's good," Sam said. "Isn't it?"

"Not here," Claus said. He pointed to the distance. A stampede of clouds rushed in. The wind blew harshly. The boat rocked back and forth. The sail puffed as the wind blew harder and the clouds came faster, trampling over the sea. They expanded over the boat. The waves pushed the porcelain back and forth—faster, harder, back and forth. Water splashed over the lip.

Claus threw his head over the side of the boat. Sam had never seen a sick bear. She threw her head over the other side. Acidic and salty. A wave hit her in the face. She fell back into the tub. Water rushed in. Claus slid into Sam. She held him. The sail expanded. The boat flew through the waves. The sail expanded. The boat rocked. What could she do? Claus took care of all things nautical. She wanted to vomit again. She tasted acid in her throat. Tried to swallow it down. She hiccupped. Some escaped through her nose. She wanted to scream but thought that if she opened her mouth, she would swallow the sea. She preferred the vomit.

Sam and Claus huddled in the tub. They tried to hide from the storm. The clouds gushed. Envelopes plummeted from the sky. They attacked the boat like rain. They surrounded the boat and soaked up the crashing waves. The wind pummeled the sail. It carried the tub into the air. The sail exploded. Deflated. The boat stopped. It continued to rock. Letters poured in. Sam pulled the drain. It let out water. It sucked out the letters. A slurp filled the tub. Thunder slammed the air. Lightning flashed the sky. The clouds fattened. Expanded. Poured. Until the clouds thinned. The letters eased. And the sun lifted from the horizon. The porcelain had cracked, and the sail had torn. Sam and Claus were covered in letters.

"Is this where Santa's mail comes?" Sam asked.

Claus twitched his nose and spat. More letters drained from the tub. Sam grabbed one. It had no address. No stamp. She opened it. There was nothing inside.

"I do not think you will find anything," Claus said.

"What thing?" Sam said.

"Whatever it is, you think you'll find it in an envelope," Claus said.

Sam grabbed another envelope and tried again.

"What do you know? Stupid bear." She grabbed another envelope. She wasn't sure what she would find, but she hoped for something. Something that would tell her what she was doing, why she was here. She wanted an answer.

"I want to fucking know!"

She stood and gripped the lip of the tub and pulled back and forth, strained her arms, her face almost smashed into the lip. She expected her scream to echo in the emptiness. It didn't. She screamed again. She picked up a pile of letters and threw them overboard. She thrashed her arms. She felt the itch on her wrists. She grabbed another letter, tore it. Threw the empty shreds over the side. Into the air. Another letter torn. More empty shreds airborne. Again. And again. She fell into the tub. "I just want to know." She lay back down and brought her knees to her chest. Claus snuggled into her arms.

"You will find what you want to know."

Sam looked into the air, partly covered in shredded paper, the white pieces glued together and slathered across the sky, a collage of torn, empty pages that never fell in the water but instead pieced together a trolley car that stared down at Sam and Claus with a large window smile and happy glass eyes that winked. The trolley turned to climb a hill—no—a mountain made of more shredded paper that almost touched the sun, but the trolley only reached halfway to heaven before the paper disintegrated and fell into the sea.

"A push in the right direction?" Claus said.

"In any direction," Sam said.

She wrapped her arms around Claus and breathed him in. His fur didn't smell like fish. He smelled like candle wax.

The letters were torn up, drained out, and watered down; the sun was high in the air again, but Sam closed her eyes, and for the first time she could remember, she saw darkness. She held Claus tighter. He nuzzled into her neck. And she welcomed the blanket of sleep.

Chapter 22

The explosion pounded Peter's door, and smoke seeped into his bedroom through the tiny crack where light shone. Another explosion, another scream, more shattered glass. He held Claus tight and pulled the blanket to his chin. This was a constant debate with Claus, whether to pull the sheets over their heads and hide or use the sheets as a shield to protect themselves from whatever stood beyond the door where his mom and the TV were supposed to be.

To the guns!

We're taking on too much water

…that's an order!

Claus dropped beneath the sheets. Peter's room lit up, the walls bright white, the ceiling blown away. All sucked into darkness. The pirate ship's nightlight lost its luster, now small and insignificant. Another blast, another bright light. The door pushed and edged and bulged and exploded forward. Peter swore splinters flew through the room but wasn't sure. He kept his eyes shut tight. The smell of smoke grew stronger; the footsteps came closer. Claus stayed beneath the sheets. The bed deflated. A hand ran through Peter's hair. He smelled tart alcohol—heard another blast, felt the bed bounce, and a hand run down his cheek. He didn't want his mom to know he was awake. Not when he could smell the drink on her.

We're going down!

***

Peter lay on the roof in a garden in San Francisco with plants in pots laid out in a
heart shape, empty on the inside. He wanted to sink his teeth into the tomatoes,
or the mint beside it, or the carrots behind them, or the radishes across from them,
the radishes that he assumed were there, but he could only see their stems and
figured they were radishes based upon what he had seen in cartoons in a life he
almost remembered. But they could have been pumpkins. Bottle in hand and stars
gone, given way to gray skies and the depression of sunlight. The door opened
with an unmistakable squeak. He didn't turn; he didn't shuffle. He laid the bottle
on the floor and stared into the gray as if it would absorb him. If he stared hard
enough, he could rise above the bottle and the roof into something better than the
truth he felt he could never understand, the truth of Sam's choice to be lost at sea,
to have followed his father to nowhere fast, leaving Peter behind. So he tried to be
anywhere other than standing over his cousin while she slept to make sure she
would wake up again because he didn't want to be taken away again, or worse,
sucked back into the bathroom.

But all he did was stare, and squint, and feel the light force its way into his
pupils and his eyes throbbed without end. He looked to the door and saw her, the
woman he would come to know as Sofia, with her tweed, floppy-brimmed hat, her
gloves covered in soil, her spray bottle, the sunglasses that covered half her face
and kept the absent sun from her eyes, eyes that could have been his mother's eyes,
in clothes that could have been his mother's clothes, long ago on a sunny Sunday
in the garden where she wasted her days away. But Sam never had a garden. Sam
wasted a lifetime of days, wasted more days than just her own.

Sofia closed the door, sprayed the tomatoes, scraped the leaves; the considera-
tion she had for the tomatoes, the care, as she rubbed the water deep into their
skin until they absorbed every drop.

The garden was hers. On the roof, with her squalid gloves and seasoned face.
A rooftop oasis, he thought. The garden swallowed her whole, he thought, and she
fed her life to the fruit—or vegetable—that was the tomato, the life she once held

dear, driven from the youth that remained somewhere around her, that she fed to the ravished fruit—or vegetable—from the water bottle.

***

Peter had never heard a man drown, the scream for help lost in the gurgle, the muted gasp of swallowing water. But he heard it now from somewhere beyond his door, surrounded by explosions and curses, gunfire and metal—from somewhere beyond his mom where she sat on his bed and stroked his hair while the loudness pounded the walls and drowned his ears as he drowned in the fog of alcohol that poured from her skin.

"You awake, darling?" she said. Her fingers were cold and dry.

He stayed still and hoped she wouldn't try to wake him, and hoped more that his body wouldn't betray him with an itch or a blink. The chill of her fingers left his face. Her hand hit the sheets with a muffled brush. She reached beneath the covers and leaned so close he held his breath and hoped she wouldn't notice his chest stall, wouldn't notice when he started to breathe again so he wouldn't choke on the smell of her. He felt Claus slide from his side, and Sam's body slip away from him. Sometimes she took Claus and held him close to her nose, breathed him in over and over until she fell asleep with a smile. Peter sometimes did the same; no matter how little he remembered of his father, he remembered that smell; through the dirt and the rain and the refusal to wash Claus, Peter still smelled his father in the fur, and until his dad came back for their planned forever Peter refused to wash Claus, and chose instead to breathe him in as long as he could, like his mom did. Peter listened for her huff; instead, he felt the fluff of Claus next to his cheek. The bed dipped around him, creaked, and he knew she was there, her arm wrapped over him. She buried her nose in his hair and sniffed. He imagined she smiled.

...fuckin' say another word and fire.

We can't take much more, Captain!

We're losing her…

***

Sofia's cheeks were flush, absent of moisture, of sweat. He imagined the woman she may have once been or the woman she reminded him of, the woman he would never know, now, in her garden hat and gloves. But she parted her lips, gave herself to the fruit—or vegetable—and sang a song he thought he might have heard once upon a time, in a bathtub while water poured over his hair and his head dipped back to keep the soap out of his eyes while his mom sang the love song that his dad had taught her, a song she may have said would help Peter grow, as Sofia sang to help the vegetable—or fruit—grow, as he felt he wanted to grow, on the rooftop, under the gray that wrapped around the city, nurtured with water instead of fearing it.

> Stay here,
> In my arms
> stay here
> for me

***

Sam's heavy breath pushed against Peter's ear, warmed him, comforted him. He breathed from his mouth. Claus did too.

"I don't believe you," Peter said.

Claus gave a dead stare. His tattoo pulsed like a dare.

"The Wolf is gone." A bright light began to reappear, slow, controlled. It didn't come through the door. It came through the window. Another sunrise, another morning to see if the light of the world would bring his father back or promise that the Wolf had gone. The sunrise a bomb, defying gravity until its light exploded in the sky and the fog lifted from the ground to show another empty morning.

***

And don't tell me that you love me,

Don't tell me that you adore me

Just tell me that you'll stay

One life, alongside me

When Peter's bottle fell and knocked around the roof, he breathed more from relief than anxiety, to the sound of Sofia's voice and the reminiscent scent of soil and earth. The mountains he had climbed, once or twice, the mountains he wanted to climb, the air he wanted to breathe, for the first time or again. Under a man-made canopy, the sound of the sprayed water settled on the plants, the plants sprouted up and around like a jungle, where Peter felt he could hide in the lush vines of the plants and watch Sofia garden and sing without her ever noticing.

Take me over there,

Take me in your longing to another place

Where I no longer have to promise

Where I no longer have to lie

Where I only exist for you

***

The wind rattled the window. The fog was ready to swarm, wrap, tumble to the horizon; it had drifted in and blown out like a useless candle. Claus looked at Peter; he could feel him. It was the howl of the wind that hung heavy over the silence, replaced the explosions from the TV, shook the walls like laughter. But Peter wasn't laughing, and neither was Claus. Peter felt him shiver behind the blanket shield. Sam snored over the wind and the walls.

"That's him now," Peter told Claus. "Right?"

The ground cleared of fog, of leaves, of pebbles, almost ready to peel back the grass, pull it over the tree trunks, and tuck them into the earth with the worms and sludge.

***

And don't ask me if I love you
And don't worry about what I think
I'm completely yours in my own way

The sun melted deeper into the fog, the ever-fog that ensnared the city. Always on Peter's clothes, in his hair, on his skin where he could taste it like the saltwater that never left his tongue. Part of him felt that if he could take a bite of that ripe fruit —or vegetable—that maybe, this time, the saltwater would dissipate or he would evaporate into the clouds of the city; as part of the fog, he could move around, float away, burn off and disappear to a place where the disappeared go. Instead, he'd been stuck in the fog for so long that often times he wondered if it made him. Each breath would release more fog to the point that he could see his breath leave his body and hang in front of him. After a while, he could see himself in his breath before it disappeared into the atmosphere, a piece of him with it, a small part of him climbing into the sky, waving goodbye to himself as his breath left and he disappeared with it, his skin paler, his cheeks redder, his shoes more broken and his toes loose. Instead, he was surrounded by it, haunted by it, living with it.

But in exchange I want to be your dream,

I don't change because of your kisses,

I want to give you all that I feel and more

***

Peter and Claus watched the sun try to rise, but it was caught on the horizon. The earth tucked into itself like a child, wrapped and warped inside, with mud slung into the air, until it stuck to the sky, and they could almost smell the brown through the window while the trees were sucked deep into the ground and left under the grass until their roots once more poked through the soil. The windows went still, and the rattle silenced.

Sam breathed deeper—deeper. Claus rested his head on his shield. Peter nudged him; the silence settled but unsettling. Claus raised his head and picked up his shield. Peter had heard it too, knew it too, felt the cold run from his toes to his fingers—the howl that was supposed to be gone and disappeared forever, that blew through lives like straw houses.

"To the guns," Peter said.

Claus nodded. They both knew. Peter's tongue was thick in his mouth. He watched the brown bleed from the sky to the earth, and the trees sprouted from the grass and were jerked by the wind, picked up and pulled out like weeds thrown into and over the horizon.

***

The water bottle empty, the garden flushed, Sofia looked about to leave, but Peter wasn't ready for the soft sound of her voice to go, the longing he heard in the song she sang that filled the sky with more than the cold.

"You have a lovely garden," he said.

Her face was covered, her hat, her glasses. She faced him. Her lips twitched. She hadn't gone yet. He wanted to keep her for a moment longer.

"How did you get up here?" she asked.

"Your tomatoes look delicious."

"You should not drink on the roof. I had an uncle that drank on a roof once."

"Is this garden all yours?"

"Is that bottle all yours?"

She pointed to the bottle with less than spit inside. He hadn't drunk the entire bottle, not all at once. He rubbed his hand over his face.

"It was already here."

"Like you were already here."

"What?"

"Basura."

"No," he picked up the bottle. "You afraid I'm gonna strip your garden?"

She reached into her pocket and pulled out a cigarette. She patted her chest, her hips, her back pocket. The cigarette hung limply from her lips. Her sweater hung over her shoulders like a loose drape. Peter pulled a lighter from his coat. He hadn't smoked in weeks, but he thought a lighter was necessary, even when he quit smoking or when he quit smoking again. He held out the lighter. Flicked his fingers. Sparked a fire. Her glasses were dark. Brown and dark. Maybe her glasses were meant more to keep the dark in instead of to keep the light out.

She dipped her face into the fire. He thought for a second that the brim of her hat might catch, but she knew how to light, by the twist in her head. The tip of the cigarette glowed.

"I was worried about birds," she said. "People come and leave rubbish. Birds come. My garden gets eaten."

"I climbed up the fire escape," he said. "I needed height."

"Height?"

"I wasn't kidding about the tomatoes."

"They are almost ready." She inhaled. "Is that bottle yours?" Smoke escaped through her nose. Peter could smell it, wanted it, mixed with the whiskey he could smell on himself, taste in his mouth, the lingered flavor that offered a respite from the saltwater.

"Yes," he said.

"You did not offer me any."

The bottle lay on the ground, the leftover spit moved.

"Nothing good left."

She dropped the ash. His feet moved and crunched the gravel on the roof.

"Next time?" he asked.

"Next time?"

"I'll bring the bottle," he said.

"I will bring the tomatoes."

He smiled.

"Peter."

"Sofia." She offered him a cigarette. He said he had quit. She smiled.

"Next time." She opened the door; the unmistakable squawk ran around the roof. "The garden needs a lot of attention. The tomatoes like punctuality."

"Who doesn't."

The door closed, her on the other side of it. He tried to brush the fog from his skin. The wind was silent. The taste of saltwater returned.

Chapter 23

Peter sat on his bed in the box apartment and felt the stamps of the box plaster the walls like wallpaper; the same stamp slapped With Love—a love he couldn't believe in anymore, one that had disappeared, waved goodbye and sank into the sea.

It was easier when he could shove the memories inside the box and forget about them—his parents, the world that they gave each other, the life they gave him, and the family they took away. His fingers wrapped tight around his head, ready to pull the skin from his face, down—out—off.

Peter forced the corners of an imaginary postcard into his flesh to make sure it wasn't real. When it dug into his skin, the paper didn't fold or crumble; his skin didn't indent. The pressure placed on his body dug deeper into his palm, ready for his blood to burst slow and dark, drip down the card, cover the words and stain his desk. But the thought of the stamps folded to the memory of his watch.

He was young the first time he sat in the tub with Claus and tried to hold onto the last gasp of air that fed his thoughts, the ones where his father was still home, still playful, still present.

The tub was full, up to his neck. He ducked into it, under it. He tried to let the water drip into his ears, to drain the deepest depths of his mind, suck out the thoughts he couldn't remember until he could soak in the tub, where he could drown in his thoughts. Where he could let his memories sink into his pores and remember. Claus perched on the ledge of the porcelain, stripped down to his tattoo. Peter watched him from below the waterline, the spasmodic surface, while Peter held his breath longer until his chest burned and he expected the room to fill with steam, till Claus dove deep into the water and pulled Peter from the wreck beneath the surface.

Peter wanted to take a breath, let the cool air into his body, but refused the comfort, lungs still heavy. Claus trod water. The water dripped into Peter's eyes. His cheeks were about to blow. He wrapped his hands around Claus, around his wet fur, his fingers pressed against his tattoo, meant to play a voice Peter had wanted to hear, couldn't remember, hidden somewhere inside the bear. He gripped Claus harder. If his own memories couldn't be coaxed out, maybe they could be wrung from Claus.

Peter was ready to twist Claus, to do as his tattoo suggested, Try Me. He was ready to try. He pressed Claus's chest and heard nothing. He squeezed Claus. Water dripped. Peter heard nothing. Claus silent. He tapped Peter. Encouraged him. Beckoned him. Try again. Press again. Try harder. Peter tried harder. Pressed harder. Compressed harder. Water trickled down.

"Harder!"

Peter twisted Claus. Water dripped from his fur, leaked from his body, from his tattoo, from his stuffing. It smelled like iron and soap. Claus encouraged him until the memories seeped from Claus's ears like pus. The water whirlpooled until Peter could no longer see his feet. The water shifted and churned with liquid memories turning dark blue. Peter ducked under the water, eyes open, into the night.

Peter in front of a concrete slab, ankle-deep in daisies. Concrete slabs littered the grass along the hillside. The hillside reached out and touched the sky. Claus's fur tickled Peter's cheek, and his nice pants itched his legs—itchy—always itchy. His mom's hair up, her neck exposed, long, fragile, new. She was wrapped in her coat, the same coat she had worn the first time they came to this place with the endless green grass and concrete stones, when she dropped to her hands and knees on top of the packed dirt, filled in fresh, and started to dig her fingers into the earth, pressed seeds deep into the ground. "Help me mark it," she had said, "he'd hate to be like everyone else," Peter almost remembered.

Now the daisies she had planted covered the rectangular surface and brushed softly against Peter's skin, under his feet. Peter didn't feel cold. It wasn't cold. Claus didn't feel cold. It couldn't have been cold. The sun dipped behind the hill. Peter heard it. Like thunder, as it crashed out of sight and the bright blue of the sky faded to a familiar burnt orange with droplets draining upwards, striped like streamers, directing the darkness, each stripe another BAM or CLACK in his ears. His mom stared at the stone, but Peter couldn't see what she stared at, if the stone was supposed to shift or morph into someone, a message, a cake, a car. Where would this stone take them if she concentrated long enough? So Peter tried to keep out the noise and stared at the stone. Claus whispered. Peter put his finger to Claus's lips, tried to concentrate, stared hard at the letters he could almost under- stand, the ones engraved in the ground. Claus whispered again, softer than a raindrop, it may have been a raindrop, dipped into Peter's ear, Andrew, the famil- iar name he had heard before, sometime before, a name Claus pressed into Peter's cheek with his paw while Peter tried to read the words on the stone that might have read Hero or Peace or Andrew or all of the above. Words he couldn't read, that shifted in front of him.

A face.

Peter wanted to see his father's face, the face he could not imagine, dim shapes where his father used to be. He held Claus tighter. His mom, Claus, him, they stared into the stone and watched the words drift away and the face rise from the stone and the flowers that had grown, to fill the gap full of the nothing that had grown bigger since Peter's father's death, his beard and his cheeks full of blue and green and yellow daisies, mixed with the faded grays of concrete that blended to- gether to make his eyes, soft eyes, even in stone, now mixed with flowers.

Peter wanted to touch his father's face. To rub his hands through his father's flower beard. The soft beard Peter remembered. The soft eyes and strong hands. Peter reached for his father's face. Touched. Stone. Hard rock. Even with a beard made of flowers, flowers that smelled of mold. His mother touched Peter's hand.

Her hand. Softer than rock. Softer than his father's hands, or the hands Peter thought he remembered.

"This is where he'll always be," Sam said. Tears ran down her face. Or it was rain. It had started to rain. It fell from the sky like a river from nowhere—from everywhere. Here, where his father would always be, so Peter would know where to find him, marked with a stone face and a lone flowerbed in the middle of a green sea that touched the sky.

Peter was unsure where here was. He looked for a clue on the ground, on his father's stone face, on the hillside, the nowhere behind him where the grass met the sky, in the rain that dropped onto his face, that came from beneath him, that rose from his feet until he held his breath, puffed his cheeks and chipmunked his air.

He rose from the tub with Claus in his hands, Peter and Claus both soaked and stone-cold. Peter took a sip of bathwater full of suds and filth to bring him back to where he may have been the last time he saw his father's face. He choked on the water instead. Claus nudged Peter, wanting to be wrung again. Peter had already done enough and gained no more than soft eyes on a stone face. The water dark blue. The cacophony of sunset shook the window.

"Love Claus," he heard the words in the wind that shook the apartment.

The corners of the room pressed inward hard and fast until the room felt broken and Peter thought his bed had snapped, the box had crumpled. He tried to rid himself of the desire to twist his hands until the past leaked from his body. If he could only wring out the half-remembered memories, let the mementos of the box absorb them. But he would rather let the memories fall down the drain, fall deeper away from him, let them slip into the sewer with the filth and the crocodiles, the rats and the roaches.

Peter wanted the watches to turn to stone—a stone face—morph into a bearable face—a bear's face—or his mother's eyes. But the letters wouldn't change, and the words he wanted to find were stuck in his stomach, ready to turn to shit. All he saw was darkness. Blackout. Blackout? He wanted to scrub the stamps away from the box lid or at least wash away the words written on each stamp. He was ready to run to the post office and buy all of the stamps with pictures of San Francisco landmarks, eager to tear them apart and flush them down the drain.

He refused to stuff more watches into a meaningless box until he couldn't move. He thought somehow the words he wrote on the stamps would have found their way to his mom and Claus; the way Claus's words had found their way to Peter. But where could Peter send useless words except to more useless nightmares?

Chapter 24

The tears in Peter's cousin's eyes were stuck behind a damn of tattooed make-up and a smile made of permanently marked lipstick.

A boyfriend had left, again, and she had found herself at the kitchen table with her hands pressed into her eyes to keep her eyes from rolling around the table like pinballs. She looked up at him with a fake smile, not forced through physical brutality but the emotional kind that crept unknowingly through the air systems like carbon monoxide suffocating you from the inside out. It was the same smile Peter and his mom had—Peter because of his mom.

His cousin's tears didn't run down her cheeks but her palms, bleeding down her wrists in imitations of lines Peter never wanted to see again.

"I was going to take a bath," she said. "You can go first if you'd like."

"I don't take baths," he said.

Peter hadn't taken a bath since his mother sailed away, too afraid to step into the rush of water and steam, afraid he would watch his skin turn to prunes and disintegrate; caught somewhere between the need to sail the infinite waters and find his mother and bear versus the fear of them—the unfettered beat of a scared and hate-filled heart that never wanted to see them because they left him wet and scared in a flood of crimson water waiting for the sharks to circle. What remained was Peter's hatred of baths and a roll in his intestines every time someone said they needed one.

"But they're so relaxing," she said.

"So is masturbation," he said. He was twelve. The closest he had come to cumming was the bullshit the boys at school slang about the sex they said they had—even when everyone knew they hadn't—and the time Peter pinched the tip of his penis and stretched it as far as he could, hoping it would extend to his belly button. It didn't.

His cousin looked at him, unsure of what to say. It was a moment between them that defined their relationship where both of them, Peter thought, wondered why she took him in in the first place. This was the longest conversation they had had without using the fart and burp of one of her boyfriends as intermissions.

"I'm learning about the effects in class," he said.

"Oh," she said. "It's good to be educated on...things." The red in her eyes looked about to crack. "I brought you this." She pulled out a stuffed lion from under the chair. "He looked sweet."

Those were the only gifts she gave Peter, hand-me-downs of broken toys when the broken relationships couldn't be glued back together. This was the first time she gave Peter a stuffed animal. It was the first time Peter held the fur in his hands since Claus had sailed off.

The quiet tears of his cousin stopped. She walked out, and Peter heard the faucet ripping through the walls. The lion's mane stood out like static beneath his crown.

"What's your name?" Peter said. "Where do you come from?"

The lion was quiet.

"Tell me...have you ever fought a wolf?"

The high-pitched moan of the walls continued. The silence of the lion stuck to Peter's clothes like cobwebs.

"Talk to me," Peter said. He shook the lion a little to wake him. "I'm sorry. Your majesty, where's your kingdom?" Silence. "King? Sire?" Peter shook him again. "Talk to me!" The walls stopped screaming. The water's rush done. Soft music seeped beneath the bathroom door.

He put the king on the table and grabbed a chair. He held it out in front of him, his other hand to his side. The kitchen almost faded. The vibrant cheer of a crowd almost drowned out the faucet. A whip appeared in Peter's hand. He cracked it. There wasn't a sound. The king didn't move. His stuffed body was stiff on the table. Peter expected a roar or a cry or a whimper or a paw. Peter expected a king—a lion—to live and jump and play. Peter tried to crack the whip once more. Another silent flick. Another empty response. The almost gleam of the wanted circus disappeared back into the drab beige of the kitchen. Peter's whip went back into the air from which it had appeared. His hand stuck to his side, the chair back on the tile.

"Please!" Peter said. He held the king close to his chest. Hugged him close. Pressed his cheek to the crown. "I was a knight once. Me and Claus…he was my— I swear we were knights."

An unwelcomed calm drifted through the house. It sent chills up Peter's arms. 'King?" The music stopped; his cousin hummed; the king stayed silent. Peter stepped to the sink—his chest barely above the ledge—and let the faucet run but tried to ignore the sound, the scratch of the water in his ears. He turned on the thunder of the garbage disposal. Bit by bit, he lowered the lion into the drain, the grind of the disposal, the tear of the stuffing, the soft fur shredded—the lion quiet. His cousin hummed through the door. All Peter said was, "Please." He didn't whisper "Release" because it wasn't a prayer he wanted or a moment he should remember. The torn smile of the lion sunk beneath the ceramic edges of the sink, stuffed into the hole until the crown disappeared.

Peter was a knight once. Now he couldn't protect a king, a fly, himself, his mother, his bear. He ran to his room, shut the door, and wished for all the clocks to turn backward, for the earth to revolve the other way, for the rain to fall up— but the answer he got was his cousin's hum muffled within the water of the bath- tub.

Chapter 25

The door-buzzer rang. When Carly opened the door, she wanted her apartment to smell like brownies. It was something her mom had told her; it puts people's guard down: if they smell sweets, it's a comfort. Something she had said would make people relax, open themselves up to whatever comes next, especially if it's a date. Not that Carly went on many dates; even fewer came back to her apartment. Peter was different. There was something about him: his awkwardness, his sweetness, the way he looked at her, with his hazel eyes, green and brown, that swirled together like tie-dye. It was the way he looked at her that first time, like he knew her or wanted to know her. With one look he saw her entire life and wanted to keep her secrets between them, like in an old romantic movie, like at any moment they could sit together, the two of them on her couch—she always envisioned her place in fantasies because she knew it; in her mind "his place" was a variation of her apartment—and the movie would have a moment where Bogart looks into Hepburn's eyes and says:

"Do you believe in past lives? "

"I believe anything is possible."

"I never like when people say 'eyes like the ocean.' Too many eyes. Too many oceans. Oceans that are blue, green, brown. Oceans so clear you can see the fish five feet away. There's a better way. "

"Is there?"

"Like a past life."

"If you believe in that sort of thing."

"There must be a better way. Like your eyes—"

"What about my eyes?"

"A memory."

And Bogart would bring Hepburn in close to him, the way Peter would hold Carly, and Hepburn would stare at Bogart with longing, because of those words, that description, a memory, like they had done this before, or had that love before, like they were meant for each other. Like he was looking back through all his lifetimes by looking into her eyes and remembering them from somewhere, but somewhere he couldn't pinpoint. And Carly would look at Peter with that same longing, like her eyes were a memory. Bogart would look down at Hepburn with that intensity only he had, except he and Peter shared it, at the moment when Carly was Hepburn and Peter was Bogart. They all stared at one another, all wanting the same thing, that same kiss that wasn't a transfer of power or an admission of lust, but a submission to love, to the memories they held of one another without ever knowing before that they had existed, until without the other person, they knew, there was something missing. Peter would look down at Carly and lean his lips to hers, and Bogart to Hepburn, until electricity brought their lips together, soft and firm and longing to reach into the other's memory with their lips and see the memories that they couldn't remember were there—their lips could remind them, like Bogart and Hepburn, their lips were the key; at that moment when their lips touched, though, Carly didn't need to remember the memories of their past lives because in the moments they were together all she wanted was to stay that way—together—and didn't need or want the past when they were apart, or a past different than what had led them to the moment where they would be together.

Carly pushed the button to let Peter up. She wanted him to look at her the same way he looked at her the first time she saw him, and she was sure that he knew her once, at some time, with that look he gave her. She couldn't imagine not knowing him ever again.

It wasn't supposed to rain. Movies and books and magazines and music made it sound like rain ended relationships. Love happened in sunshine; rain was meant for breakups and arguments. The rain outside wouldn't keep Carly from Peter or him from her. The brownies were almost done, and the scent traveled to every corner of the apartment. She was never sure if it was because of what her mom had said or because it was true, but the smell made her more comfortable. Carly's mom would make them when her mom had a bad day, and when Carly was younger, there seemed like more days with brownies than days without, days with swollen wrists and bruised shoulders, punctured skin and gnarled fingers; Carly somehow safe in the park, at school, a friend's, somehow not around until her mom's body was bandaged and the smell of brownies and her mom's—Carly knew now—fake smile crowded the house. It always made Carly feel better, even after they ran, from that fucker of a husband, the big man who had to make himself feel bigger by beating his woman because she was disrespectful somehow, that he justified in his fucked-up drunk way. A way Carly promised herself she wouldn't allow to happen to her, be a part of someone's drunk justification, a stupid justification that they, nor she, could make sense of.

Sense is a hard thing to make, especially as an artist. But Peter looked right at Sunflower Star fields and knew it, watched it glow in the darkness and expand from person to person, absorb the darkness and lift into the air like the sunflowers were comets, falling to the earth in a starless sky, sunflower comets that glowed and fell and lit up the dark—in people's lives—to give some form of guidance, if only for the moment—and Peter found Carly in that darkness. And she found him in the light of the fog—as the light in the fog—with an awkward smile and a self-conscious conversation, and the only person who looked at a work made of glow-in-the-dark sand without needing to make sense of it, even if he had to clean it up.

She opened the door, and Peter stood in the hallway with his clothes so soaked they stuck to his skin, his hair matted down and black with wet, with that awkward smile on his face.

"Smells like brownies," he said.

"Come in," Carly said.

"I stepped in a puddle," he said.

"Must've been one hell of a puddle," she said.

"Better than stepping in a poodle," he said.

"The bathroom is just there," she said. "I'll see if I have some clothes." She pointed to the door, four doorways but two doors, the bathroom and the front door. She grabbed his hand; it was cold. She wanted to wrap her hands around his until she could feel the blood pump through his veins, warming him up.

"Lovely home," he said. "Sorry, I'm flooding it."

"Not even," she said. "Go dry off. I'll get a fire going."

He wrapped his other hand around Carly's, his hazel eyes looked into her, his skin ice against hers. He looked at her. That look—again—searching history to find her when she was right in front of him waiting for him here. She was a spark, or an explosion, in his eyes, a burst of light, the realization that it was her in front of him, the history he looked for wrapped up inside of the girl he wanted, for whatever reason he wanted her, knowing that she wanted him too. He pressed his wet body against hers, the water through her clothes and on her skin in seconds. But she didn't care. The water from his hair, and his face, dripped down on her face. But she didn't care. Because of his lips, wet, soft, for her, with a hint of hesitation, his eyes closed, holding the thoughts of her that he had found. The lips she wanted, and she took them, and she loved them; he kissed her the same way he looked at her, with need instead of want, with worth instead of insecurity, like the kiss was how he could express himself; the words were filler. His lips were lush and left her feet unstable, and the water dripped, and his lips kissed, and his skin cold, his skin soft, his lips soft, his mind on her, her on his mind—Peter—a stranger—? No, Peter, a person she had known in lifetimes before now, through all the time-lines that ever were, because they fit together, in each other's eyes, in each other's arms, in each other's lips, in each other's hearts—somehow.

He pulled away.

"I love brownies," he said. He walked into the bathroom.

"I'll look for something you can wear," she said. A clank. "You okay?"

"It's ok," he said.

"Are you ok?"

The door opened, and Peter stood in the doorway in her robe, a bright blue robe with toothpaste stains on it that looked like bleach. His socks were dark blue, saturated, and in his hands. He flung them over the shower-curtain-rod.

"Hope it doesn't take too long to dry," he said. "Might get funny looks walking home in this."

"It's San Francisco," Carly said. "You'd fit in on the bus. Dinner's almost ready."

"I could use a drink."

"Sit," she said.

He sat on the floor, just above chest level to the coffee table with his back rested on the couch. He leaned his head back onto the cushion. She poured two glasses of wine, red wine because he said he liked it better. She did too; it was heavy and rich, good for the rain, and a robe, she thought. She handed him the glass.

"You could sit on the couch," she said.

"Where would I put my head?" he said. He didn't look at her. He looked past her. She put her glass on the table and walked across the room to the fireplace.

"Help?" he said.

"Think I can't lift a log?"

"Trying to look useful," he said. "Hard to do in a bathrobe."

"Harder to do with wet hair on my cushions."

He lifted his head, that awkward smile returned. The unsure smile, a little bit of blush in his cheeks as the fire started to build momentum and the crackle filled the fireplace.

"Sorry," he said. He took a sip of wine.

"Not even," she said. She sat next to him, her elbow on the couch, wine in her hand. "Thought you liked the high ground."

"I like lots of things," he said. "Like wine. Food. Travel, you know, the usual. And the high ground."

"What else?"

"That painting," he said.

He gestured to the painting above the fireplace: Cerberus, the three-headed dog that guarded Hell. The left head smiled, the right head cried, and the center head bared its teeth—all the heads dripped with drool and stood on a mountain of broken bones on the banks of the River Styx. Someone once told Carly it looked like it smelled like sulfur and putrescence.

"Yours?" he said.

She sipped her wine and nodded. She didn't hang much of her own art around, thought it suffocated her thoughts, and left her too much time to worry about a line, or a grain of sand, or a smudge, or the possibility of a smudge, but this one was different. Not because of the content, but because of the title and when she painted it. She had been reading Dante's Divine Comedy in high school, she and her mom had just up and run from that drunk fucker of a father, and this was the first time she created something that made her feel better, that she transferred emotions to, as if her thoughts made their way through to her fingers and her fingers to the brush, the brush to the paint and the paint to the canvas. All of a sudden, there stood Cerberus in front of her, but not guarding Hell, as he did, but guarding her, her emotions, because he was her, and the Hell that he guarded was her mind, where she couldn't allow anyone access.

"Cerberus," he said. "Fan of Styx? The river or the band?"

"It's called 'Self Portrait,'" she said.

"I see the resemblance," Peter said. He rubbed the watches on his wrist and sunk into a faraway stare.

The oven chimed. The brownies were done. So was the chicken. She never asked him if he ate chicken, but at least she knew he wasn't a vegetarian because he had asked for her bacon the first time they met...the first time she met him.

He ate bacon; she assumed he would eat chicken. He said he wouldn't eat anything soy. She didn't blame him.

She had set the dining room table for them, placemats, plates, forks on the left, knives on the right, even put up a few candles to try and make it romantic, the pop of the fire and the rush of the rain helped, but the candles weren't needed, not really, there had been candles on their first date, at least the first dinner date, that ended at the restaurant with their first kiss, when his lips first tasted like need, and his eyes flashed bright with her. At breakfast, he had been thoughtful. At coffee he had been curious, dinner he had been wanted—needed—and when she felt his lips, she knew he wasn't another drunk, knuckles ready to prove his manhood; she wanted to swim in the depths of him, tell Cerberus to let this one through, like Dante, let him into her mind to see if he could make it through the depths of her. And she wanted him to. They didn't need candles for that. They didn't need the dining room table for that. They didn't even need to be fully dressed for that. She put the chicken, garlic bread, and spinach salad on the plates and brought them to the coffee table.

"The table is set, though," he said, but he didn't move.

"This is better," she said.

"I'll get the silverware."

He refilled the wine glasses while he was up. Carly crossed her legs and smelled the garlic and the butter. She couldn't not use butter. Another cooking tip she took from her mom. Peter put the wine and silverware down, took a seat, took a bite, and made a sound like a cow in the grass.

"Crazy good," he said. He was still chewing.

"Family recipe," she said.

"Your own family," he said, "or someone else's?"

She took a bite of chicken and pointed to herself.

"Then I might have to say that I love your family," he said.

"That's a big commitment," she said. "My family might be scared away."

"I do leave creepy messages," he said. "But if your family makes chicken like that—" he took another bite.

He devoured his food and she ate hers. It was nice to see someone enjoy her food, someone other than herself, someone other than a guy who comes into her apartment, comes into her bed, cums into her, without a look of the place, without a taste of her food, with more than a taste of her body, but it hasn't always been their fault—it was hers—hers and Cerberus'; another reason why she kept that painting where she could see it, to remind her that she had a guard, a help, a reason to keep the depths of her deep down in the darkness, because if someone were to swim in those waters, they could drown, never be seen again, and she would be the cause, she would be the end of them, and that could be the end of her. Like Guy. A docent at the D'Orsay.

She was nineteen. He called her "mon chouchou." She would try to speak with her eyes what she couldn't say with her tongue—the things Peter said with his eyes—she wanted to be absorbed by Guy's lips when he spoke to her, about her, touched her, with his fingertips, his lips, his breath. It was short-lived. He was in love with Ernest Barrias's 'Nature Unveiling Herself to Science.' She thought she was too, the sensuality of a full-figured woman undressing herself to the world, a different world, a different perception of what was and what would be; she thought she loved how it looked, like Guy—until she found him being science and a Spanish tourist named Franco being nature. But she hadn't been ended, and Guy hadn't been swallowed, at least not by her. Instead, she stormed, inside and out, stormed away from Guy, and swallowed the clouds whole until Cerberus reared his ugly heads, larger, stronger, fiercer than before: "In his original darkness," Guy had said when she tried to teach herself German so she could read Kierkegaard as Guy had told her to do, but she should have been learning French. Later she found out it was Franco who had fed that line to Guy, anyway.

The plates clanged when Peter put them in the sink. She wasn't sure if he liked the food or was eager to get to the brownies. It was nice that he offered to do the dishes, though. The robe swayed when he walked to the kitchen, and how he swayed his hips so the robe swished even more. The rain had calmed. Not stopped, but settled to more of a mist than a storm. The window made the outside world look wrapped in cellophane, hazy cellophane covering the bay.

"Any other art?" Peter said. He put down a plate of brownies and two bowls of ice cream, both with whipped cream; one had more than the other. "Just because you have whipped cream doesn't mean you want a whole heap of it. Pick." Carly chose the heap. He picked up a brownie and shoved it into his bowl. She did the same.

"Not much here," she said. "Hard to stomach your own work sometimes."

"Hard to stomach work in general most times," he said.

"Why is that?" she said. She took a bite of her now-sundae.

"Guess people are inherently lazy," he said.

She shook her head. The ice cream was cold in her mouth. Almost too cold.

"Why a janitor?" she said.

"Is this the, 'You could be so much more' talk?" He didn't sound annoyed, more like he had expected the conversation eventually. He took a bite of his sundae.

"Not if you want to be a janitor," she said.

"You ever want to erase history?" he said. "Not erase but clean."

"Like with turtle wax?"

"That works," he said. "I generally use a whole-lot-of-Windex. It works for me, the Windex, I mean. Clears the smudges away, at least on hard surfaces, not so much on skin—trust me on that one."

"Not even—"

"Sometimes there are the things you want to remember—"

A nice way to say it; sometimes all Carly could think about was blood and spaghetti sauce: when she came home from the park and saw her dad eating spaghetti, noodle by noodle, mom in the kitchen, wouldn't turn around, drops of blood or spaghetti sauce on the tile; when mom did turn her hands were bandaged and her smile was broken. The drunk-fuck-father at the table slurping the spaghetti noodle by noodle. Carly hoped the mess on the floor was all sauce.

"...lots of times there are things you want to forget. Or maybe just rather not think about. I can do that." Peter said.

"Your superpower?"

"If you only get one, might as well be a good one."

"How long have you had it for?" Carly said.

"Still hoping for it."

"So you can't do it."

"It's a work in progress," Peter said.

"How much progress?"

"It's a space to myself."

"A stolen fortress of solitude?" she said.

"Cleaned," he said. "Cleaned of all fingerprints. Face-prints. Clean of all the oily smudges that were touched, rubbed, and smeared all over the museum as if no one had ever been there before me. I clean away the history of the space. 'Tomorrow's a new day,' type of thing. Then it's just me. Me and the museum, without any other people, without any of the smudged problems of these people's lives that they left behind with them at the museum. Just me...and my problems." He laughed and took a scoop of ice cream.

"The Exploratorium is a big space to fill with problems," she said.

"I got enough to fill it," he said.

"So does the human race."

"If I could clean away someone else's past, maybe I could do my own."

"Looking for a clean slate?"

"Just a less cluttered one."

"Buy a new one?"

"Who's got that kind of money?"

"Find a new one?"

"Who's got that kind of luck? I'm just looking to clean off the one I have."

"How's that going for you?"

"We're back to work in progress."

Carly finished her ice cream. He offered her the rest of his. Whether he expected she would take it or not, she did. He smiled. It wasn't the awkward smile; it was more of a smirk, with his lips tilted at the edge—his eyes burning into her; her stomach fluttering on its own.

"What was your childhood like?" Carly asked.

"Short," he said.

"Your height?"

"That too."

***

One time Peter wandered into his mother's room, the closet full of his father's clothes, the clothes that still smelled vaguely of spruce and sweat; the clothes that Sam couldn't get herself to throw away; the clothes that she sometimes wrapped herself in at night so the smell that remained of Peter's father would brush against her skin and she could close her eyes and pretend he was with her, his arms wrapped around her tight. When she would wake up, she would see that they were her arms, her arms in his clothes, his clothes that started to lose the scent of him, replaced by the scent of her.

Peter blamed himself for the smiles he couldn't create, the ones he didn't remember of his mother's because Sam hadn't smiled that way since his father died. Peter was too young to remember what that smile looked like. Shame mostly came up from under Peter's feet and sank into his skin like some form of moisture that his body couldn't prevent. So Peter ran away from it. He kept running away from it. But the more he ran from it, the faster it came, until running wasn't enough.

One afternoon he walked out of Sam's room in the red and green plaid shirt, sleeves draped down to the floor and the Birkenstocks like clown shoes that poked out of the bottom of the shirt as it trailed behind him. His mother sat on the couch, legs folded beneath her, glass of wine to her lips. Peter had gone so far as to draw a beard on his face with scented markers to see if the brown marker smelled like his father, but it smelled like cinnamon, and Peter was hoping for bark. Sam's eyes were huge, like the glass she looked through when Peter came out of the room. Peter said her name, her full name, because he remembered his father saying her full name, but Peter was young and had a bit of a lisp; it sounded like Tham-anta. Andrew was the only one who ever called her Samantha. It had always sounded too formal to her—she was anything but formal— except when Andrew said it. He would say it soft and delicate, which made her feel delicate, even if he were angry, somehow the way he said her name was like a cushion around her or a safety-net below her, but no matter how he said her name, he was the only one who said it that way; Peter didn't know how his father had said her name, just that he did, but in Peter's imitation he didn't see the smile he had hoped to see, the smile the streetcar had in his mother's painting. There was no smile. She sat and stared at him. Eyes as large as a magnifying glass, to get a better look at him, to read his marker-bearded-face, to see the stitches on the clothes that he wore, made in Cambodia, or Nepal, or Vietnam, or China—giant eyes that could see right through the clothing Peter wore, from the person he tried to be, for himself, for her, so she would wrap Peter in her arms like she wrapped herself in the empty arms of his father's shirts, because she was his mother and seeing her without a smile was watching the blue sky crack, shatter, and fall into the sea leaving an empty void in its place. She was his mother, the person who was supposed to love him the most, care for him the most, the person who was supposed to hold him in her arms and tell him that everything would be fine, even if she couldn't tell herself. That was what he needed to hear, the words she couldn't or wouldn't tell herself, and in turn wouldn't or couldn't tell him, even if he didn't know that that was what he needed to hear at the time because he was too young, dressed in his father's clothes, the clothes that had lost the smell of his father; Peter stood there with the clothes dragging on the floor and a cinnamon beard on his face.

"Tham-anta." Her big eyes too busy with the boy he was and not the man he tried to be.

"Sam-anta. The moon is calling." He pointed out the window, his finger barely visible in the sag of the sleeve. He made a phone with his fingers and put it to his ears. "He says the cow is a liar and never jumped over him.'"

Sam put the glass on the table. A drop bled down the side and stained a ring into the tabletop. She raised her arms out to Peter, made the motion for him to come to her. He clopped over; the Birkenstocks almost tripped him with every step, the shirt a plaid train. She held him at arm's length.

"You smell like cinnamon," Sam said. "How are we going to get this off of you?" She rubbed her thumb over his beard and smudged it.

"Raise your arms," she said.

He did.

"The moon said the cat was never a good fiddler," Peter said. Sam lifted the plaid off Peter, his man façade reduced to his tiny body in batman underwear, traces of his father reduced to the chemical smell of cinnamon.

"What were you doing?" she said.

"Is a wolf a dog or a cat?" Peter said.

Samantha crumbled the plaid shirt and held it close to her nose. Her eyes closed from the magnifiers they were, now that Peter no longer resembled the man he wanted to be—for her. She dropped the shirt to the floor.

"Like a tiger," he said. "A tiger is a cat."

Sam picked up Peter and set him in her lap. She hadn't smiled though, still, not like the one in the painting, not since the car accident. But he was wrapped up in her now, the warm comfort of his mother.

"Claus said a wolf is a dog," Peter said. "I think Claus could jump over the moon. If he wasn't so angry."

Sam held onto Peter, close, his naked skin against her softness, and he felt safe. He felt like she said the words he didn't know he wanted to hear, even if she hadn't said them at all, even if the words that came out of her mouth were, "You're going to need a bath, darling."

"Claus first," he said.

"The same time?" Sam said.

"Yes," Peter said. But he wasn't ready to leave the comfort of Sam's arms, the safety of a world he didn't know wasn't safe. He pressed his hands to Sam's arms and whispered release, to paint her into forever, and this moment, into forever. She and Claus were all he had left, he knew, but sometimes he wondered if she did, if she could, without the smile she once had, could she ever.

"The same time," he said. But Peter wasn't ready for a bath.

***

Carly couldn't tell if the rain was still falling. The fog had rolled in and covered the city. She wasn't sure if she could see the apartment across the street or if it was a reflection of her apartment in the fog.

"To a clean slate," she said. She raised her glass.

"Speaking of clean," he said. "I don't want to clean away everything."

Not even, as if he had to tell her: there was that look again, that everything look, that look that let her know it wasn't about erasing history, but about protecting himself from his past, from his vulnerabilities, his Cerberus. He couldn't want to erase history, she knew, because of that look. The look of them, the way we were, are, and will be—together. She knew he had a secret. They all did, and he wasn't ready to share it, for the same reason he tried to clean it all away. He just wasn't ready. She wanted him to be but knew he would get there, eventually, ready to tell her what he was trying to clean, why he needed it to be clean, the thing that drove him to travel the way he did, the thing that drove him to stay here as long as he had. But that look, she wanted to stay in that look.

He put a small glass jar on the table; it had a lid and swirls of yellow, black, green, and red. The layers glowed in the dim firelight.

"Remnants of sunflowers," he said. "I told you I didn't want to clean it."

Carly wanted to stay in that look.

Chapter 26

It was rare for Sofia to have a quiet moment without the brass and bass of the radio loud in the air, her voice cloaked by the mix of music that surrounded her. She had spent so many years in a shroud of noise—radio, television, her thoughts—that since Valentina disappeared, the sound of silence sometimes confused her. Peter breathed deep and even in the silence of the car. Sofia counted the seconds between his inhales and exhales. He hadn't spoken since they got on the freeway. He hadn't said much since they left Muir Woods. Peter had told Sofia he wanted to see the Redwoods. The tallest trees in the world. She had been in San Francisco for this long and had never been to see them. After twenty-odd years, she should have seen them by now. She had always wanted to go with someone—a friend—to share in the majesty together.

The nature outside of the city reminded her too much of Gaston and his ranch outside of Buenos Aires. She wasn't ready to think of him any more than she already did. But if Sofia were honest with herself, she would admit that she had been too tired. She had been running since she put away the alfajores the night after Valentina didn't come home. If Sofia were honest with herself, she would admit that Peter made her less tired, gave her a reason to leave her apartment beyond the market and exercise. That is the problem with silence, Sofia thought. You can't help but be honest with yourself.

The car ride to Muir Woods had been full of sound, the engine's roar, the hum of the car on the freeway, the rush of the wind through the window and the burst of music from the radio, strings and violin, the thump of drums; for Sofia, it was the comfortable noise of an enclosed space.

"How long have you wanted to see them?" Sofia had said.

"Was reminded of it recently," Peter said. He tapped one of his watches. "I remembered one of mom's paintings. It was a giant redwood with a split trunk. The split was wide and almost halfway up the tree. A man posed in the split. The branches spread high up on the tree and twirled down in a swirl of leaves that looked like hair. The hole in the tree had an outline of teeth. There were eyes hidden in the bark. The man was blurry, almost faded. The tree looked like a face—my mom's face. She had only painted that one self-portrait, the one of her in San Francisco, but this face was similar, like in the way an aged photo looks. You can see the person is the same, but things have changed. Maybe the portrait of her in San Francisco was the only one she painted when she was happy."

"Perhaps it was not her," Sofia said. "As the tree?"

"We should go," Peter said. "I think it'd do us both some good."

They left early in the morning. When Peter got in the car, he handed Sofia the box she had seen on his bed in his apartment. Stamps created a mosaic of the world on the lid. Sofia had a desire to open the box, but fear was a hard feeling of which to rid herself. She worried she would find something in the box she didn't want to know. And fear overtook curiosity.

Sofia had hoped that the marine layer would burn off throughout the day. As they left the city and drove farther north, the marine layer wasn't a layer but pavement made of clouds that hung lifeless in the sky. Peter drove. The radio blared. Sofia had grown accustomed to the sound of people's voices in a swarm of instruments. She picked out a person's voice amongst a tumble of vocals. The drive to Muir Woods was no different. Peter was learning to do the same. He turned down the music far less often than he had when they first met.

"Think you will see her there?" Sofia said.

"It's like the fog just sits there," Peter said.

"She will be in the tree?" Sofia said. "Think there will be a face?"

Peter honked the horn. Traffic had been steady on the way up. He had said he wanted to go early. Sofia didn't understand the rush. He had waited this long to see the trees. They weren't going anywhere. Sometimes he can be impatient. Sometimes she forgot he was still a child.

"I think it'll be nice to see how big these trees can get," Peter said. "They are supposed to be beautiful. Crazy big."

"Yes," Sofia said. "They are supposed to be."

"There is one up north that you can drive through," Peter said. "It's not every day you get to drive through a tree."

"It feels like there are more and more places where that is all that you get to do," Sofia said. When she looked back at her life, there were too many times when Sofia sat as a passenger along for the ride, stuck in the seat watching her life pass her by, unable to get out, unable to stop the seconds and linger amongst a cherished moment—another hug with Valentina, her soft skin and passion fruit hair. Another kiss with Gaston, his warm hands and passionate stare.

The song on the radio changed. The high-pitch of an accordion filled the car. Sofia tapped her thigh. Peter tapped the wheel. The mix of red and green trees passed the window.

Sofia unlatched the lock of the box and lifted the lid. A mound of watches. The stamps atop the letter had writing on them. It said, "With Love."

"Who are these for?" Sofia said.

"They were from my mom."

"And what are you going to do with them now?"

"Bury them," Peter said.

Sofia clapped at Peter's impetuousness. How reckless children could be when the repercussions were easy, she thought. Sofia looked at the watches stuffed in the box.

"These do not look like garbage," Sofia said.

"One man's trash is another man's—" Peter said.

"Treasure?" Sofia said.

"So the saying goes."

"They do not work?" Sofia said, noting the broken faces.

"They work…differently," Peter said.

"Will you be throwing these out the window?"

Peter rolled up the window. Sofia closed the lid and let the music move them forward.

When they made it to Muir Woods, Peter parked the car, eager to get on the trail. Sofia had never seen him this excited. In the quiet of the forest, she understood his excitement, his impatience; Sofia knew that Peter expected to find some sort of closure in the forest. He carried the box tight in his arms. Peter's chest covered the words he had written on the stamps. Perhaps if he confronted his mother's inspiration for her painting, he could let go of her ghost. Life isn't that easy. If it were, Sofia would have gone back to Buenos Aires long ago, taken Gaston's face in her hands and kissed his soft lips. She would have walked down the streets of the city and sat on the same benches her daughter had sat on, walked through the same parks, ate passion fruit, drank hot chocolate, studied political science, buried her locket in the soil of the pampa Valentina loved so much. Sofia would have let go of all the empty space that swallowed her from the inside out; if that were how life worked.

The deeper they traveled on the path, the stronger the smell of moss. The leaves smelled wet. The smell of bark surrounded Sofia, sometimes mixed with the sour scent of charred wood, as if smoke had taken over the air for a second. Peter moved through the trail with quick feet. His shoes scraped the dirt path. His shoes left diamonds in the dust. The tick of cameras filled the area. Tourists photographed one another. Tourists with peace-sign fingers. Smiley faces. Bucket hats. Mickey Mouse sweatshirts. Hiking boots. Tourists that hugged trees and kissed the bark. Some kissed one another under the canopy of the redwoods. Maybe Sofia could hug one, feel how far around the trunk her arms could go. If passion fruit grew on redwoods, Valentina would have had no problem watering the tree from the rooftop.

"I found it," Peter said. Disappointment replaced the shutter of cameras. Peter stood at the crack of a tree where the bark split wide enough to let couples stand inside the wound, showcasing the height and width of the wound.

"They are the largest trees I have ever seen," Sofia said. "Thank you for bringing me. They are lovely."

Peter didn't go inside the split. He pressed his hand to the outside bark. His grip had loosened around the box. Sofia leaned against the rails of the trail.

"They are nice," he said. Sofia wasn't sure if he had seen any of the other trees. "They are big."

Water streamed nearby. Sofia heard the trickle and drops. Peter pressed his other hand against the tree. He looked inside. It was as if his hands refused to let him enter. They protected him from what might have been inside, but more importantly, what wasn't.

"There's a stream close by," Peter said. "Naturally." He laughed a little. A strained laugh. A disappointed laugh.

"Do you want me to take a photo of you?" Sofia said. "You can climb inside."

"Does it sound like the water is getting faster?"

"It will be a nice photo."

"I don't know," Peter said. "I thought I'd find…anything."

"We can take the photo together."

"I didn't expect an answer," he said. "There isn't an answer. Does the water sound like it's rising? I just thought, maybe, that this time there would be something different. I thought this time, if I went somewhere that mom had painted, somewhere that had affected her, maybe I could get rid of that feeling...this feeling."

Sofia put her hand against the rail. She wanted him to continue, but she didn't want to push him. He had been closed off for so long, to everyone, not just to her. She knew how that felt. It had taken her years to feel ready to open up. She knew he hid something. She knew it was about his mom. She could tell by the way he spoke about her or when he would avoid her. She knew from the way he looked at Sofia when she spoke about Valentina, like he wanted someone or needed someone to miss him the way Sofia missed her daughter. Sofia and Peter had been alone before each other. Being alone for so long boarded them up to the point that to tear down their own walls they had to punch bare-fisted through concrete. Sofia's walls had been torn down—almost. Peter had helped. Another person escaping from a previous life, from people, from memories, from ghosts. What they needed was each other. When Sofia let the first crumb of her wall drop to the ground, it was as if she had taken her first breath in ages, the first time she had taken a step without the weight of her past shackled to her ankle. It had been almost as painful as when she built the wall in the first place. There was something about Peter that had let her know it was time.

Peter took time. Maybe he hadn't known that time was what was needed or that a wall had been built in the first place. But here he was, with his hands against the wall, ready to tear it down, body stuffed in the large split of a redwood, scratching at his past with his fingernails.

"That worry that the water is always there, rushing, rising, and chasing me. That she'll catch up to me no matter where I run. I thought that this time— maybe—if I came here and saw the tree, that I could escape, just for a minute."

Sofia walked toward Peter. She put one hand on the bark and her other hand on his hand.

"I know she won't come back," he said. "She's gone."

Sofia nodded her head. He rested his head on her shoulder. She held him close to her. His breath shallowed. He held her tight. He was warm. She hoped she was as warm to him as he was to her. The sound of the water subsided. The shudder of cameras returned. A group of tourists stood in line, waiting for their turn to enter the crack in the bark. Some took photos of Peter and Sofia. Sofia and Peter stepped away from the crack and let other people settle into the split. A small man with a comb-over and glasses, sandals and socks held out a Polaroid to Sofia. She shook her head. He thrust the photo toward her. It already looked faded. It was of her and Peter. Just now. In the center of the tree. His face buried in her shoulder. Her cheek rested on his head. A small smile on her face. Her eyes closed. His eyes the only visible part of his face. She said thank you to the man. Sofia and Peter walked back to the car.

In the quiet of the ride home, Sofia watched the red and green of the forest fade to the suburban sprawl of the freeway. She pulled out the photo of her and Peter. She couldn't blame him for his want to rid himself of some of the world that he carried on his shoulders. How often had she tried? She would never stop trying. He shouldn't either. His eyes avoided the box in the back seat. The case loomed large over them both now. She didn't reach for the radio the moment the car started. This time wasn't her moment to fill with sound. If Peter needed the quiet, she wanted him to have it.

"Sam told—" he cleared his throat. He struggled with his mom's name. Sofia had witnessed the struggle first hand, when she had said a word so often it began to lose meaning. The struggle came between the desire to hold onto what the word meant and to let the word turn to an empty sound that could fall out of her mouth for whatever reason. She had held tight to Valentina, to daughter, the sound of them, the meaning of them, because they meant the same thing. Sofia heard the way Peter hesitated when he said the name Sam, the uncertainty of the word on his tongue because he had to hold onto the words: Sam and mom, because they were one and the same. Sofia wanted to put her hand on his, to tell him she understood, that as much as he wanted to run away from the hurt of the words, he didn't want to let the meaning of the words slip away.

"My mom told me a story," Peter said. "About a baby's heartbeat." Sofia imagined Peter as a boy lying in bed beside his mom, his eyes heavy with sleep, the room filled with the smell of his hair after a warm bath. He'd ask to hear the story again, the one he had heard every night for a week. After his mom started, Peter would interrupt, saying he wanted to tell the story, eager to recite the words exactly how his mom had.

"A baby's heart beats so fast because it counts all the angels that touched its heart in heaven." In the car, Peter's face was passive. In Sofia's head, where Peter spoke as a child, he wore a veil of tired excitement. He watched the road as the Golden Gate came into view. "All the good memories the baby had before it was born were captured in its heartbeat. Smiles, laughter, stories, warmth, caring—handprints of angels."

Peter would ask why people's heartbeats slowed when they aged, Sofia thought. Once again, Peter would drift in and out of sleep, unable to drift fully before his mom answered. She would respond with two reasons: One is that we lose the handprints of angels on our hearts because the older we are, the more we forget.

"But as we lose the memories of the angels," Peter said in the car, "we get something better; the second thing. We start collecting the handprints of people who have touched our hearts over the years." Here Sofia imagined Peter's mom pausing and rubbing her hands through Peter's hair. "Some more than others, but there will always be people that touch your heart. Your heartbeat is the collection of their handprints."

Outside, the lights of the Golden Gate Bridge imitated the stars in the sky, the stars the fog had covered. By the time Peter and Sofia entered the bridge, they could have been driving through the galaxy. She patted Peter's shoulder, unable to say any words, not because she couldn't but because the quiet in the car still belonged to him—even if she knew what to say, she would have kept it to herself at that moment. Until he breathed. A deep breath. Where his chest heaved. His arms relaxed.

"I laughed when I heard about Valentina," Sofia said.

Peter looked at her.

"Not right away," she said. "The next day. Right before I fell asleep. It was like laughing until you cry but in reverse. I had not cried yet. Not at that time. Not out loud. I felt my body tense and throbbing, but no tears would come. It was almost seven-thirty in the morning. I had been up all night and finished cleaning the kitchen. I left the alfajores out, in case she came home. I lay next to Gaston. He stirred a bit but seemed to be sound asleep. It just came out. A laugh. It was a laugh that came straight from my belly. I could not stop it. It came out and kept coming. I was worried that I would wake Gaston, but he did not move. I was in bed, in my pajamas, exhausted, in despair, unsure of where my baby was, and I could not stop laughing."

Sofia laughed a bit now. Peter smiled. Sofia laughed harder. Peter's smile widened.

"Sometimes you cry until you laugh," she said.

They drove through the stars of the Golden Gate and back into the city. Peter touched Sofia's hand and whispered what sounded like the word, release.

Chapter 27

Sofia was nineteen when she married, responsible for a new home, her new husband, her new family, her new life. Valentina was now nineteen, but Valentina was not the same. She had no responsibility, a rebel boyfriend too much of a boy for marriage, both of them too immature for the real world, too involved with class and politics, not worried enough about their future, job, family, home. She shouted about the oppression of the working class, the inequality of Argentina, the brutality of the government, her parents' self-inflicted naiveté.

"How are classes?" Sofia asked. Gaston huffed.

"The university is abetting in the strangulation of Argentina."

Philippe must be putting these thoughts in her head.

"That's silly of you," Sofia said.

Gaston had given up on Valentina when she decided not to attend church anymore. She had been fourteen.

"Why do people believe in God?" Valentina had asked.

"Because God is good," Gaston said.

"But how is He good?" Valentina asked.

"Where did that come from?" he asked. He looked at Sofia. She shrugged but sometimes asked herself the same question. "He created the universe, feeds the hungry, helps the poor. You know all this."

"He also causes famine, floods, plague, murders," Valentina said.

Sofia watched Gaston's face.

"He answers prayers," Gaston said, his green eyes darker.

"Whose prayers?" Valentina asked. "Not my prayers."

"Our prayers," Sofia said. "He gave us you."

"I didn't realize I was prayed for," Valentina said. "I don't want to go to church anymore. God has no prayers from me to answer."

Sofia knew Gaston's stare, the mustache twitch, the silence. Sofia hated that silence.

"You don't go to ask God for things," Gaston said.

"Yes, you do," Valentina said. "Whether it's for money or forgiveness, it's always something. I don't want to have to be forgiven by someone who wreaks more havoc on the world than I do."

Sofia never wanted Valentina to feel that stare, to hear that emptiness. But she couldn't control Valentina any more than she could the sun. Gaston had grown less and less interested in his daughter's opinions after that day. Now Sofia wondered if he listened to Valentina at all.

"Our professor said that the impetus of modern thought is active conversation," Valentina said.

"Would you like another empanada?" Sofia asked Gaston. He reached across the table.

"He hasn't been seen since."

Gaston twitched his mustache.

"Did you hear about Mrs. Flores?" Sofia said. "She lost Maria in the metro for twenty minutes. She found her at a newsstand and had to pay for the six chocolate bars Maria had eaten."

"A man that says, 'as many people as necessary must die in Argentina so that the country will again be secure,' can never be a good leader," Valentina said.

"The empanadas are delicious," Gaston said.

"He's willing to sacrifice his own people," Valentina said.

"How can a child eat so much candy?" Sofia said.

"Jorge Rafael Videla is a criminal."

Sofia bit into an empanada. She half hoped that the crunch of the crust would overpower the conversation, but it was a half-hope because she knew no matter how loud the crunch, Valentina wouldn't stop.

"The people shouldn't stand for this!" Valentina said.

"What people?" Sofia said. "Children like you that look at war stories and think of fairy tales? We have seen wars, darling. They are not pretty."

"The youth of this country understand sacrifice," Valentina said.

Gaston's eyes were sharp.

"You are spoiled and ungrateful," Gaston said.

"The longer we wait, the less perfect the world becomes." Valentina stomped to the door and slammed it closed behind her.

"Who spoke of perfection?" Sofia said. What was wrong with the lives they led? They were comfortable, they were happy, they were together. What was wrong with comfortable?

"I'm going to bed," Gaston said.

"Love?" Sofia said. "She is impulsive. Like her mother."

Gaston kissed Sofia on the cheek and went to the bedroom.

Valentina had constant complaints about the government since she started University. "Their blatant disregard for human rights and the Argentine constitution." Valentina had constant complaints about Sofia and Gaston. "You don't understand and never will!" But Valentina always returned home. She would open the door quietly. Maybe she didn't want to wake her parents. Maybe she didn't want to chat. Gaston was always in bed by that time. Sofia would wait for her daughter to come through the door. No matter the time. She would brew maté. Bake alfajores. Sofia knew that Valentina loved the smell of browned butter and dulce de leche. Valentina would sit at the kitchen table, rest her head in her hands.

Sofia would poor tea, stare into her daughter's green eyes, eyes she took from her father, but Sofia knew that Valentina had always been more like her.

"I'm— "Valentina would say.

"Eat," Sofia would say. And she would kiss Valentina's forehead, sip tea, eat the cookies, and sit with her until she went off to bed.

But tonight, Valentina didn't come home. Sofia had brewed the maté, baked the cookies, and waited for her daughter to creep through the front door. Now she sat alone, her hands twisted into the pockets of her bathrobe, no comfort. No warmth. The clock struck late. And later.

She watched the front door. Her leg shook. She tapped the table. The apartment smelled like butter. She saw a shadow pass across the glow from under the door. She jumped to her feet. She ran. Grabbed the handle. Opened the door. Valentina—

"Philippe," Sofia whispered.

His beard was brown, and spotted his face rather than covered it. It was a philosophical beard, not serious, a student's beard. And Philippe thought himself an intellectual, someone who could tear down governments with his thoughts. Someone who could impress girls with his thoughts, girls like Valentina. That's all Valentina was, a girl. Philippe looked pale. It was strange for him to be at Sofia's home at all, let alone this late in the evening, or was it now morning?

"Come in," she said. Philippe stayed silent. She couldn't hear him breathe. Sofia made him sit. She poured him some tea. She waited for the color to return to his face.

"Tell me," she said. She knew. With him there. With Valentina not. In the dark where the night met the morning—she knew.

***

You can smell Philippe before the door opens, that mix of sea and fruit that makes you think of the Caribbean, but you've never been to the Caribbean. You've never been outside of Argentina. You yell at your parents again before you rush out the door and are happy they will not talk to Philippe. You grab his hand and hop down the stairs. You do not stop and kiss him until you make it to the street and feel safe from your parents' scrutiny, your mother's scrutiny, who would not condone such behavior from a proper woman, though your father has admitted otherwise in the few stories he has told you. You kiss Philippe and are ready.

Philippe asked you the first time months ago, before you could smell coconut when he entered the room, when all you saw were the patches of his beard, when he stood on campus and struck up conversations with everyone, and you felt no more special when he spoke to you than if you were a cashier at the theater. But he came to you and asked you to dinner, and you accepted, not because he was the first man to ask, and not because your definition of a man was limited to the ability to grow a beard or the patches of beard that Philippe grew, but because he asked you a question that wasn't a question: Come to dinner with me.

And you ate, and talked, and kissed, and repeated, and after weeks in this cycle, Philippe told you that he spoke to people on campus to see who questioned the government and worried about Argentina's future, and you had never thought about the government or Argentina's future because you were preoccupied with your own future. But when Philippe said he had a meeting, you asked if you could go, and so he never asked you, you asked him, but he asked if you actually wanted to go, and you said yes because you did, and not because of the way he kissed or the coconut smell that you were becoming used to, or that his breath always tasted like fresh mint, or that now that he was in your life, it was hard to imagine an empty face where a patchy beard once stood, or the absence of the warm arms that held you, or the voice that was soft but with a gravel edge that made your spine tingle.

You went to the meeting and stuffed yourself between the corner of the can-sized room and the bodies inside. You tucked yourself as far down as you could because you felt out of place among the bodiless voices that clouded the room and spoke of the president as a beast and a warmonger to his own people, and the future is here were the words that you started to inhale in your corner with your knees pressed to your chest as you hugged yourself to keep from running because you had never felt a part of the world, or what would change it.

Philippe stood on the table at the far end of the room and towered over the people while the cloudy words of the crowd dissipated, and the breaths you took were full of only air. His voice started low, so you leaned forward to try to hear the words that dripped from his mouth, but you couldn't until the gravel in his voice grew louder and pushed everyone back into your corner, because of what he said, because of how he said it, because he stood so tall that his head tapped the ceiling. You absorbed the words, and the crowd absorbed you, and the room absorbed the crowd. For us and for those not here. For us and for those to come. And Philippe raised his fist in the air, and the room stood and raised theirs, you with them, unable and unwilling to ever put that fist down.

When you walk into the room, the cloud of words does not hang over your head. Instead, you walk into the cloud and let it absorb you, familiar with the cigarette smoke and the thickness of it. You walk through the crowd, and it is your turn to stand on top of the table and wait for the room to quiet, and you look at the corner you had fit yourself into months ago, and now you stand above the cloud and watch it disappear into silence as the room looks to you and your words. And you feel them shape and form in your stomach until you feel sick with them and they need to be released. Shaped into a ball and pulled through your lungs, you are ready to scream them because we are what they fear. But you never say them.

The door pounds. The room looks around. A crack. A pound. A cave-in. The room fills with more smoke. The room turns gray and dark. The room screams, and your eyes fill with smoke and your lungs fill with pepper. You cough. Your thoughts burn. Your body burns. You cough. You hear the police enter, banging their batons against their shields. They yell at the room to get down. Unlawful Assembly. The corner stuffed full of bodies, bloody, teary. Police bat their ribs and their wrists as the bodies protect their bones like glass from a rock—and shatter—

and you watch them and their bones because you can do nothing else. The crowd has scattered, and you want to scatter with it, with the fist that you never want to put down, with the eyes that burn and the lungs that don't work. You scream for Philippe but hold onto the table because you are not sure where you can go. The smoke fills the room. You try to duck beneath it to see if the room has a pocket of air where the cloud of words remains, a space where you can see the future and breathe.

A brick. Your nose bursts open. Blood leaks into your mouth. You taste it. Feel the baton against your ribs. They crack. Break. You turn into a ball. Protect yourself. Scream. Stuck. Your fist has fallen. You look for Philippe. From under the smoke. Through the batons. Through the shields. You see him—the patchy beard. The coconut smell gone. But he is there. By the window. Open. To let out the smoke. To clear the room. But he jumps.

***

"I didn't want you to question," Philippe said.

"Stay the night."

Philippe was asleep before Sofia woke Gaston.

"I knew her mouth would get her in trouble," Gaston said. He rubbed the sleep from his eyes.

"Don't say that," she said. "Not now."

"What can we do?" he asked.

"Let's go to the station."

Gaston grabbed a taxi to Avenida Independcia. It had been two hours since Philippe came to their door. Sofia heard the conversation again. And again. and again and again and again. Gaston rubbed her back. She stared out the window and watched the city go by, but not the city, the blur the city had become, the buildings and streets and light-posts muddled into one long stretch of dim light that streaked by the window with Sofia at the center of it.

"She will be fine," Gaston said.

How could he know? But he must know, because Valentina will be okay. She must be okay. How could she not be okay? They arrived at the federal police station. Sofia was still in her bathrobe.

She walked through the front door and placed her hands on the desk. Gaston followed her. Sofia gripped the wooden divider. If she didn't, she would fall off the earth. If the divider weren't there, she would have screamed at everyone in the station, her fists tangled in shirt collars, spit from her screams plastered to people's faces, ready to tear down the walls of the building with her fingernails if she had to. The officers paid no attention.

"Excuse me?" she said. She tapped the wood. She tried not to break. No one listened.

"Breathe," Gaston said. He rubbed her back. She shrugged him away.

"Officer?" Sofia said. No one looked.

She broke.

"Where is my daughter!"

The sound of her voice scared her—shrill, from somewhere else, not her. The officers no longer ignored her.

"May I help you, Miss?"

"My daughter was taken," she said, "by mistake."

"I don't know what you're talking about." The sergeant turned to walk away. Sofia tried to grab him. Hands pulled her back. Gaston. Gaston. His silence wouldn't help.

"Where is she!" Gaston pulled her away from the divider.

Sofia had heard rumors about the government disappearing people. She hadn't believed them, though Valentina had said so. It couldn't have been true. Sofia didn't want to believe it could be true. She couldn't believe that it could be true. She felt the world spin. She crouched to her knees. She was ready to vomit. All over the officer. All over the station. All over the city. Gaston spoke to the officer. Sofia couldn't hear the words. If she heard, she couldn't understand. Gaston lifted Sofia and took her home. It was a moment that could have taken a second—or a lifetime.

"They didn't have a raid last night," he said.

"Did they tell you where she is?" How could he be so calm?

"They said maybe she stayed out."

"They don't know our daughter," she said. "You don't know our daughter." Gaston's mustache twitched, his green eyes dark. He turned towards the bedroom. Sofia could make out the scar on his face as he walked away. The scar she once thought showed tenderness, love that he had for her, the scar that she wanted to turn away from now, not look at, not if he believed the police and not her.

"Now is when you say something!" She wanted to run to him and press her face into his chest, not just for comfort, seclusion, from the world that she felt might tear her away. He needed to say anything. Valentina will be okay. She is okay. She will be home tomorrow. Tell me anything but let me know that our daughter is safe, that we are safe. Wrap your arms around me until our baby comes home, and we can wrap our arms around her, together.

"I'm going to bed." He made no noise as he walked to the bedroom. If he did, Sofia couldn't hear it and the hush rang in her ears.

Valentina would come home. She had to come home.

Sofia cleaned up the tea but left out the alfajores. Maybe Valentina will want them later—when she comes home.

Chapter 28

Autumn was new, harsh, and cold. The clouds suffocated the sun and left a bite on Sofia's cheeks. Her heels hit the concrete and echoed off the buildings. The voice in her head eclipsed the pain in her heels, the voice that whispered Valentina's name. Both the voice and her heels pushed her forward. She had walked Bartolomé Mitre five days a week for the past eight weeks. Forty-five out of sixty-one days, her heels ringing down the quiet road. One thousand eighty hours fighting the urge to throw her shoes at the gray pillars of the Ministry of the Interior. Eighty-seven thousand eight hundred forty minutes swallowing the scream she wanted to echo in the hall. The receptionist told her to wait, again, and she knew she would, for another eight hours, because she hoped for an answer, some small piece of information about her daughter's whereabouts.

The room swallowed her, empty except for a desk, with a sky-high ceiling and people that vanished into the distance. But Sofia sat and waited for her name, hopeful that the curly-haired, red-lipped receptionist between her and Albano Harduindeguy would let her know that it was time to find something.

Time passed in silence. The occasional passerby filled the emptiness for a second. She had to explain the mistake the police had made. Her daughter was a student. Nothing more than a student. But hours passed and the only sound, "Take a seat and Mister Harguindeguy will be with you shortly." Shortly. The seconds felt like days, every day a deeper pit of hell, where the fire burned hotter the heat consumed her. Shortly. God wouldn't have found these days to be short. The receptionist said the same words every day. Did she believe them? Sofia could see the woman at home after a short day of work, alone and unmarried, twenty-one, maybe, with a soft voice that hinted a smile, her dark hair up in curls, her bright lips waiting for her boyfriend to propose, every day dressed up in anticipation of a ring, to quit this job and keep a home with a baby soon on the way, and after the baby's born, her husband home every night for dinner, until their baby was all grown up and at a university where the police mistake their child for an undesirable and the woman has to sit in this Godforsaken lobby every day for months just to find out where her child may be! Or maybe she has a child, a bastard boy of Harguindeguy's, and the woman's stupid belief that soon Harguindeguy will leave his wife for her and her baby boy—their baby boy, and she'll never have to worry about her son in the wrong place at the wrong time, which is why she can afford a smile in her voice every day because her son will always be safe, when Valentina was taken by mistake because of that stupid Philippe, and Valentina's stupid want and her stupidity to follow Philippe somewhere she never should have been.

She shouldn't have been there. She shouldn't have been there.

"She shouldn't have been there," Sofia said to herself, unable to keep the words inside any longer.

"Where was she?" a hoarse voice said. The woman sat a chair away. She was heavier than her voice led Sofia to believe. Her hair was auburn. The color of autumn in the country, the country where Sofia, Gaston, and Valentina would spend holidays, away from the noise and the humidity, away from all the problems of the world, safe near the ranch Gaston loved, the soft smell and sound of horses, all wrapped up in the rainbowed leaves where they fell to the floor. The smell of autumn, but Sofia couldn't smell autumn now in the hall with this woman. Sofia smelled roses and myrrh.

"I didn't know anyone else was here." Sofia wasn't certain how many people constituted an assembly, if warnings were given out, or if people were rounded up immediately and locked away. If they see me behave like that, they will know that my daughter would do the same.

"Where was she?" the woman said.

"I don't know," Sofia said. She clutched her black bag. The leather creaked under her fingers. She smoothed her hair and looked at the floor. Her bones felt hollow. She wanted to drop to her knees and confess to this woman, who wore a black dress like Sofia. Perhaps she mourned the loss of a child too. Perhaps she was a test to see if Sofia was strong enough to withstand the torture. A test from God. A test from the Minister. She wanted to fall apart, to deconstruct her body, brain first, separate it from her tongue, from her ears, from her lungs, her heart.

"Do you go to church?" the woman asked.

Watch the floor.

"That was rude of me. I was on my way to church after my appointment if you'd like to join me. My name is Mercedes."

Since Valentina had disappeared, Sofia lived in church. Church and the Ministry of the Interior, back and forth, between holy spires and negligent bureaucrats. Between the soft glow of candles and the fluorescence of mass electricity. There were still a few hours left in the day. There was still a chance the receptionist would call her name. What if she had waited all that time only to be absent when her chance arrived?

"They won't call your name," Mercedes said.

"How do you know that?" Sofia said. Her voice burned. Mercedes smiled, full of empathy, as if sad to see Sofia waiting in this chasm of the unknown. She grabbed Sofia's hand. She gave it a light squeeze. How long had she waited?

"I think I could use confession," Sofia said.

They stood. Mercedes was smaller than Sofia had expected. She seemed powerful, dragged through fire and ice but come out whole, not whole, but together. She was older than Sofia. Or looked it. Mercedes put her arm through Sofia's and they left, hollow.

Bartolomé Mitre was still cold, but Sofia felt a bit warmer.

Mercedes hailed a taxi and told the driver to take them to the closest church.

The ride was quiet. The distance between Sofia and the Ministry grew, and Sofia felt the knots in her stomach unravel. She stayed silent, afraid she might talk too much, might talk herself into trouble, with a woman she didn't know and a taxi driver who would hear everything, would inform the government because taxi drivers were notorious for informing on others, weren't they? The taxi passed Casa Rosada. The President's mansion made her wretch. She caught the bile in her mouth. The taste stayed in her throat.

Mercedes entered the Iglesia San Pedro Gonzalez Telmo, a church Sofia had never been in. It was smaller than her church. The architecture still beautiful. Yellow paint. White pillars. Statues that looked down and judged, deemed people worthy to enter the hallowed ground. Textiles and colored glass on the spires and the upper tiers of the building. It made God beautiful. His place wasn't just on earth but in the beautiful things He inhabited—and perhaps the not-so-beautiful things.

Sofia entered the church with her head down. She tried to breathe deep. The blue and white tiles on the floor led from the door to the dais and lifted into the sky because the farther forward she walked, the closer she came to God. But it was an illusion. The tiles were flat. The floor wasn't angled. She kneeled and lit a votive candle. Her prayers had changed, first for Valentina's return, then for Valentina's whereabouts, and now she prayed for a meeting. A meeting would get her access to the first two. She hoped that her prayers rose to heaven. They were light and needed guidance. The smoke of the candle pushed a prayer in the right direction.

Myrrh and frankincense crowded the air. The smell buried itself into Sofia's dress. It made a home in her skin. She moved down the aisle to Mercedes. Christ looked down on them from the far end of the church, hung low, his feet extended. They could touch him. But Sofia couldn't touch him, wouldn't touch him.

"Six months," Mercedes said. Her voice was hoarse and tiny. It unsettled Sofia. "My son and daughter-in-law. I went to the Ministry every day for six months. They wouldn't help me. To understand what happened to my son and his wife."

She didn't cry. "They won't help. I see women—mothers like you, like me—there for the same reason."

"Valentina," Sofia said. "I've gone every day. I didn't know what to—"

"I know," she said.

Sofia didn't want these secrets. She didn't want to keep her daughter a secret, a shame, a mistake.

"Valentina was a student," she said. She told Mercedes about Valentina's activism, about Philippe. She told Mercedes about Valentina when she was a girl, her precociousness, her sweetness, her hobbies. She told Mercedes about Valentina's brown hair, about her pigtails as a child, and about her eyes, her green eyes, her green eyes she shared with her father. Mercedes listened. She clutched Sofia's hand. Sofia felt safe, in Mercedes's hands, in the house of God, in the eyes of Christ. She spoke until her throat was raw. The bells rang. The quiet of the church broke. Sofia breathed in the quiet. The memories were a block, hard around her body, hard to breathe, harder to stand, impossible to walk.

Where did Mercedes get the strength? Why continue? She had other children to return to. Sofia didn't.

"Give it time," Mercedes said. Her voice was a whisper. "We can all get there together."

"We aren't allowed—"

"Why wouldn't we? Would you want to?"

The words hit Sofia without grace, without mercy. They had been strangers. They hadn't existed to each other before today.

"Help?" The word hung over them like a cloud, waiting to rain down guilt or anger. Sofia stood from the pew. Her heels hit the tile. Mercedes didn't let go of her hand.

"Sit back down."

"I don't—"

"My son was taken from my home. He was taken in the night. Every night I go home. To where Néstor was taken. To where his wife was taken. I climb into the sheets with my husband. We dine in the same kitchen. We lounge on the same couch. In the shadow of my son. You want to know. We want to know." Sofia sat down. Mercedes released her hand. "We deserve to know."

Sofia closed her eyes.

"We are not alone," Mercedes said. "You and I. There are others like us, mothers like us, whose children have been taken, accused of one thing or another, taken and forgotten by the people who took them, but not forgotten by us. They are our children. They will never be forgotten by us."

"What can I do?" Sofia said.

Mercedes looked like she might cry.

Chapter 29

Music and the scent of fried meat filled the kitchen. Gaston came in from the bedroom. He wore light-blue pajamas. He always wore pajamas on Sunday unless he went to church. He didn't go as often as he used to. As if his absence from church was a small rebellion against the faith he had always clung to, the God he had always believed in. Even if Gaston didn't attend church as often, it never felt as though his faith had faltered, never felt like a crack had formed between him and heaven that slowly grew until one day it would become a canyon that separated him from being saved. Sofia wondered if he ever felt as lost and alone as she did.

Almost a year had passed since Valentina's arrest. Gaston didn't talk about it. He didn't talk much at all. He sat at the head of the table. This was his home. He would always sit at the head of the table. Sofia had brought in the paper. He turned down the music. He said good morning. Sofia told him to sit. He sipped his orange juice his tea and straightened the paper. Sofia set the plate of sausage and eggs on the table. She refilled his tea. She buttered his toast. She sat.

"What's this?" asked Gaston. He lowered his newspaper.

"The paper."

Gaston pushed his plate away. He slammed the newspaper on the table. He straightened out the creases and stuck his finger in the page.

It was an advertisement; on any other day, he might have passed over it, might have thought that editorials were a waste of time. But today, he happened to read the right page, at the right time, or scrolled through all the pages and found the ad the Mothers had written, the ad that the Mothers had discussed, but as far as Sofia knew, had not decided to publish.

Come home soon: Néstor Gallo, Salvador Braverman, Carolina Noia.

Close to the bottom—Valentina Morales. She wanted to shred the paper, to throw her plate across the room, to slam her glass to the floor and watch the pieces scatter, but it wasn't just an ad for the mothers who were a part of the group. It was also for those that weren't, for the women whose children or husbands had been taken but didn't know there were others like them, others ready to stand, even in silence, and tell the government, tell the world, that they would not hide themselves away—and Sofia was with them, a part of them. Even now. Even though she hadn't known about the ad's publication. She had been happier since the marches of the Madres de la Plaza de Mayo. She liked the name. Mothers. She was still a mother. In search of her daughter, their daughters, their sons.

Women that circled the Plaza de Mayo and demanded answers in silence. They all had agreed that their husbands should not be involved. It was too dangerous to consider. But Sofia was exhilarated when with the Mothers. She felt needed. She felt strong. She felt loved. She didn't want Gaston to question. He didn't want her to participate in the march, or the demonstrations, or the meetings. This was much more than a list of names. So many names that hadn't been mentioned, the names of children whose mothers' sent letters to the group, signed by women around Argentina who demanded to know the whereabouts of their families. How she wished the list shorter—down to zero, or selfishly, at least shorter by one name.

She imagined all the mothers of the unnamed children, imagined the ad cut from the paper, a mother writing her child's name at the bottom of the list to add their child to the names of those who would return home, those beautiful children who would never be forgotten, as if their child's name needed to be on the list to be remembered—to have been disappeared. Sofia didn't know the list had been published; she didn't want Gaston to know; he wouldn't understand. She needed this. And right now, she needed to act like she knew about the paper.

"Why is our daughter's name in it?"

"Because I put it there," she said. "Because that is our daughter, and I refuse to pretend she doesn't exist."

"Did we agree not to get involved? Did we not think it would be too dangerous for the men—?"

"We who? You sat in silence. I told you the decisions the Mothers made in concern for our husbands and the rest of our families. Well, this is it. You and me."

Sofia pushed the paper from the table and stood up. She took her plates. Threw them into the sink. The plates shattered. Wrecked. Mixed with chunks of chewed sausage fat.

Gaston shoved his way into the kitchen.

"And if they come for me?" he asked. "What if they see her name and decide that no husband is safe?"

"And what if they come for me?" Sofia said. "What if they decide that the men aren't the only dangers? They didn't think it ridiculous to take our daughter. I want answers. I chose to put her name there." It was her choice. Valentina or Gaston. And she chose. She wanted Valentina's name out there, for all of Argentina to see, to be witness that her daughter had existed.

"We took a risk from the beginning. But not you. You stayed silent. You always stayed silent."

"And what would you rather have? Another missing body? A corpse—"

"Don't ever say that! Don't you ever say that!"

Sofia slapped Gaston. Her fingers spread across his cheek. The shattering of a once-strong substance. She had never hit Gaston before. She had never thought of hitting Gaston before. She never wanted to hit Gaston before. This is where their lives had brought them. The threads that bound them together had been turned to glass, and with that slap, she broke the final piece of them, and without him to tether her to earth, she might not last much longer, already feeling the pressure of

a world without the threads of them, together—left in the company of the unknown of what happened to Valentina.

Gaston stared. His cheek bright purple. Sofia's hands over her mouth. It
couldn't have been more than a second. Sofia ran to her room, changed clothes,
ran from her home. She ran down the stairs and into the street. She ran over the
cobblestones of San Telmo. She made her way to church. She wanted to be alone.
Surrounded by crowds of people. But alone. Hiding.

The shadow of the steeples lingered over the street, darkness from a house of
light. The church bells rang midday. The chapel held a crowded silence, the sound
of a crowd that tried to be quiet—a shift in the seats, a whisper to a neighbor. Sofia
walked to the votive, dropped to her knees, and lit a match. She froze. Should she
pray for Valentina? For the disappeared? For herself? For Gaston? She traded the
match for the confessional.

The door creaked. It was another noise in the crowd of noises. She kneeled
before the grated window and crossed herself. She never did like confessionals.
They were too small, too crowded, too dark. She preferred open space and candlelight.

"In the name of the Father, and of the Son, and of the Holy Spirit. My last
confession was..." Sofia kept her head down and her palms together. She didn't
care to hear what the priest had to say. She wanted to talk. She wanted to apologize.
But she wasn't ready to apologize to Gaston. "I have been an unfit mother and an
unfit wife. I have let my family down. My daughter has left me. My husband has
left me. I want to leave myself. Is that possible, Father? Can I separate from myself?"

"Your husband left you?" the priest said. "Was he a Catholic?"

"He hasn't physically left," she said. What a stupid question.

"Then why did you say he left?" he said.

"He's not the man I married." She didn't feel comfortable talking about Valentina. Could she trust a priest? This is what her life had become, to question

whether she could trust a priest, a man of God. What could a man of God do that God didn't do Himself? God hadn't saved Valentina, or Gaston and me from disintegrating. What could a priest do? Even if she trusted him. "Our lives have changed. Our family has changed. This city has changed." The priest cleared his throat. "He doesn't talk anymore. I don't know if he'd notice if I left."

"These are not the questions of a devoted wife," the priest said. "Your doubts will consume you. Is there anything else?"

"This morning…" She cleared her throat, "Before I came to confession, we had a fight. I slapped him."

"Are you sorry for your transgression?"

She could still feel a slight tingle in her fingers. Gaston had been wrong. He had changed. He should apologize to her. How could he say such a horrible thing about their daughter? About her daughter.

"No!" she said. "I'm not sorry. I have no reason to be sorry. He should be sorry."

"I cannot give you penance if you do not believe in your guilt."

"I don't want your penance. I want my life to be put back together. Can God help with that? He hasn't so far."

Sofia stood, opened the door. A loud thump filled the room when the bodies shifted. Sofia moved the hair from her face. She patted her curls and adjusted her hat. She lit another match at the votive. The priest wouldn't carry her prayers to God. She turned to the flame, attached her prayer to the smoke like a letter to a balloon. If it lifted high enough, all her prayers would be answered. What if her prayers were too heavy to get to heaven? Gaston was so certain of providence. But I'm not.

Too much had happened to prove otherwise, that providence was a myth, a fairytale, like the stories drawn in glass, fairytales to keep people inflamed with hope of what God could provide, or what the church could provide, as long as Sofia lived a righteous life, a justified life. How had she not? Where in her life had she strayed from the hopeful sheep of the church, from the pasture of God? When did she stumble into the forbidden land of the hopeless? Because that's what she had become, hopeless, and what was left when hope was gone, when the hole in her soul had grown so large that hope fell out and all that was left to fill the hole was emptiness?

Smoke rose from the candles, gray and thick; it lifted slowly to the ceiling, and Sofia knew it would never get past the roof. That should have been her first prayer, to let the rest of her hopes through the roof and up to heaven. She imagined all her prayers stuck in the roof tiles, huddled together and crowded like coins in a fountain, cluttered and waiting to turn from wishes to reality; isn't that what she was taught? That when a wish came true, the coin disappeared from the well? She had marked a coin once as a child with her father, marked her wish with red paint and threw it into the fountain. He asked what she wished for, and she said a new bike. Two weeks later, Sofia had a brand-new bicycle and rode it to the fountain to see if her coin was under the water looking back at her. It wasn't. Years later, she learned the fountain was cleaned out every few days—wishes stolen and never coming true, she now realized, like the votive prayers, bloated and stuck between the ceiling and floor, ready to crush everyone in the church. She had enough weight on her body already; she didn't need the addition of unanswered prayers, especially her own. She wanted to take them back. All the prayers she ever had. All the candles she ever lit, all the hopes she had that never came true, the life she should have had, the family she should have had, the daughter that should never have been taken.

Sofia extinguished the candle. The smoke of other candles continued to rise. Her prayer snuffed out while others rose into the crowd of smoky litanies above her. One by one, slow, quiet, with little more than a whispered end, Sofia snuffed the remaining candles. For every prayer she had that was never answered, she extinguished another light, another's prayer, determined to take it back, to take them all back.

Most of the day had passed her by. The sun fell behind the buildings and left shadows over the streets. The crowds of people a flood of smiles unfazed by the expanded shadow and the rapid sunset of summer. Sofia sat in a café. She drank café con leche. She watched the families.

Little girls pressed their faces against a window and almost licked the glass. They wanted to touch the dresses, to try the dresses, to be women, to be desired by the boys that paid them no attention. They were young and innocent.

Little boys ran around their mother and almost stepped on her heels. They poked one another, they screamed obscenities, they imitated their fathers' walk and tried to be grown men, but they hated suits and thought girls were silly.

Valentina would have been done with school in a few months. She would have had a degree. She could have worked. Built a family. Traveled. She could have taken a year to see Spain, or France, or Italy, or America. San Francisco. She could have roamed the world. Gaston had stopped roaming ages ago. Because Sofia had made him. Because she wanted him there for Valentina. But it wasn't for Valentina. She wanted him there for her. She missed their first night together, and every night after, when he kissed the back of her head, wrapped his arms around her stomach and pulled her into him, folding over her like a blanket.

Sofia was ready to apologize. Not for the slap. She had taken Gaston's passion away. He missed his ranch.

She stood from the table. The crowds had dissipated. The shops closed. Sofia walked home. The gas lamps flickered down the cobbled streets, a different life than the sunlight. The noise of bars carried laughter and shouts, guitars and accordions. She half expected to find Gaston frozen from the morning, wrapped in his pajamas and waiting for her to return.

***

Sofia crossed the entry to a room full of light. She heard the kettle, but it was late for tea. She stepped farther in. Gaston stood in the kitchen near the kettle. Sofia met his eyes. Her reflection in the glass cupboards showed her swollen brown eyes. Sofia, like all the Mothers, was determined never to cry in public. Never let them see you cry. They may think they've gotten the best of you.

"You're home," Gaston said. He poured the tea into a cup and brought it to Sofia. "Sit, please."

She took the teacup and a seat on the couch. She tried to say something but instead sipped the tea. Gaston stood with his hands in his pockets.

"Gaston, what happened?" Sofia tightened her fingers around the teacup. Gaston's teacup stood lonely on the table. Sofia wished she could speak to him, to apologize for the life she made him leave, the life she wanted in Buenos Aires, in San Telmo. If she reached for him now, touched his hand, felt his warm skin, now more than ever, if he wrapped herself in his arms and he pressed his lips to her forehead, she would melt into him and give up Buenos Aires, San Telmo, the Mothers—Valentina. She would whisper into his skin, let's leave this place forever. Just us. To somewhere that we can make ourselves whole. Like we used to be. She watched him pace but said nothing.

"You haven't heard," Gaston said.

"I came straight home from…a cafe." She wouldn't tell him about her time at church, now or ever. She didn't want to believe that she had the audacity to erase other people's prayers. "What happened?"

"It's Mercedes," he said. "The police took her. She is gone."

"Now?"

"They raided her apartment in Villa Dominico today."

They had felt safe. They had felt strong. How could they sit there? How could she sit here?

"Her neighbors sent the message. It's too late." Mercedes was strong, small but untouchable, Sofia had thought, the person brave enough to have brought all those women together; the woman proud enough to lead all these women into a police station and demand the release of one of their own. She had looked straight into the officer's eyes like a bulldog, ready to rip his throat out, or maybe like an angry, disappointed mother, a woman that the officer saw his own mother in, a group of women that reminded the officer of his own mother, so much so that he released the woman who had been arrested. Mercedes had been their savior that night and a savior to how many other women since the start of the Madres de la Palaza de Mayo, Sofia among them?

Sofia rested her hands in her lap. Her eyes puffy, her face stone.

"They took Léonie Duquet and Alice Domon," Gaston said.

"But they're nuns! They're French." If nuns could be taken, who was safe? The quiet end of candles replayed in Sofia's ears. The church, even if a lie, had been the safest place, safe enough to hide, or meet, or—a place that might have encouraged the Mothers to bring the government to justice. That idea had dropped from heaven, crashed hard, and broken. Another hope tortured into submission, another argument for the hopeless. Sofia wasn't in church anymore; her prayers hadn't been answered. They were too heavy, after all. When wings of prayers are broken, it's time to realize how heavy hope really is.

"There are no limits in the end," Gaston said. "I have given you too much news for one day." He took Sofia's hand in both of his. She felt how warm his pockets had kept his skin, how gentle his fingers could be when he caressed her.

"I can make us some alfajores," she said.

Gaston gave a slight nod, but he never ate the cookies, Sofia knew. She would make them for herself if she made them at all.

"Take all the time you need," he said. He patted her hand and went to the bedroom. She sipped her tea and dipped her finger into the hot drink before sucking the moisture from her finger. She didn't know how much time had passed. The dim light of the room never changed. The city remained quiet.

When Sofia finished her tea, she walked to the bed where Gaston sat with a book in his hands, again silent. He watched her move. She felt heavy again. She couldn't see Gaston's face but felt the glow of his eyes. Had she left a bruise or cut into his skin? Soon it would heal to another scar, one that would remind her of their argument, or their reconciliation, what she was capable of or what she wanted to fix desperately. She slid under the covers, his body next to hers, and almost sighed with relief because he hadn't left, because maybe he understood. Maybe she still had the energy to leave this nightmare, hand-in-hand, let him lead the way away from all of this.

"I'm sorry for the life I made you leave," she said.

"This is the life I chose. Have faith."

Sofia couldn't afford to live on faith any longer. It ended up hurting too much. Another mother. Two sisters. It was only fitting that God lose some of his children too.

Chapter 30

You smell shit in the air and when they take the blindfold off there are two of them; you can see the silhouette of their faces merge but you imagine how they look, like stone, rotten from the inside out; the smell isn't you, even though you can feel the shit run down your leg—it's them, rotted, and one tells you that you must talk, tell them everything, and he implores you to spill what you know of the subversives you were with and the plans you all had, but you know you aren't a subversive and you know you're scared, you're covered in your own filth, and grime has crusted your face, and you hope that you'll be set free after this, but the man calls you back with a knee to your face and you bite your tongue and spit blood—it tastes like metal—and you want to scream, you want to tear out his eyes, but your wrists are cuffed behind your back and the men grab your hair and drag you across the room, roll you over and tie your wrists to your ankles while you drool, unable to hold all the blood in your mouth—the rope burns and digs deep into your skin; you tremble and you're cold in the concrete room that you couldn't stretch in—if you weren't already bound, and you aren't sure if you'll ever make it out—you think days pass; they shave your head and you try to lick the hair off your shoulders because you think it might taste better than the dried blood that has dressed your lips since the moment you woke up in the concrete room; they take your blindfold off once in a while and fill your mouth with water and a lemon, you savor the citrus, you savor any change from dried blood, and you want to feel fresh water because you're tired of washing your hands with piss, and the water is a nice change from your bone-dry saliva, but the blindfold is quickly replaced, another demand is made and another knee to the cheek—you feel your face crack in half, but they aren't finished and they pull your eyelids trying to peel your skin from your body, scalp you from your green eyes back until the only remnant of you is your sallow muscles that no one would be able to identify—you scream but it doesn't come out right, you sound more like a rat than a person, and you think how quick you have devolved into an animal—they release your wrists from your ankles, turn you over, lift you onto a mattress and for a second you feel relief until they re-bind your wrists to the bedpost and strap wires to your skin and you feel the wet of freezing liquid hit your stomach followed by a hellfire pulse through your body that swallows you from the inside and gives new meaning to the fire in your eyes because you think they have lit an actual fire behind your eyes—you think smoke escapes from your lungs instead of sound, once, twice, three times and swallows you whole, and three times you feel like you breathe fire, but you don't, and you have survived but they aren't finished with you as they drag you back to your room, the smell of dried blood and dripping filth fills the cold, damp air, but you welcome the bitter cold as if the cold outside might help the fire inside, but it isn't helping and you don't think you'll ever make it out alive and you aren't sure how long it is since you first arrived or if people know where you are or how they can help you, or if they can help you, and when they pull down your under-wear and pull up your shirt you hear the guards' belts unbuckle, and you wait for the searing pain of your clitoris splitting open, but instead feel a burn on your skin; the guard screams, "The bitch shocked me!" The other guard laughs, a hard grav-elly laugh, until he coughs—and maybe you shouldn't have stopped going to church, and your father had been right in his silence—a slight pinch in your arm—you drift to sleep.

You are in a plane but have no idea where you are or where you are going; the choppiness of propellers cuts the wind, the heavy scent of exhaust fills the com-partment, and your nose burns, but it's a burn you are happy to feel, and your head hurts and your cheek aches from when it was cracked, and your tongue is swollen and bloody almost all the time now and your hands are tied together and you notice the searing pain in your shoulders as you move your arms for the first time in God knows when—you think about home and you wish you had been able to have one more alfajor, another quiet conversation with your mother, but know it is too late now, and someone pulls you up by your arms, their giant hands wrapped around your tiny body; you close your eyes and hear the noise of the passing air outside—someone has opened the door, and you smell the sea and feel the rush of the wind and hear the propellers crush the air and the hands push you. You fall. And you whisper good-bye.

Chapter 31

Peter and Claus sat in the kitchen, safe from the wind. Outside trees bent. Branches flew. Leaves disappeared. The walls shook. The window rattled. Peter held Claus tight and scoured the horizon for signs of life, or resistance—for what caused the wind to pound against the house. The Wolf? Big and bad and hidden behind the trees in the distance, camouflaged in the morning. The watch he wore had bright red straps too big for his wrist. He stuffed a napkin between the time-piece and his skin to keep it from slipping.

The trick is to spot the Wolf early and blow as hard as you can, Peter's dad often told him. And there's Claus. Small but fierce. He'll protect you better than anything. Claus had protected him, Claus had always protected him—from ghosts, pirates, ninjas, bad dreams, car accidents, loneliness. As long as he and Claus were together.

Peter and Claus had watched the wind from the kitchen since sunrise. It was their favorite part of the day, when the world suspended into silence, asleep, when the light of morning fought the dark of night, when Peter could sometimes hear the measured breaths of his mother. The wind blew through the sunlight, swift and forceful. The Wolf was patient, more patient than the last time they met. The Wolf's eagerness had been his downfall, prideful and arrogant, with his big, bad breath and his big, bad attitude. Peter and Claus, small but fierce, they fought for good; they fought to protect the weak. The Wolf was haggard and old from constant battle with pigs—his huff and his puff. But he was determined, and he was back, big and bad.

The window shuddered. A whirl of leaves pushed past and caught the glass with hopes to hold on or take the house with them. The sound thundered through Peter's ears like a storm of past battles on the shores of his memory, Claus in his arms.

The puzzle pieces he tried to put together—the car door caved in. The windshield gone. His mother's scream. Pulled from the back seat. His father still. The noise. Peter couldn't remember the noise. The ambulance arrived. His mother held him. He held Claus. Claus let him know it would be ok. It was the last time Peter saw his father. The back of his head. He was silent. He was still. The wind was hard. Claus wanted vengeance. Peter knew he did.

"He's stronger," Peter said. Claus's face was the answer Peter wanted. "This time, he won't come back."

Peter grabbed his sword, light and shimmering. Claus waited at the table.

"We can't win if we don't fight." He grabbed the doorknob. "A trap?" He hesitated. He hadn't thought of a trap.

"Claus, you're brilliant!" Peter let go of the doorknob. He ran through the kitchen and opened the door to the backyard. "That's why we couldn't see him. He's not out front."

Peter's blood pulsed. A flimsy screen door separated him from the Wolf. Claus was eager to get his claws on the Wolf. Peter could tell by his silence. Peter held up his sword, ready for the beast. Claus stood close. He nodded. Their war faces swelled thick in the air. Peter slid the screen open; together they ran onto the battlefield.

The wind pushed Peter back. Each step a fight to stand. Claus kept low to the ground. His fur flew in the wind. Peter's hair rushed in his eyes.

"He must be close." His sword was almost weightless, as if it were made of plastic. A branch flew at Peter. He ducked. Leaves attacked Claus. The sun was cold and useless. Peter swiped his sword at debris. No birds in the sky. A howl.

From the wind? From the Wolf? Peter followed the sound. He continued to fight the wind. Claus covered him. And Peter found the Wolf.

"Behind the tree," he pointed. "Come out, Wolf!" The Wolf stepped from behind the tree. Barrel-chested. Fanged. Spit dripped from his chin. Decay swirled in the wind. He looked at Peter and touched his ear, or what was left of it. A reminder: Peter's mercy. When he and Claus had found the Wolf's cave, snuck through the darkness and the smell of death that filled the lair, with the Wolf asleep, Peter knew, because there was no wind, the quiet sound of darkness and presumed safety all around. Claus had spotted the Wolf first, his teeth bared and ready to wrap around the Wolf's throat, but Peter held Claus back, told Claus to do what heroes do. Peter woke the Wolf with a slice to his ear, his sword then at the Wolf's throat, the choice: leave and never return or die, a deal heroes gave villains, and the Wolf had chosen, but here the Wolf stood, ear tattered, mouth open, teeth dripping with poison. The deal broken. Peter ready to finish the deed, to show that the rejection of his kindness was not acceptable, the deal the Wolf didn't deserve. Now Peter didn't have to keep it.

The Wolf took a breath—deep. A howl came from his lungs. The huff lifted Peter from the ground. Claus roared. Peter hit the ground. He ran at the Wolf, sword raised. The Wolf swiped at Peter. Slashed his pajama armor. Claus followed. Attacked. The Wolf's stomach. The wind blew. The Wolf threw Claus. The Wolf's fur caked in blood. Peter ran. His chance to strike. He always struck right. The Wolf countered the first time. Peter swung left. Claus ran to the right. The Wolf lunged for Claus. Missed Peter. Peter blew out his anger—harsh, big, and bad, and dug his sword into the Wolf's stomach. The Wolf tried to huff, or puff, or snarl. Peter looked into the Wolf's eyes, gray like the clouds that formed in the sky. He opened the Wolf's mouth, reached his arm down the Wolf's throat, past the putrid teeth and smell of decay, and pulled out the Wolf's lungs. The Wolf fell to the floor, silent and still.

Claus roared. Peter screamed. They had defeated the Wolf. They were free of him forever. Claus had his vengeance. Peter had his freedom. But the wind continued to blow. Peter and Claus crossed the battlefield and entered the house. The wind knocked the windows and the walls. Claus had fought hard. They deserved a rest.

Peter wanted to wash the stench of wolf's blood from his body. He heard a splash of water in the bathroom. His mother took long baths. After his father died, Peter sometimes heard her cry in the tub and imagined her tears as raindrops helping to calm her. It didn't help. She was so sad so often.

"But what could I do?" he asked Claus.

The house rumbled. The waterfall from the faucet reached beneath the door and swarmed the hallway.

"Mom?" He knocked on the door. "Mom?" He knocked harder. The rush of the faucet answered. Peter's toes went wet. Water seeped and pooled through the crack of the door. Peter pounded the door. He grabbed the knob and twisted. It was unlocked.

The water from the hall sucked back into the bathroom. It drifted from under his feet and back onto the stained tiles. And it grew. Higher. Dammed inside the room. The water rose. Higher. The wind shook the walls. Harder. The door banged. The numbers on Peter's watch blurred. The walls shook. The windows clanged. The water rose. The watch face cracked. The walls rattled. The watch hands stopped in the water—the water that swirled with pink that dripped from red that hung from sorrow.

The water spilled over the tub like a cascade, around the copper claws of the tub, around the porcelain base; more water, over the tub, into the flood, up and up, until touching Sam's limp fingertips, her hands covered in syrupy red that leaked from her wrists and dripped into the water. The water rose to Peter's chest; his toes rubbed against the tiles for traction; a mast raised from the tub's center, emerged over the lip of the tub, higher, until it poked the ceiling, and grew thick and metallic, with a crossbar at the top. The ceiling disappeared and the sun shined down onto the water that rose and the faucet that ran. A sail dropped and dressed the mast, ready to catch the wind that had never left, even with the Wolf gone. Claus loved to watch ships leave port because it was the start of a new adventure. But Claus had disappeared. He had been right next to Peter, but Peter was too busy watching the tub set sail to notice Claus's absence, and now the water was at his neck and burned his eyes, the sound of the faucet harder to hear. He called for Claus when the water was calm, the tide an easy push back and forth, the tub almost close enough to swim to, if Peter knew how to swim. The far wall of the bathroom opened like curtains, and the tub drifted to the open sea, while the sunshine reflected the emerald sea. The sail caught the wind and took the tub, the trees overrun by the new ocean that started in the bathroom and pushed past the horizon, the leaves a layer of film splattered across the top of the sea. Peter was stuck in the ocean, unable to break the surface where water met air; he sank deeper to the floor, the floor where sand and coral overtook the tile, where fish made homes and swam around Peter's limbs like an aquatic jungle gym—on the ocean floor where he called for Claus. Bubbles escaped from his lungs; the sound of Claus's name drowned in the depths. Peter closed his eyes, the burn of salt water too hard to handle; in the darkness, he called for Claus again. The bubbles now a gurgle in the sea, the dense water, and Peter imagined the sound carried in the bubbles to the surface's brink, when the bubbles breached the film of leaves and popped, his cries for Claus would scream into the sky, and Claus would swim to Peter and tell him what to do. But Peter couldn't wait. The weight of the ocean ready to crush his chest or burst his lungs. He preferred the Wolf to the water; he could fight a wolf. Peter pressed his feet firmly to the ocean floor, pushed hard. His body rocketed to the surface, broke the water, through the film, the harsh sun a welcomed change from the dark water. He breathed.

"Claus!" He said. Panted. Breathed. The water rose. The boat sailed farther away. He wanted to swim to it.

"Claus!"

"You can't win if you don't fight." Peter heard Claus. "Don't get caught."

Peter flapped his arms and kicked his feet and strained his neck—his muscles ached, his eyes burned, he screamed and hit the air and found Claus on the boat with his mother, and Claus waved, his grumpy face soft. Peter held the watch to his chest without knowing how Claus got on the boat or how the watch slipped from his wrist to his hands, broken, silent, still. The harsh wind blew. The Wolf was gone; it was never the Wolf, Peter now knew. Sam twirled her fingers in the cool water. Claus waved until the tub drifted to the horizon, met the sun, and departed.

Chapter 32

Gaston pushed himself onto Sofia, his lips perspiring and heavy. His body persistent. His ambition, his confidence, his gaucho pride. She pushed him away. His lips away. His body away. His pride away. And their past—away. Their life together that only they knew. When Gaston had kissed her with soft lips, with his mouth reminiscent and not compulsory. Now the more passionate he made himself, the more nostalgic she grew. With the nostalgia came anger; with anger came a lost rose and more nostalgia. A life full of have-nots and could-have-beens. Valentina—a life of the hopeful and the wish-there-were, the perhaps and the dream. But Gaston pressed his lips to Sofia's and she felt the pressure of his body, the heat of his breath, the touch of his mustache, the force of his hand, as it moved close and closer and closer. But all she wanted was to break away.

***

Gaston stood before the flame and stoked the fire. Each thrust of the poker made the wood crumble and spit sparks. Sofia had ironed his suit that morning and now it looked worn and wrinkled and too large. He stoked the fire again; one hand thrust the metal, the other limp by his side. Sofia wanted to hold it, to twist her fingers between his, lift his hand to her mouth and kiss his flesh. The last time he held her hand, she led him to the couch and folded herself into him, the calluses of his youth present but smoothed over by time.

Gaston threw a photo into the fire. The smoke hit her lungs harshly, and she coughed.

"I didn't realize you were home," he said.

"How was your day?" Silence. "How long have you been home?"

"A long time." He looked at the fire and plunged the poker into the wood. The ashes of the photo disintegrated. He threw another onto the flame. "Where have you been?" The first time he had asked in months. "With them? Those bitches?" He spat into the fire. The slur in his voice, his lazy tongue when he called them bitches. She found the bottle of whisky on the mantle above the fireplace, empty. He hadn't been drunk since Valentina's birth, or maybe it was her christening.

"I'll make some dinner," she said.

"Don't bother," he said. "I've eaten." He reached for the whisky and found the bottle cold.

"What do you keep throwing into the fire?"

"Nothing that concerns you."

"It all concerns me."

"You parade around town with these whores—"

"They are my friends."

"They are shit." He forced the poker into the burnt wood. He faced Sofia, his green eyes, the rest of him shadow. "They are demons. They steal memories until there is nothing where life had been."

"I will make you some maté." There was no reason to argue, not like this. Gaston had spent so long in silence, so long hidden from the world Sofia lived in, the world she believed had blown to rubble. Maybe these were the words he had needed to find to join her in this broken world so they could rebuild it. It wasn't an argument. It was a release.

"Everything is wrong!" he said.

Gaston threw the bottle. Into the flames. The crash. The shatter. Shards flew out of the fire with the sparks. The flames ballooned from the crash. Gaston remained a statue.

"Everything went wrong."

"Sometimes everything goes wrong," she said.

Gaston threw another photo onto the fire. He had been strong for her for so long, when they were young and she teased him, when she was pregnant, always strong and quiet but there—for her, with her. Valentina's disappearance hurt him too. This was how he dealt with it. First, silence. Now, this. He needed his moment of escape. She went to the kitchen to boil water for tea with half a hope that after tonight Gaston would return. She heard the crackle of the fire.

The water was quick to boil.

"Everything is all right," she whispered to him. Her hand stroked his back; the memory of her wrapped around him, fingers dug in, his back bare. Another photo into the fire. Sofia found them familiar. Nostalgic colors. Crisp edges. The flames tore into the corners first. Melted the faces. Tore at the people inside. They were not nothing. The fire ate it. Consumed it. Erased it. The scent of burnt paper filled the room and bled into the walls to tear at her home, building layers of absence where concrete once was.

Valentina. Gaston. Sofia. Pigtails. Trench coat. Smiles. Family. Burnt. Ashes. Sofia wanted to vomit smoke.

"Our daughter. Our family. Our memories?" Sofia said.

"The demons have taken everything."

"You have given it up," Sofia said, "watched it burn, photos, bridges, us. You have given it away." She wanted to burn his clothes, blister his skin, to stab his heart with the red-hot poker. "You are not a man."

Gaston's eyes set dark and deep. "You have nothing but a group of stupid women; nothing but nightmares where you wish your dreams could be."

For the second time in her life, for the second time in their marriage, for the seconds she allowed his words to burn, she slammed her hand across his face and felt the fire make a home in her fingers. She hated him for his words. She hated him for his stare. She hated him because some part of her knew he wasn't wrong. But he wasn't right either.

His rigid fingers wrapped around her neck and pulled her to him with blank eyes and heavy breath, with lips terse. His heart punched her through his chest, the whisky clung to his skin, the putrid smoke filled the room, and despite her desire to feel the sting of her fingers on his cheek once more, she closed her eyes and tried to find a remnant of them in the kiss he forced on her.

She counted the seconds and waited to feel him come back. His body creaked, his tongue sandpaper—and the seconds took forever to pass, his lips rigid, hands cold, and the fire dying.

She pushed him away.

"You need to leave," she said. He stared, his eyes lost. He was silent. "The man I loved is missing. You have pulled away from me and I don't know where you have gone."

She threw herself against him. Her arms pressed to his chest.

"You need to leave now." She wanted to pound her fists into his heart; maybe it would beat for her again. She wanted to rub her hand across the print she made and linger, feel the sting, remind him of her. He couldn't stay, because of who he was and because of who he wasn't, the man he had become that was so far from the man she wanted, the man she needed him to be, the man she needed to be tethered to, a life she could rebuild or move on from, or a life she could move on to, a life worth living, a life that he could no longer give her or help her toward because he couldn't survive himself—he wouldn't survive.

"You need to leave."

It came out of her in a breath, and she wanted it lost in the ether. Gaston grabbed her wrists gently. He guided her away from him. He held another photo in his hand and looked to the fire. Sofia wanted to grab it, wanted to seize him, to steal the photo from his trembling hands and swallow it, make it a part of her forever. He placed the photo in his pocket, turned from Sofia and the faded fire. He reached for his coat and hat and walked out the door.

The shadows of the furniture flickered on the wall. There was a chance the door would swing open, that the words weren't real, that at any moment she would watch herself hang her coat, set her bag down and try again. Or Gaston had forgotten his bag, his wallet, his lighter. The door would open and she would run to him and forgive him for his indecencies, his insecurities, his maladies. Except she wouldn't. She waited for herself as the shadows passed into darkness. She waited for Gaston as the fire turned to ash. She wished he had fought to stay.

She found a small photo of her and Valentina where the whiskey bottle had been. Sofia's smile—Valentina's smile, two smiles that had changed forever, and the photo more than a memory—her last memento.

Chapter 33

Peter thought it romantic when he opened the door to the roof and found the table set under lights that flickered like stars, but the stars weren't visible behind the dark clouds in the sky. The music was soft enough to hear the sounds of the city rise from the streets. Sofia had set the table. It was her idea when he mentioned that he wanted her to meet Carly, the two women in his life. The two people in his life not packed away in memories and stuffed under his bed. The two people in his life that didn't haunt him—these were the women in his life, and he wanted them to meet, needed them to meet; he needed them to like each other.

The garden surrounded the table, the vines and bushes and the roses, the table set in the heart of the garden, hidden in Sofia and Peter's private jungle. Carly took a deep breath next to him as she walked through the door—all stairs, no elevator. The night absorbed her, the night and the roof and the garden, and for once, or for now, he didn't mind the thought of one place.

"You ever feel like it's meant to remind you where you are?" Carly pointed to Coit Tower.

"No," he said. It was never the tower he looked for but the bridge, the Golden Gate, if he ever needed to be reminded, but not of where he was, but for how he could leave.

"I guess it's—"

The door opened loud.

"You must be Carly," Sofia said. She held a bowl of salad and tongs. The table had been set for three, each plate with a picture of a rooster in prominent profile.

Sofia set the bowl on the table, walked to Carly, kissed her on one cheek then the other. A warmer welcome than Peter had received when he first met Sofia. A warmer welcome than he had gotten when he met Carly.

"My name is Sofia. It is very nice to make your acquaintance."

"I've heard so much about you."

"You are a liar. I know Peter. I am sure he has said little of me."

"That's not—" Peter said.

"He praises you. At least your empanadas. He says you make the best."

"I hope he did not make you think that I would make empanadas tonight." It was hard to know what brought Peter closer to Sofia, the empanadas or the company. No reason it couldn't have been both. Each time they ate together he put his life in her hands. Not the life of his heartbeat and brainwaves. The life he found more important, the life that he hid in his watches, the life she said she saw behind his eyes, the space that Sofia and he shared knowledge of. Every time she made him dinner, the space became less cluttered, the weight of the watches lighter, all the memories that had chased him since childhood felt slower, and he felt ready to plant his feet close to Sofia and settle in a place called home. The food didn't hurt, though.

"I wouldn't have—" Peter tried again.

"That's what he told me. You make the best, and you would make them for us tonight."

"I didn't—" He didn't.

"He knows that I only make empanadas for certain occasions." He knew.

"That's what—"

"He made it sound like this would be one of those occasions." He may have.

"I cannot allow him to lie to such a pretty girl. Perhaps I can manage a few." Sofia turned to the door and closed it behind her.

"She seems taken by you," Peter said. Another day Sofia saved Peter from himself, another day more restful than the day before. Peter moved the hair from Carly's cheek, pushed it behind her ear. It was his favorite touch, to watch a girl's eyes brighten when his fingers reached her cheek, when his skin touched hers, to reach the strands of hair that dangled around her face like ribbons, to push those ribbons away and watch her cheeks flush, her eyes cast down because she wasn't sure where to look—at him, made her blush; in his eyes, made her weak; at his mouth, made her lust. Carly did all three; he watched her eyes, the blue eyes that looked like the sky, the forever blue that he remembered. He moved the hair from her cheek and saw it all—and her, like he hoped she would be—waiting to give in.

The door opened again. "I happen to have some," Sofia said.

Carly moved her head away.

"Lovely," she said.

"Perhaps Peter did not lie as much as I made you think."

"No one thought I lied."

"There was a second there I wasn't sure," Carly said. She dipped her head to the side and stuck her tongue out. Teased him. Invited him into a secret space they could share. It was a space he was ready to stay forever in, under the stars Sofia had hung, with the food Sofia had cooked, with the girl that somehow knew him through all the gray in the city. The girl he felt played the same game he played for so long that for a while, he hadn't been sure if he knew how to stop the game at all, until Carly came along. He realized maybe he didn't need to stop; he needed to learn how to play the game differently. And she could teach him. He could learn Finnish if she taught it to him, if he needed to know it to speak to her, to stay with her, because that's what he wanted to do, stay. With Sofia, with Carly, on this roof, in this moment—forever.

"Please, sit." Sofia motioned to the table.

The table was full of too much food. Sofia offered salad. Peter waved the salad away. He poured the wine.

"Peter told me you work at the Exploratorium, yes?" Sofia said. She motioned for more wine. Peter poured more. The glass almost full. "What is your favorite item there?"

"I think the bubble screen," Carly said.

Sofia took a sip of her wine.

"She just got off work," Peter said.

"It's a tub of soapy water with a guillotine contraption set in," Carly said. "When you release the cord, a squeegee drops. When you pull the cord, the squeegee rises and makes a screen, a window bubble. I love when it pops."

"You like to make children cry?"

Carly laughed. A bit of wine dripped down her chin. She wiped it away.

"I don't think that's—" Peter said.

"Not even; I work at the wrong museum if I do. The bubble stretches and pulls and widens. It's like watching someone unwrap a whole box of cellophane and stretch it over the sun, wrap it up like leftovers and save it for later. Haven't you ever wanted to save a sunny day for later? You know it will rain soon, or the fog will roll in; God knows the fog will roll in. The kids want the bubble to last for as long as it can. They have this look in their eye, like confidence—all of them have the same look. It's like they're certain the bubble is strong enough to last. I can imagine some of them want to wrap themselves up in it. I know I would." She let out an embarrassed giggle. "I'd try to take it to school for show and tell. In that moment, it becomes more than a bubble. It's something magical to them. Then it pops."

If Peter could have wrapped all the sunny days into one ball of cellophane, he'd still be able to fit that ball into his backpack—maybe. But he didn't need to test the theory because most of those sunny days were already wrapped up in his watches, boxed and stuffed under his bed. How many times had he wanted to stop a sunny day and swim in it, the sunshine or the sky, to touch the sun because somewhere, at some time in his life, the sun became the key, the artifact that could make the world spin backwards, make time spin backwards, until Peter could burst into the bathroom and stop the water from rising, or call out to his father and keep the car from crashing; until he could touch the sun, flip the switch and turn time around the other way. The watches would stop time instead. He had enough sunshine stopped in his watches to build his own sun, maybe, and let it shine on the roof right now, flip the switch, turn back time and bring Sofia and Carly with him.

Peter buttered a roll. He waited for Sofia and Carly to finish their salad. He wanted them to hurry.

"But the pop is your favorite part?" Sofia put a forkful of salad into her mouth. Peter heard the crunch of the lettuce.

"It's their faces," Carly said. "Their bubble bursts. Sometimes hundreds of tiny bubbles scatter and the kids chase after them and try to pop them one by one, or swoop their arms to gather as many as they can before popping them all. They want to save one gigantic bubble and pop the millions of tiny bubbles. But when that big bubble pops, there's sadness, a bit of uncertainty. Questions. But the questions fade—"

Peter reached for an empanada. He didn't want to wait any longer. Sofia said he would have to wait another year to eat one, and now that they were in front of him and he needed to take one...or five.

"How rude of you to not wait for us to finish," Sofia said.

"I—"

"What do they do next?"

"They make another bubble."

Sofia didn't smile. She didn't frown. Her lips faltered. Peter noticed it. She hid it with a sip of wine, took a small bite of her salad. The unshakable hope of children, the unquestionable lunacy of children, their willingness to try again and again in failure or in triumph because they believe the impossible possible, and they will prove it. That's why they make another bubble, Peter thought. A child is always full of hope; the world will work in their favor. That's why Sofia's lips faltered, because the world hadn't worked in her favor—or his.

"The empanadas," Sofia said. "Carne," she pointed, "y cebollas y queso." Drool flooded Peter's mouth and he tried to hide it with a hard gulp. He reached for the plate and offered Sofia and Carly empanadas before he slid two of each onto his plate.

"What's your favorite museum in the city?" Carly asked.

Sofia took another sip of wine.

Peter took a bite. He sucked in all the cold air he could to try and stifle the heat. Another taste bud burnt in his empanada craze. He grabbed Carly's hand and squeezed it. It was the first moment he hadn't hesitated to hold her in some way, the first moment his mind didn't turn over the possibilities of her touch, of his touch, of her reaction, if she pulled away, kicked the table, melted, swooned, or if he would have done the same. He thought only of what he wanted, and what he wanted was to be close to her, so close that next to her wasn't enough, the type of close that came with old age and the knowledge of how she brushed her teeth, up and down or side to side, of the twist motion she made with her wrists when she put her hair up or tied his tie—when he wore a tie. It was the type of close he would wait centuries to achieve, all frozen in time, between the seconds, between him and her. It was a close too far away from now, so instead, he grabbed her hand, he grabbed her hand, and he squeezed.

"I saw fire jugglers at the Palace of Fine Arts," Sofia said. "Muy lindo. The atrium was lit like a palace, Roman or Greek. The night was clear. Clear nights like that one are rare. There were three jugglers. Two had chains, with balls. The balls were on fire. They circled themselves and each other. The fire waved around their heads and their arms. You could feel the heat. The statues in the atrium looked down at them, at us. Like we were a part of the show, like they judged us.

"The man in the middle had a baton? A...stick, like a police stick. He waved around the fire-stick, twirled it in his fingers. I thought his hand would catch fire. He pulled the fire-stick around his back, against his chest. You could see the sweat drip from his face. I could not take my eyes off of the statues that watched the man—and me…and the crowd, like they waited for him to explode, or for us to explode. I thought they were ready to jump through the hoops of fire."

Sofia had jumped through so much fire in her life Peter was amazed she didn't have any scars. At least on the outside—but the scars on the outside are the easiest to get over.

Sofia took a bite of her empanada. She drank a sip of wine, stared into the glass, almost empty.

"What do you think of the empanadas?" Sofia said.

"The best I've ever had," Carly said.

"Have you eaten them often?"

"I didn't lie," Peter said. "The best."

"What happened to the fire-jugglers?" Carly said.

"The crowd lost interest after a few minutes. So did the statues. I could not take my eyes away. Some people cannot take their eyes away from fire. Some bore very easy." Sofia gripped her wine.

"Peter, will you please bring another bottle?"

"I brought two."

"A smart boy," Sofia said

"He's well trained," Carly said.

"I do not train. I teach," Sofia said. Peter accepted the space between Sofia and Carly as if they fought for control of him. He didn't care because he wanted them both, in his life and in each other's lives, with him in between or bringing them together, trained or taught, Carly and Sofia were his, and he was theirs. The lights flickered in the garden, with the wine and the food on the table disappearing as the fog sank deeper into the city.

Chapter 34

The rain fell fat and heavy. Carly walked in the street and made no effort to protect herself from the storm; Peter close behind her. The raindrops clung to his eyelids. He'd blink them away. They'd come back. He'd wipe them away. They came back—thicker. He caught up with Carly in the middle of the street. He felt his shoes sink under the water that rushed down the hill. Neon lights flashed in the storm like lightning, but the bars were empty. Carly and Peter stood alone in the street with the storm for company.

"It's very beautiful," she said. She watched the flash of neon. Peter imagined her counting the seconds until the next flash, waiting for the pound of thunder to see how far away the storm was. But they were in the thick of it. The rain started to feel like rocks. "The water is so calm," she said. Her voice was soft in the hard rain. Another flash from the sign.

There was a painting inside a tattoo parlor, a ship on the horizon, almost tipped over the edge of the earth, ready to fall into the unknown. But before Peter could find his mother or his bear in the art, the flash was gone and so was the painting.

The water was at Peter's ankles. Could he reach a point where he was so wet he wouldn't notice?

"There's always another storm," he said.

Carly's hair twisted. Water flew from her body. It ran down her face, her skin. It hung tight on her clothes. Peter wanted to shrink. Carly's eyes cold.

He had wanted to tell her the truth from the start, the morning she had been born from the fog and walked into the diner. The moment she sat down at the table, part of him wanted to let the truth fall out. I'm Peter—my mom and my teddy bear haunt me, but God, I want to know you. But that wasn't what he said. He never came close to those words, to the truth he wanted to tell Carly, the truth he felt she deserved because she existed, she wanted him, to be with him—or deal with him—she deserved to know because he wanted to spend the type of forever with her that meant eternity, not life, the type of forever that gods had, front row tickets to watch the sun explode in a future that people couldn't imagine; but Peter could, if Carly were next to him, or near him, knowing the life that troubled him because he didn't want to hold that weight alone anymore.

He missed the window for truth, the small moment he could have—he should have said, No. Sam is not at sea, not really, not ever, let me explain.

Carly, Peter, and Sofia had sat on the roof under the imitation starlight Sofia had made, dinner done, and the over-satisfied lethargy close. Sofia brought out the candles, said she wanted to include our new friend.

"What's the tradition?" Carly said.

"We light candles," Sofia said. "For the lost."

"No one said we aren't lost," Carly said. Her voice was soft and simple. A tight smile, the words warm without understanding. Peter wanted to hold them, or her—or both—until he was warm enough to burn away the fog.

"Of course it is for us," Sofia said. "It is good to remember."

Peter had wanted to forget so much so often, but Sofia was right, he knew, he thought about all the forgotten memories, the memories he tried to squeeze from the back of his mind, those of his father's face, the way his voice sounded, how his mother smiled before his father was gone. It was good to remember.

"Who are you remembering?" Carly said.

"Anyone who is worth remembering," Sofia said. "Those that we loved enough to have hurt us when they left. A daughter—" she took a sip of wine. "Or a mother, perhaps." She looked at Peter and took another sip. "Anyone."

Quiet. Maybe Carly hadn't noticed or did notice but thought the toast was about his mom's being at sea, far away in physicality, the pain in it, but still reinforced the lie. But there was a sudden stillness on the roof, not a peaceful frozen but a broken stillness, where the world rotated and leaves shook and fog settled, but Carly didn't move; she stared at Peter, through him, to the place revealing his thoughts like a slide show, and she saw the photographs of his mom in the bathtub sailing away.

Sofia lit the candles, a quiet flicker, the broken feel of the air remained, and Carly excused herself from the roof, from the fake stars and quiet candles, down to the street where the fog shifted to uncontrollable rain, to uncontrollable sadness. The lights burst on and off because the world knew, because Carly knew, and Peter hadn't told her.

"You're soaked; we're soaked; we could get something to drink." He wanted the drink for himself, to warm himself after her cold stare crept between his ribs and froze his lungs. He wanted to wade through the street, almost a river, and disappear from her. To run back to Sofia and ask her why? Was there a reason she had alluded to the secret he kept or that she kept because those were shared between them, for them, shoved deep inside the closet of their histories for so long they were hidden in dust and old clothes? But their secret lives had crawled out of their tiny, hidden space and almost crashed through the door. Peter was tired of pressing his body against the door to hold the secrets in. It wasn't Sofia's fault. He should have told Carly. He didn't move.

"You didn't have to tell me," she said. "I knew. I knew you hid something about your mom. I knew you weren't ready to tell me, but I thought you would. I hoped you would. You didn't have to say anything. But you did. You said something to Sofia, to Sofia, and not to me. Not even—the way you looked at me, I thought it meant—I thought it was…more. Not even—you didn't tell me."

Peter rocked in the water—up to his knees. "I wanted to." He wanted the words to fall from his mouth and drop into the water, float downriver with the trash, but they dropped to his feet. He tried to lift his legs but felt them stuck beneath the water, tied to the ground by the words he had said, too heavy to float away. He sunk deeper into the street.

"You said she was at sea. I knew she wasn't at sea, Peter." Her anger stuck to him. The water rushed past his body. It tugged. He was ready to let go and see where the water would take him, but he couldn't, and it wouldn't take him anywhere, not while each word tangled around his legs, weighed him down, caught him. "You could have told me. She's dead. She died. Did you think I would laugh? I would point at you, laugh, and call you an orphan? You couldn't trust me?"

He reached his hands through his hair. He pulled. He wanted to scream. She hated him now. She couldn't trust him now. If he opened his mouth wide enough, he could swallow enough water to drown quickly, save Carly and himself from the harm of his mistakes, mistakes he had made or would make in his life, his life pieced together by frozen memories and mistakes.

"You didn't have to talk about it. You could have said anything."

"Like what?" he said. "That I was young? That I found her in a tub of blood and water? Is that what you wanted me to say?"

Carly froze; the raindrops caught in mid-air, the river stuck at his chest. He wanted to press his hands to her and release, to freeze her into forever, like his mother did, which he knew he couldn't do—with the neon sign, he saw on her face, the difference between the tears and the raindrops fixed to her cheeks, the strands of hair stuck to her neck, the drops of water that refused to sink into her skin or her coat. The storm wrapped around them uncomfortable, and her eyes sharp where softness had been.

"I know she's not coming back. I didn't fool you. I didn't break you. I'm the one that deals with it."

"Do you?" The water began to fall again. "Or do you just pretend to?"

"It had been enough," he said.

"What had been enough? Pretending?" Peter wanted to nod. The water was at his neck. He didn't want Carly to sink in it, to be taken by it. "It's not real," Carly said.

He was almost underwater.

"It was real enough."

She grabbed his arm. The pressure of her fingers over his coat. He wanted to keep her hand there, to bring her closer to him and wrap her in his body, protect her from the rain and the flood and the tub always on the horizon. The neon light flashed.

How quickly we find excuses to run, Peter thought, *from ourselves and each other*. Carly thought it was easier or safer to spend time with herself rather than with the people she cared about. Then she would end up alone. Peter had done it. Sofia had done it. Carly was doing it—he was doing it—he had done it for so long he didn't know if he could stop. And now, as the rain fell and Carly's words seeped into his skin, he knew he wouldn't stop. He would break away before he could get hurt, like Carly did, like he had done, even though he knew it was too late. This time. The heavy pain had wrapped around his body the moment he met Carly, the anxiety of possible hurt squeezing tighter until it eventually suffocated him.

"You don't touch broken things." He tore his arm from her. He wanted to keep the imprint of her palm on him, but it would fade. Instead, he gave into her argument and pushed her away like she tried to push him. It was the trait that Peter understood defined his life, where one half of his heart had been shattered by loss while the other remained intact, even if slowly shriveling from neglect. He preferred the familiar pain of loss to the unbearable pain of heartbreak. And so he tore himself away, because it's easier to be alone.

"I don't want to be fixed. Broken is all I have left," he said. He rubbed his hand over his watches. The water rose again. His words constricted around his ankles and made it impossible to move. He wanted to say sorry, to wrap his arms around her and float away together. He wanted her to know him and his life, but when he finally moved, she was already floating away, like his mother had done.

"It's not the things you said. It's the excuses you made." She drifted farther from him. The neon sparked. The rain looked like sunflowers or stars falling to the earth to tell him it would be okay. He never heard the words; too soon, the world went back to black. The rush of the water rose above his head. He couldn't see Carly anymore. His eyes closed. Body under. His legs cold. The rain swallowed the street. She was gone. He thought he saw the tub—his mother, Claus—reach over the hill and ride the river down to him. Reach over the tub and pull him inside. But he would rather swim away. Rid himself of the tub and go after Carly. Claus was supposed to look out for him, but he had left in the boat with Peter's mother, and Peter chased away Carly, the remnants of her gone in the rain, and the tub always near, no matter how far he ran. He let the water run over him, run through him, and when his words disappeared, he floated away with the storm.

Chapter 35

Sam pointed into the distance. The sky was still blue.

Claus saw the boat, a shell of a van with no roof. Its sail blew hard, expanded, contracted, expanded. The boat came closer.

"Where is the wind?" Claus asked.

"There's no wind?"

The ship edged closer. Sam watched Claus. Claus watched the sails. In. Out. Like breath, deep and concentrated. If it was that easy to push the sails, Sam would have tried long ago, but wasn't sure she hadn't already tried.

The boat pushed closer. The bright pink base, the green butterflies painted on the side. The roof had been torn off and the sails hung high off the mast that was stuck in the center of the mutated van with its crushed front end that seemed familiar.

A howl broke the silence. Claus grabbed Sam's hand hard. Hard. His furry paw. His tense grip.

The boat pushed against the tub. A ramp slammed down onto the porcelain.

"You are dead," Claus said. A wolf, matted and dark gray fur dangled off his body, loose and long, bits of dried blood flaked from his chin and swirled in the air with the smell of rancid death—long death, death that had been buried underground long enough to decay, absorbed by the mud and forgotten, death. The cross of a sword pressed against the Wolf's chest.

"No more than you," the Wolf said. He touched the stub where his ear once was. His fangs were green. Spit fell from his snout in long strands puddling on the floor.

The Wolf stepped toward the tub. The cross of the sword deep in his chest, shining with a plastic handle.

"You know who I am," the Wolf said, staring into Sam's eyes; his eyes black, a color Sam hadn't seen in the endless sunlight.

"Don't come any closer," Claus said. He pulled down the sail and wrapped it around his fist, a shield made of sailcloth.

"I've been searching for you. I'm here to say hello, lungs and all." The Wolf took a deep breath; he took another step on the ramp towards the tub.

Sam stepped back from Claus, unsure where this wolf had come from, unsure where she could hide.

"Leave," she said.

"It's never that easy wherever you are," the Wolf said.

"And where are we?"

"Somewhere different."

The Wolf reached his claw into the tub. It was half the size of Claus, like jagged glass. Claus slammed it with his sailcloth shield. The Wolf screamed; he stepped back. Larger than Claus—so much larger than Claus. So fearless a bear. A guardian. She needed to be guarded.

"Was that necessary?" the Wolf said.

Claus raised his shield again, made himself ready.

"Is your visit necessary?"

"Absolutely," he said. His fangs showed. "Can't have a job unfinished." His chest inflated. All the air around the sea sucked deep into the Wolf's lungs. The sails fluttered. Water pulled from the ocean. Sam's hair almost pulled from her head, sucked into the Wolf's lungs with the air and the water. Claus almost lifted from the boat. The whole world Sam knew about to be inhaled. Water flew with her hair, ready to be drawn into his lungs. Claus's foot was trapped under a rope. Sam held to the mast.

"A breath will only push us away," Claus yelled.

"What?" Sam asked.

The Wolf breathed deeper.

"Everything will be okay," Claus said. He held up his shield.

"What?" Sam held tight to the mast, tried to press her chest against the metal, felt her feet almost lift in the wind.

Claus covered his eye. The Wolf held his breath. Sam closed her eyes tight—tighter, and braced for the blow. She heard a sigh. A thud. A scream.

She opened her eyes. The Wolf's jaws were wrapped around Claus's tattoo, around his heart: Try Me. The Wolf tore into Claus. His teeth clenched; the tear soft; his growl furious, grave, rasping.

The Wolf's eyes pressed against Sam's chest, cold poured down her spine, hitting every bone. The Wolf pressed his teeth deep into Claus; Claus screamed. The Wolf growled; Claus didn't bleed. His shield dropped. Limp and weak in the Wolf's mouth, less than a child, a child's toy, defenseless and small in clenched jaws. Sam searched the tub for a knife, a razor, any object that could stop a wolf, that could save a friend. She found a bar of soap and Claus's pajamas. She let go of the mast, grabbed the galaxy pajamas, wrapped the soap in them, and swung it around her head like a mace.

She slammed the mace into the Wolf's head. Clunk. He tore his teeth from Claus. She swung the mace again, watched as the Milky Way slammed again into the Wolf's head. Clunk. Claus was silent. The wolf turned his head. His eyes black. His teeth sharp.

"You won't feel a thing," the Wolf said.

"I'd rather feel everything," Sam said.

She swung the mace. The soap slammed into his jaw. Snap. It echoed in the sky. The Wolf fell to the floor. Claus was still. Sam dropped the mace. She picked up the Wolf. Lifted his body. Strained. Tightened. Yelled. She pushed it over the lip of the tub. The water splashed.

She felt the drops on her lip as she watched the Wolf sink deeper into the water. She could taste the salt. She could taste the cold. The Wolf dropped out of sight. She added him to the reason she didn't like deep water.

She turned to Claus, quiet and torn at the base of the tub. His heart tattoo swollen. She placed her hands under him and could feel his warm fur. She lay next to him and pressed her face into his—cotton and mothballs. He stared into the sky, and she followed his eye, to the blue, to the empty blue—to where the sun hung high, a bright lightbulb hung far beyond reach, for a long time, Claus had said, a long time Sam could now feel. The long time could end, somehow; the sky not the far away empty blue it had been for as long as Sam could remember, an outline of the lightbulb was close, in the sky, while the string hung low, low enough for Sam to pull, to turn off the sun and change the long time of day to a different time. She felt the coarse hairs of the string. She jerked down.

The sunlight stayed but a crack, an echo, pulsed through the emptiness that they lived in, felt in the sway of the boat and the pulse in the sky. Like when ice breaks on a lake; when it separates between legs, continents adrift, a body stuck between them. She focused on the sun. The large crack divided the center of the bulb. Another splinter of separation. To another. And another—until the sun shattered. Bits of glass dripped from the light and floated through the sky. Claus pushed his forehead to hers. The glass fell like snowflakes. She opened her mouth and let the glass melt on her tongue. The distant light faded to deeper blue, to darker blue, to night—a night she hadn't seen in a time she wasn't sure of but knew it had been long. But Claus, with his nose pressed into her neck, a nose she now knew was cold and wet, careful and caring, with not much time left.

"I always miss the snow," he said.

"Like candy."

"Yes, my favorite kind, it disappears on your tongue."

She grabbed Claus's paws and wrapped them around her neck.

"There is nothing to worry about."

She could feel him. His soft fur. Everything must be okay. His warm fur. She could feel him.

"I am fine." His breath slowed. His eye closed.

Sam dug her face into his cheek. The night deepened. The silence thickened. She wasn't sure if she sailed in the water or the sky; both were dark, and both were clear.

Then the mountains began to shape above her. They rose in the sky, stretched beyond her sight, beyond the horizon she had thought was the end of existence. Perhaps that was the world where something could be, and they could be something. The mountains stretched, and she thought she saw a face mold into the rocks. A face she recognized. A face she thought could save them, her and Claus, if they could reach high enough into the sky. And with a sudden jolt of warmth in the darkness, set beneath the mountains flooding over her like exploded paints, she remembered the promise she hadn't kept and the life that had eluded her for too long, when she sunk into a couch, overtaken by a deluge of alcohol with the faint sound of a tearful voice beyond the bedroom whispering, hopeful, longing, and young.

"I told him I would be there," she said to Claus. "I wanted to give him time. He was just a boy."

"He wanted to protect you," Claus said. "He wanted to be strong."

"Stronger than I ever was."

Claus closed his eyes and started to drift. Sam whispered more words into the felt of his torn heart, trying to speak it back together, the face in the mountains now clearer with a prominent, granite beard and beckoning smile.

Sam wrapped Claus's arms around her, his paws tight around her neck, his furry face against her chest. She wondered if Claus could feel her heart. If he counted her heartbeats with his and wondered why there was a difference.

Sam reached for the mast and climbed. The metal cold against her palms. She gripped them tight and felt her fingernails pinch into her skin. She climbed the mast. The boat rocked. The mountains stretched. The water rested. The second boat drifted into the distance. Sam concentrated on the mountains in the sky—on the face in the sky that smiled and encouraged her to climb. Her hands ached. She felt sweat drip down her neck, followed her spine and crept slower and lower. She was close to the peak. She could almost reach.

The crossbar. If she could only stand on the bar and jump, she and Claus would be saved. If only. She lifted her feet onto the bar. She held the mast for balance. If she could jump into the mountains, they would be saved. If only. She felt Claus nuzzle deeper into her chest. Her heart fast. His heart slow. She reached. If only.

Chapter 36

Sofia set dinner on the roof again. The music soft in the night sky.

"There is more space," she said.

Her apartment had felt too small. Every time Peter opened the door, he entered an apartment of decreased size; it still felt bigger than his. He was happy to be outside, out of the box, whether his apartment or Sofia's; at least on the roof, he could pretend to fly. He offered to help with dinner. Sofia said no, looked at his empty hands and sighed; for the first time in all their dinners together, Peter had forgotten the wine. He sat on the roof's ledge and looked into the street: empty.

Peter thought of the plane ticket on his desk. The ticket he had stuffed in the box since he moved to San Francisco with the thought of rest, his feet, his shoulders, his past, if he could have put it all to rest long ago. He had postponed the departure date so often he almost cancelled the ticket altogether—because of Carly, because of Sofia—because of how he looked at Carly and because of the promise he made to Sofia. The look couldn't get him to hold onto Carly because he couldn't bring himself to say the words he needed to say, even when he wanted to say them. The promise he made to Sofia became another broken promise in his life of shattered mistakes, in broken forevers, because everyone Peter knew made excuses to run away: the only thing he was taught to do. The departure date was soon. It whispered adventure. He would be in Nepal, away from failure and away from ghosts. He would feel cold, crisp, thin air, not the overstuffed air of San Francisco he wanted to suck into his body, imagining all the crap that lined his lungs, which would soon make him choke. He would soon stand at the gates of heaven and look over the world from a chair made of clouds and feel as the gods must have felt on Olympus. He could watch the world rotate beneath him where he stood in the sky, and from that high up, he could see a world without horizons, where he wouldn't have to run anymore.

A glass of wine waited for him on the table. The light glanced against the red hue, turning the crimson color ruby across the table.

"You must drink," Sofia said. "We are celebrating."

Peter didn't reach for the glass. Sofia turned from the table and handed him his drink instead. He took it from her. She clinked the lip of his wine glass with hers as a soft breeze blew, rustling the leaves of the herbs and vegetables around the garden. Sofia swayed her hips to a rhythm Peter couldn't hear, perhaps shaped by the way the leaves danced in the night air.

"Celebrating?" Peter said.

"I will be selling my empanadas," Sofia said. She swayed her hips to the ever-present music in her head and sipped her wine. "They will be a big success, I am sure."

"To success," Peter said in nearly a whisper. He took a small sip of the drink and placed the glass back on the table.

"Tonight, we have chicken," Sofia said. She had her back to him. She chopped vegetables, or strained pasta, or made salad. How could he just leave? All children leave. They could also return. When had he returned to anywhere? He had never had a reason. He had never had someone on the opposite end of a postcard. Now he did. He had someone he could write to. He had someone to return to. Simple, all he had to do was come back. It shouldn't be hard; it wasn't hard to say. It was hard to imagine. Not because he had never returned, but because his mom never came back—his dad never came back, or Claus. Because that was what Peter screamed at the tub, on the dock of the bathroom, alone, the tub sailing into the horizon while Claus waved, Sam silent, Peter's hand in the air and the watch held to his chest: Come back! It should be easy to come back, but it was just another thing he was never taught how to do.

Peter sat at the table. Sofia and Peter shared their lives—the lives they were living and the lives they had lived. She would rather see him go than be the reason he stayed, he believed.

"I said chicken," Sofia said.

"Great," Peter said.

"You do not look yourself."

It was hard to choose the right words when any word he chose could hurt.

"Everything is—"

"Do not say fine," Sofia said. "I have known your faces for too long." She stopped swaying her hips and took a sip of her wine. "This is not your 'everything is fine' face."

"Carly and I didn't work out." Wind blew through dinner, under the tarp and over the roof. The tarp twitched. The music hummed low.

Sofia came to the table and poured Peter a glass of water. Her apron was tied around her waist. She wrapped her arms around Peter's shoulders. She kissed his cheek.

"It is her mistake, cariño." The wind picked up. Leaves swayed and cracked.

He couldn't remember the last time someone told him the world would be okay. He felt like the world had crumbled. He wanted to fall apart, to turn to dust and mix with the rubble of the crumbled world, be blown away by the wind. Sofia walked away. Each footstep sounded like thunder. She was going to the other side of the table. Not gone. She wasn't leaving him. She wouldn't leave him. But he would leave her. After the promise he had made to stay, after he had watched Sofia break a bit more after she received the letter. It was his nature—was it his nature? To run, always, even after he found a place he could stay, a place he should stay, with someone he needed, someone who needed him. The world wasn't too broken to fix, and maybe part of his world had been glued back together now that Sofia was in it, but Carly wasn't a part of it anymore because of him, another life his mom had stolen from him, another tear in the world he tried to rebuild that ripped and tore the longer he stayed; running was easier. He didn't have to see it all fall apart.

"It's not okay!" Peter wanted to run into the storm and drown in the rain, but the wind had pushed away the storm, the ever-wind that Peter once thought he had gotten the better of, gotten rid of, when he killed the Wolf, but the wind never left, was never defeated. Peter was never the hero he thought he had been. Maybe the wind could have taught Peter a lesson; the wind always came back.

"I bought a ticket." Peter reached for the wine.

"You bought a ticket?" she asked. The rush of the wind made it hard to hear. Wind in his ears. Words in the wind.

Peter looked at the tablecloth. He couldn't look at Sofia. He would be another disappeared in her life. But he had made the choice to leave. Sofia leaned against the table.

"I already…had the ticket, really," he mumbled.

"Where are you going? " she asked.

"Nepal," he said. He was surprised the word didn't get stuck; he was physically repulsed by it all of a sudden, in his throat, sour from the sound of it, the taste of pennies in his mouth from a word, a place he had wanted to run to, that he still wanted to run to, but now the sound of Nepal, the idea of Nepal sickened him, and he half hoped she didn't hear, that Nepal had been taken with the wind, too.

"I am sure you will have a fantastic time. I think the Andes are just as nice. I never climbed the Andes, but I crossed them to get to Chile a number of times. They were—" Sofia dropped the knife. A hollow knock. "All you do is run."

He ran. He admitted it. Sofia, of all people, knew that, but she ran too. She knew people ran because she ran, because it's goddamn hard to sit in a pot full of pain and boil in it; every piece of broken heart added to the water brought the temperature up. All he could do was kick the pot over and run. She did, ran from

Gaston. Ran from Valentina. Why was he wrong to run again, and again, or again, to keep his feet pounding pavement long enough for the world to forget about him and the mom and the dad and the bear and the broken history he ran from. He ran to forget because maybe it was better to not remember, despite what Sofia said.

Peter stood from the table. "You have been running for twenty-five years." He tried to yell over the wind. "You left, got comfortable, and stayed."

"Ghosts do not stay where you leave them," she said. "They follow you whole. I left to not be reminded. Life hurts."

"No," he said. Another gust of wind. Leaves torn from their trees, swirled around the roof and blown over the side. It wasn't life that hurt. Death hurt, living was unbearable. To live with a heavy world packed tight on his shoulders, stuffed full with all the pain the dead and broken, memorable and unmemorable, and failures that living created dripped down like oil from the world on Peter's shoulders and soaked him in it, unable to ever get clean because all that slick oily shit was his—his life, his world—and he didn't want to struggle any longer like Sofia did every day. "You hid. You hid in your cramped apartment. You hid in this stupid fog. And you hid behind your stupid cookies and empanadas."

"Leave," she said. Her voice was soft. Almost unheard. "Eres un niño estúpido."

A child. If he could be a child, if he could reach into the sun, turn back the world and hold himself for a while—to be a child with the unbroken sense that there was a life ahead, but for a child far ahead was far away, so far away. Childhood was so beautiful, but he wasn't a child anymore, as much as he wished he could be because that was another life ago, another life taken by a bathtub sailing away, full of lives that should never have left. Sofia was not Sam. Sofia gave him a sense of life he could hold onto in the fog and the flood. She was the reason he had wanted to stay. He wanted life to be okay, but he fucked it all up, and it all fell apart because of him. The wind rushed over the bass and brass of the music.

"He dicho ve!" The force of her words carried by the wind almost pushed Peter off the roof, almost carried him away like he wanted, but couldn't carry him far enough.

The wind pushed harder. Hit branches. Twisted vines. Tore leaves. Picked up pots and moved them around the roof. The tarp flapped and caught the air, picked up, a hot air balloon taken away, off the roof and into the fog. The radio crashed to the ground. The music gone, the wind louder. The pots inched closer to the roof's edge. The heart formation twisted and transformed until the heart was gone. Where the heart once stood was stained dark and smeared from the moved pots, the pots now at the roof's edge. The pumpkins or radishes, mint and basil, toma-toes—the rose bush, almost bare from the force of the wind. Peter should have helped. He wanted to help. The wind, hard. Unforgiving. Lifted the plants and vegetables. The rose bush. Up. Out of their pots. Soil and all. Up. Off. Over. Away.

Peter rushed out. He didn't look at Sofia. He didn't look at the plants that were now gone, that had brought Sofia and him together, that had disappeared with them, like Valentina, like Sam—like him. The door slammed. The building shook. He fumbled for his keys. He opened his door. Walked through it. Leaned against it. He had pushed Sofia away. The wind had pushed her garden away; there was no reason.

He lifted his head and saw the ticket. It's closer than you think. He rested his head against his knees. Too many people had abandoned her. He was another one. Another in a group of broken promises.

The box lid littered With Love turned into a painting and bled onto the walls to form a mural, as if the colors had decorated the room all along. A small boat waded in calm water with the tops of palm trees leaning into the scene.

The storm is never over, is it? Peter said to the shadow of the painting. The hope that maybe Sam could hear him, bring her life back, or his life back, give him the protection he wanted and never had, the warm protection of his mom, the warm protection Sofia had given him that he was running away from. Sam would never give him his life back, he thought. Any hint of a bear he hoped to find peek-ing out of the boat had left.

The apartment blacked out. A quick sizzle that said the city was dark, and Peter with it. In the howl of the wind, he walked to the bathroom, turned on the faucet, and listened to the rush of the water as he drew himself a bath.

Chapter 37

The sweat dripped down Sofia's forehead. She waited for the festivities of Corso de Buenos Aires to start, for the horns to blow, the guitars to hum, the drums to bang, and the crowd to dance, in place, in the street, with one another—just dance. Valentina sat on Gaston's shoulders. She waved her little arms in the air and towered over the crowd of people that clapped and cheered, urged the parade to start and make its way down Avenida de Mayo. Valentina's fingers raised to the sky. Her tiny hands that couldn't wrap around an entire glass of milk or juice, tiny hands that tilted a drink down to her mouth because she couldn't lift it; her tiny hands now raised up to heaven, high above the hands of the crowd, ready to be touched and blessed by angels because of the angel she was, all her fingers pointed to the bright sun, to the blue sky, ready to touch God before the parade ended.

The rat-a-tat of drums began, the crowd swayed, arms up, bodies pressed together. The sun ruthless. The crowded heat worse. Humid. Wet. The Murga made its way down the street, a solid wave of purples, blues, and yellows rolled down the avenue and far to the edges of the city that Sofia could see, colors pushed deep into the spaces of the city that she knew, colors that pushed from the spaces that she didn't know. The drumbeat: rat-a-tat-tat, the Murguistas dressed like jesters, ready to entertain and dance for the royalty of the crowd. Sofia rubbed Gaston's back.

Bodies pushed against her. Gaston grabbed Valentina's hands, clapped them together to the rat-a-tat-tat of drums and the splash of cymbals. Sofia wanted to watch Valentina, her laugh, her stare, her focus. Sofia didn't care about the wave of colors and the drumbeat or the awe of the crowd. She wanted the awe of Valentina. The Murguistas danced; their colorful pants and hats mimicked the build-ings, built high and painted bright to the point of camouflage. They jumped, scrambled in circles, kicked their legs over people's heads. Sweat dripped from their bodies like fountains. Valentina giggled at their dance and their costumes and their music. She clapped without Gaston's hands, reached for the stilted giants that hovered over the crowd. Bodies, screams, hands everywhere, all over, wrapped in the air or warped the air, Sofia wasn't sure but wrapped around her, pressed against her. Hands on her arms. Sweat on her neck. Screams at her back, in her eyes, large mouths open and empty, tongues out, teeth sometimes missing, coffee breath and excitement sinking into her hair and her eyes. Sofia wished she could feel Valen-tina's body laugh, the tiny hiccups of uncontrollable joy, the type of warmth that brought easy sleep. She wanted to laugh at the costumes and the music and the dance but couldn't take her eyes off of her little darling, her sweet darling girl, her white rose, bright smile, green eyes that shined on the festival, eyes that made the heat less harsh.

The Murguistas had feathers in their hats, which waved out of sync with their high kicks, low kicks, jumps, and steps, feathers that stretched higher into the sky than Valentina's tiny fingers and almost tickled the bottom of heaven, the way Sofia ran her fingers down Valentina's feet as Valentina kicked and screamed and giggled and said again, again. The fringe of the Murguistas' colorful pants twisted and shimmied and whirled and devoured the Murguistas' movements again and again. Sofia wanted to dress in those pants and press a peacock feather into her hat and stand in front of Valentina to be the one to make her clap and laugh and smile, to always keep her baby girl smiling, a smile that would see no pain, no hurt, no heartbreak, no life broken down and beaten up by the world that didn't deserve a girl as sweet as her Valentina, a world not ready for a soul as darling as her baby girl. Sofia could steal a feather, a long green one, like Valentina's eyes, with bursts of purple like Valentina wanted in her eyes, Sofia could imagine, and use the top of the feather to tickle her darling girl, her tiny feet, to keep her smile awake—alive.

The smell of sweat and churros drifted through the crowd. Sofia's feet hurt, her heels hard on the concrete street. She wanted to eat a churro, drink a coffee, sit with Gaston and Valentina, rest her feet, escape the crowd of random hands and rancid screams for a second—for a lifetime. The dancers continued, moved down the street through the parted crowd, the music pulsed, beat: rat-a-tat-tat, the people clapped and cheered, and she couldn't leave the parade, not yet. Gaston had never missed a Carnival.

"Celebrate before you liberate," he said. One last chance to sin, to enjoy the sin, indulge in the sin before repenting, before Sofia needed to prove to God that she and her family were pure and good and righteous, or at least strived to be.

Gaston wanted to dance and drink and be merry before carne levare. But he never gave up meat. When Lent came, he would give up chocolate or wine or both, but never meat and never flesh. Forty days without her husband would be a punishment. Sofia never kept Lent. She always gave up a week in, but she didn't consider this a weakness. It was silly that she tried for even that long. She tried for Gaston. If God were all-knowing and all-forgiving, then He would know that she always felt bad about her sins and confessed to the priest often enough. It felt nice when she decided to give up chocolate or wine or some other habit, but when the temptation came, she always gave in. Gaston knew. He liked that she tried. That's what he told her, and would kiss her cheek and hold her close and she would think that God had a nasty sense of humor.

Sofia looked into the crowd. The Marguistas had pushed down the street. The mass wave continued to pulse in the heat. She couldn't find Gaston. She couldn't find Valentina. Her white rose's hands weren't reaching up to the sky, weren't pressed together to urge on the stilted, colorful dancers. Where had they gone? Why had they left her in the overheated mob where her sweat felt like it puddled the streets and would eventually extinguish the sun for good? It was hard to breathe. Her chest heaved—another bead of sweat fell. All of them down her leg, almost stuffed into her stockings like a swamp. Did they run from her, hidden by the crowd? Would she be left paralyzed and punished by her inability of willpower?

"How wonderful," Gaston said. She heard his voice but couldn't see him. A hand, a soft hand, pressed to her back. She turned. How had she missed them? Valentina wrapped around his shoulders. A wide smile draped across Gaston's face. They were here. They hadn't left. How quickly anxiety can press its hands to your mouth and smother you. But they were here. They hadn't left. The Marguistas danced. She took a breath. Lent was coming. God had a nasty sense of humor.

Perhaps when Valentina was a little older, old enough to question why she had to commit to Lent while her mother didn't. Hopefully, that question would never come. To freeze this moment and stay here, with Valentina in her colorful dress. Where Sofia could breathe again. This moment where her family lived and loved—complete, and she felt drunk like on her wedding night, but now with more than just Gaston, with Gaston and Valentina, the loves in her life, the lights in her life; Valentina, the little joy in a large world. Valentina, happiness—to live without her would be to live without life, an empty life, joyless, empty of all the reasons to live, the happiness built from hugs and smiles, laughter and kisses, from watching Valentina dream in the moonlight that peeked through her bedroom window while she dreamed of unicorns or candy, princesses and dragons, someday if not already. Someday, Valentina would have those dreams—larger dreams— that would absorb her whole and guide her life until all she ever wanted had been reached, and the cloud of dreams would disappear into the ether because, at some point, all her dreams became a reality, and it would be far better to stay awake and live in truth than sleep and see nothing. Sofia's life was a dream, a dream she never wanted to wake from. Someday when she was old and ready to let go of life, she could look back on her loves, Gaston and Valentina, and choose to wake, to let go of the dream she had lived and the love she had cherished. Valentina would be grown, in her own dream, with loves of her own life, with a baby girl with curls in her hair and a world in her laughter. Valentina would know then what Sofia knew now, that dreams could carry you, could take you anywhere, could make you laugh forever, anywhere and everywhere, like Valentina, now, on her father's shoulders, as she made the sun shine brighter but seem softer, and the rowdy crowd celebrated her with cheers and dancing, with rat-a-tat-tat drums and blended screams, cele-brating her sweet curls, her smile—much better to freeze this moment. Gaston's smile. His full mustache. His strong back. Better to freeze this moment before the nightmares could ever set in.

But the moment would never freeze. Could never freeze. She'd never survive Lent, no matter what she let go of.

The Murguistas passed them. The loud motor of papier-mâché floats rumbled, cars transformed into large faces and masks drifted past. People stood on the top of the motorized heads and waved, poked out from ears or eyes and screamed to the crowd. Gaston brought Valentina down from his shoulders, and Sofia grabbed her hand and held onto the soft, warm skin like a lifeline.

"I could use a drink," Gaston said.

"Yes," Valentina said. "Yes."

"You want something sweet?" Sofia laughed over Valentina.

"Yes," she said.

"She has a new favorite word," Gaston said. "Let's see if it stays that way."

"I could use something sweet, too," Sofia said.

They found a café. Gaston ordered maté and a sweet empanada stuffed with caramelized apples with cinnamon. Sofia ordered an alfajor for Valentina and a churro for herself. They shared a hot chocolate. When the desserts came to the table, Valentina stretched for her father's empanada, switching between her cookie and the flaky crust of her father's afternoon snack. Sofia decided then she would make empanadas for her daughter, hoping Valentina would react as eagerly for her family recipe as she did for the empanada in front of her. Sofia took a bite of her churro and savored the crunch, the sweet and spiced flavor from the cinnamon sugar, and watched as Gaston fed another bite of empanada to Valentina. She gig-gled in the fading sun. Gaston smiled at the way his daughter's curls bounced when she ate the food she enjoyed. Sofia held Gaston and Valentina in her eyes and let the colors of the parade and the remainder of the crowd pass them by.

Chapter 38

The rocks dug into Peter's shoes and prodded his skin as he stood in the undertow. The sky was empty except for the sun; it would be gone soon. He held onto the basket. The wicker burrowed into his palms, full of empty faces that smiled at nothing.

He was twelve when he first stole a picture frame. He walked into a department store and wandered by a wall covered with photos, a prominent display of faces he could have known once upon a time, all looking back at him with smiles, in a scene he could have been in, a place he could have known, in a life he could have had. He looked into each photo and searched for a familiar face, a face that taught Peter to catch a baseball or fly a kite. Faces that sat around a picnic blanket and ate grapes and cheese. Instead, he found tea parties with little girls attended by giraffes and elephants, but no one he knew, no faces he once loved, no bears welcomed to tea. He found coffee shops in strange places, empty of life but focused on the steam of a coffee cup with a tower in the background, a place he was supposed to know but didn't.

He pressed his face to the photos, as if distance was the problem, as if the background of the photo would show a new perspective of the narrative Peter could fit himself into or find himself in because the photo had been of him and his father or mother or both all along, and Peter had just looked at it wrong. He scoured the photos row by row, back and forth, in search of a memory he wasn't sure he had, filling his eyes with flowered frames, right angles, obtuse angles, children's writing, cartoon decorations, and wooden frames that, upon closer look, were plastic like all the others. That is where he found the first photo—a man in a white shirt with a smile to match—the trees blurred in the background. The man's arms lifted into the air, his son at his fingertips. Peter almost remembered the man—almost remembered the moment as his own. He grabbed hold of the frame and rubbed the fake wood, smooth and cold. He pressed the picture to his face. He wanted to smell the man, to hear his voice and know that it was his photo in the frame. Peter wanted this moment for himself. He slipped the frame under his shirt and felt the plastic against his skin. He walked out the door.

Peter felt the water soak into his skin and absorb his ankles as he sank deeper into the sand. The tiny cuts from the rocks on his soles burned from the seawater. The water was colder than he thought it would be. Waves crashed on rocks and sprayed the air. The sun dropped slow in the distance, burned the horizon. The sea surrounding him grew higher with every step he took. He thumbed through the photos and made them all face center.

It was supposed to be once, just once. He had returned to the store weeks later. He stood before the wall of photos, a family tree he thought he deserved and displayed for the world to see. He found photos of family pets and family vacations, first swims and first bike rides, fathers and daughters, mothers and sons, graduations, and spring breaks. It all depended on the type of frame that held them. He had hoped that the first time would be the only time, that the photo of the man that could have been his father, of the boy that could have been him, would satisfy him. It felt good for a moment. It felt real for a moment: a moment in time is like a paper airplane in a rainstorm, his mom once said. He didn't know what she meant at the time. He still wasn't sure, but he knew that the one photo wasn't enough. He placed another under his shirt: a mom and dad watched their son ride his bicycle, hands clapped, smiling faces. Peter didn't know how to ride a bike. Maybe this memory would remind him. He felt the happy moment against his stomach and hoped this time it would last. He walked out of the store.

Peter placed a note into the basket:

Dear Mom,

Are you lost?

With Love.

The water hugged his chest, making it harder to walk, and the water lifted him and he tasted the bitter salt and smelled the seaweed. He placed the basket in the water, photos to the sky, letter to the center, and let the undertow take the basket to the horizon.

He was almost fourteen when he stopped. He entered the store, always the same store, hood up, hands in his pockets—he stood out in his attempt to blend in—the same wall. Most often, the same photos. A family for a moment between the shelf and his shirt, but empty when it hit the air outside. He found another photo. A boy in a bathtub with goggles and a rubber duck, his mother on the lip with her pants rolled to her knees and a sponge in her hand while his dad watched from the doorframe and smiled. It was all in black and white, except for the duck— it was blue. Peter grabbed the frame, painted like fake wood. He pressed his nose to the photo and tried to smell the soap but smelled gloss and plastic. He looked around and waited until the crowd covered him. He slipped the photo into his usual space and made for the door. A man stopped him. He wore a nametag on his white button-down shirt. Peter didn't look at the name. The man's mustache covered his mouth. His eyes were too dark brown and looked like shitty water under his glasses.

He asked what Peter was doing. Just looking, Peter told him, and said he was just about to leave but wanted to look at the new frames that came in. The man said he'd seen Peter around, that he came in quite often and asked if it was always to look at the frames. Peter said he came in now and again, and he liked to look at the frames; he liked to see how they were filled. The man said that maybe Peter should stop coming around so often. Peter asked why he would do that. Lately, things have been going missing, the man said, and he'd hate to misjudge someone so interested in photography; people might get the wrong idea.

The man rubbed his hand through his thin hair. Peter wanted to ask why the man thought Peter was into photography but stopped himself; he realized what the man meant. I'd hate to be misjudged, Peter told the man, and perhaps I should come less often, just a bit less. He pressed his fists into his pockets. The man smiled; it looked fake and stupid under his mustache. Maybe a little more than a bit, he said. Maybe, Peter said. With his hood up and the photo stuck to his sweaty stomach, Peter walked out the door and felt the emptiness return with the air and realized no matter how many photos he found of people that could be him and his family, that could be the memories he couldn't remember, they were only plastic.

Peter's hands sank beneath the water as he waded his way back to the shore. His watch slowed, and he could almost hear the gears crust with salt. The sand was shattered glass beneath his feet, sticking to his skin. The basket moved towards the sun, and Peter hoped Columbus was wrong, that beyond that horizon sloshed a waterfall dropping into space, where the world ended, and the ocean fell fast and silent into the center of the sun, and the water would steam; the basket full of faces would turn to ash and dispense with the memories he never had but always wanted but couldn't convince himself of.

The sunlight flickered as it set in the distance. The picture frames glared when they reached the sun hung tight on the horizon like a clothesline, while a flock of seagulls struck silhouettes in the sky and broke the emptiness. The crash of the waves spoke softly, drowning the sound of the sunset—a whisper. Peter smelled the fresh sea and tasted the remnants of salt on his tongue and the crunch of the glass sand under his feet. He rocked the world still, clothes wet—watch broken. And he breathed the world back into motion; the seagulls flew, the waves fell, the photos drifted, the night came.

He woke up as his apartment in San Francisco shook. Just as he was ready to give in to the water in the tub and the waves of his memories, a soft knock from the door pulled him back. He drifted from the bathroom without thinking. The carpet was coarse on his bare feet. A breeze brushed over his wet skin. A photograph rested on the rug. It must have been pushed through the crack between the door and the floor. It looked faded. It showed Peter and Sofia in the center of a tree, his face buried in her shoulder with her cheek resting on his head. Her eyes were closed. Redwoods surrounded them. The room continued to shake. Peter shivered in the draft, but it wasn't from the cold. The darkness had crept in over the city, over his room, over the bath. But for once, Peter was unafraid of the dark.

Chapter 39

Sofia stood by the hostess stand. Candlelight lit the restaurant. The power had been out for too long, the city lit by candles and powered by kerosene or gas generators, but Sofia wouldn't miss tonight, even in darkness. She had even bought new shoes, which Gaston probably wouldn't see now that the lights were off. She wasn't sure what felt more awkward, the new heels or the new stockings. She hadn't needed nor wanted either before reading Gaston's letter.

The hostess led Sofia through the narrow trail of black and white tiles, squeezed underneath and between the mass of tables and chairs, people and cloth. The restaurant compacted like her apartment, an appropriate coffin to be buried in, she thought, a good time to be buried too, with the man who started her life in this direction, in a way, with one word—darling. Maybe it could all end with the same word, stop her heart and bury her in this restaurant, the last box she wanted to be in ever again.

The restaurant had a collection of trees that blocked the diners from the doors. The high ceilings reminded her of her old apartment in San Telmo, but that home had been built up and out, plenty of space in every direction; the restaurant had been built only up. She was early. She didn't want to be surprised by Gaston, how he looked, how he changed, or hadn't, in twenty-five years.

Sofia's hands shook. It's because I haven't eaten all day.

Sofia looked through a break in the trees. Dim light but enough to see through the leaves. See Gaston when he walked in. If he walked in. If. She hadn't thought of 'if.' The possibility he might not show up, might change his mind, not want to see her, can't see her, even after twenty-five years. Even after he wrote her. If. She never thought of 'if.' She assumed if she came, he would too. He would. He had to, because he sent the letter, because he wanted to, because she needed him to. She needed to be released from the nightmares that brought her to San Francisco, that pulled her away from a life she had loved and ran to a life that she hoped to disappear in, by choice or by demand, and Gaston would be the one to let her go, to let her let go, to let her rest or live in peace, she hoped, after all these years, after all the lost faces, after Valentina—after Peter.

The clutter of conversations mixed with a clatter of pots and pans. She saw a brown suit enter the restaurant, the man's face obstructed by leaves and candle-light. The hostess pointed to Sofia. Her stomach ached, the type of ache that started in her bones and moved outward and upward towards her mouth until swallowed or thrown up. She wanted to run. She had changed. She was older. She felt it in her skin and her bones. She felt it in her wrinkles. She felt it in her hair, in her feet, in her thoughts. She should stand up and leave. Her legs wouldn't move. The man in the suit moved closer. Sofia didn't recognize him. He was shorter. Bland. Paler. Walked stiffly. Sofia tried to find a memory of the man she knew, the man she loved once. The dark hair she had known or the scar she had loved. He looked away. He walked past. Towards the bathroom. Not Gaston.

What if he had changed enough to be unrecognizable to her? Gray hair or bald? Squat and rosy? Half deaf?

The waiter placed a chocolate soufflé on the table next to Sofia. She could almost taste the velvet. She wanted to dig her pinky into the whipped cream. A habit she never outgrew, never wanted to outgrow—a habit Gaston had loved, that she didn't want to change. What if he didn't recognize her, or couldn't believe how she had changed? Would he expect her hair to be full and brown? Her skin smooth, her smile bright? What if he walked into the restaurant, took one look at her, and walked out?

"Good evening, darling."

That voice. A bit rough—just as soft. His darling. The name she thought she'd be buried in, or at least could be, cloaked in it maybe, like a gown, the word she would hear one last time because she needed to, from him, one last time before she let go. He was here. The word was said. Darling. His darling. She was here, still, not gone, like she thought she'd be after the sound stabbed her, but it didn't stab her. It warmed her. An armful of books, a youthful glow, a try again tomorrow—all the dreams and thoughts that the word held draped around her with his voice. Darling. His darling—

"I have not been your darling for many years," Sofia said. Gaston's eyes glowed, a green she remembered as his—his and Valentina's.

"Sit. Please," she said. Her shawl dropped around her shoulders. The crowd of conversation drifted away. The scar around Gaston's eye had faded. His mustache was full and angular. His hair was longer, and parted, and silver. But he was the same.

"You were never one to wear black," she said. He loved brown and gray. He said it reminded him of horses or the wild. Colors that reminded him of a life he would have rather lived, she thought. Except for green or blue. Dark blue. It reminded me of you, he had said, and the night sky. But one makes me think of the other.

"I was never one for suits either," he said.

Sofia hoped she looked half as good as he did. She liked him in his black suit. She liked him in his black tie and his white shirt. After twenty-five years—she liked him. His voice. His face. Loved even, for all the memories that they shared, before they lost all their time together, the lingering sensation filled with nostalgia and possibilities—love. She knew it was love.

"A cane?" she asked.

"You look lovely, darling. That shawl. It was a birthday gift from me and...."

It was Sofia's twenty-seventh birthday. Gaston had placed the box on the table next to a purple cake. Valentina was seven, stood next to Sofia with big, bright eyes. Sofia reached for the gift with a wide smile.

"It's a shawl!" Valentina said.

"It was supposed to be a secret," Gaston said. He grabbed Valentina, wrapped her in his arms and laughed.

"...from us," he said. Sofia wasn't ready to say that name either—Valentina. Not out loud. Not to him. The last time she saw him: the ashes of the photo edges and burnt faces, Gaston's, Sofia's, Valentina's—Sofia wasn't ready to say that name to him.

"How is business?"

"Exports are in demand. We have to find ways around the government."

"They do get in the way," Sofia said. She fought the urge to spit. It was a reflex after all this time; she swallowed it down.

It had once been hard to see her daughter in Gaston's eyes. It was harder when she watched her daughter fade from his eyes and Sofia's thoughts of his eyes. She should go. This was a bad idea, and she couldn't remember why she came in the first place.

"There comes a time a cowboy must kick off his boots and hang up his hat."

"You went back to the ranch?" Sofia asked.

"You knew I would."

Sofia nodded. The waiter offered drinks. Sofia ordered the filet of sole. Gaston joked about the parilla but ordered the paella. Sofia smiled, ordered a glass of Malbec.

"You always hated an office," she said. "It made you—"

"Horrible," he said.

"Irritable."

"I could have tried harder."

"I never would have asked you to. But yes, you could have tried." Sofia took a sip of wine. She had not lost her love of Malbec.

"What happened to your leg?"

"Got bucked during a drive," he said, "outside of Cordoba. Snake came out. Horse went up. I went down. Lucky the cows didn't run. Broke my femur. Never healed proper. At least I have this friend." He patted his cane and its silver topper. The extension was a horse's head; its mane glistened in the glow of the restaurant.

Dinner arrived, and Sofia told him of life in San Francisco and the boy across the hall who ate with her, who she wasn't certain would be there for the next dinner or the dinner after. The boy who kept running, who couldn't stay in one place long enough to bury the ghosts that ran after him, the boy that hadn't learned. The boy she loved, whose eyes had stared at her from the refrigerator because she couldn't bear to lose another photo, whose face she would never see again, maybe, but she hoped she would, if she could let herself hope at all.

"I want to expand to North America," he said.

"Is that why you're here?" she asked.

"It's a reason," he said. He pulled out his wallet and took an old folded photograph into his fingertips. Wrinkles textured the faces when he opened it. *Just like the wrinkles on my face*, Sofia thought. It was the last photo Gaston had of the three of them, the one he never had a chance to burn. He stared at it for a moment and placed it on the table. Sofia remembered those smiles, more like dreaming than memories. "I...I want you to come home."

Sofia dropped her fork. Home? What home? The home that burnt down in her mind the moment he threw the photos into the fireplace? The home that carried the ghosts of her baby girl, her laughter and baby shoes, passion fruit smells and curls, of their failed marriage that carried Sofia's hate, Gaston's anger, her broken heart, beaten hopes, forgotten prayers that held who he used to be but wasn't anymore?

"It's been too long to ask me now."

"We are still married, Sofia."

"Not in my eyes," she whispered.

"In the eyes of God," he said. The table stuttered. Their neighbors stared. God didn't answer prayers, not her prayers, not their prayers. God couldn't even give them an answer to what happened to their child? He couldn't keep Sofia and Gaston together. Why should His eyes matter?"

"The God that broke your leg? Or the God that gave us our baby? Or the one that took her away?

"That was man," he whispered.

"And God allowed it."

Silence. Sofia remembered that silence. It had filled the last years of their marriage. It haunted her sometimes. A silence that suffocated.

"I would very much like to be with you again," he said. His voice ached. Sofia could feel it.

"Why now?"

Time doesn't heal everything.

"She broke her toy," Gaston said. "When she was four or five. You remember the train that she loved? The wheel fell off and rolled around her like a tumbleweed. She looked up at me with her eyes, her big green eyes—filled with tears, ready to break. I shushed her like you would shush her—my finger to my lips. I picked up the wheel—the train. I sat down with her between my legs. She watched me replace the wheel and screw it back together. I put it right in her hands, and she smiled. A knowing smile, like I could fix anything. Everything. And I knew I could. I believed I could. Until that day she never came home. That day that I watched a part of you break away from me, a part of you that would never come back. That day that somewhere deep down inside, in a place I never wanted to admit to myself or out loud—"

He reached to grab Sofia's hand but pulled back.

"I couldn't fix this," he said. "I knew I couldn't fix this.

"I look in the mirror and understand what you saw when you said goodbye. I want her back too." If he could ever understand what Sofia saw when she told him to leave. The anger in his eyes, in the space that used to remind her of Valentina, the unbearable slow disappearance of the last physical presence Valentina had in Sofia's life—in Gaston's eyes, a small glint of her daughter had remained, her baby love in the eyes of the love of her life—until the day the photos hit the fire and the whisky hit Gaston's brain. The last part of Valentina disappeared with the rest of her; Sofia couldn't live with him, with who he had become, without Valentina—not then. But Gaston saw it now, the spark that had disappeared. The trace of Valentina in him, what had held the best part of him, as if with the loss of that spark, the best of him died. He had found it now, maybe, or at least understood it had gone.

"She's not coming back," Sofia said.

No matter how hard she held her hands together, she knew he wouldn't leave. Life happened. It tore them apart, and he wanted to sew them back together. He was a good man. She was tired of loneliness. Back to Argentina. It couldn't be so different from before. Gaston seemed to be fine. Maybe she should go. Peter would leave for Nepal soon. She should go.

The soufflé came to the table. Sofia put her pinky in the whipped cream.

"I need to think about it," she said. Gaston slid the photo he had held onto towards Sofia. She brushed her fingers against the photo's edges but couldn't bring herself to touch their faces.

"It is yours," Gaston said. "We both have our memories." Gaston smiled. Sofia had missed that smile, handsome and boyish, even with age. His eyes bright, the brilliant green returned. The spark that had been lost now present in the candlelit restaurant. In his eyes. Gaston's eyes. Valentina. Valentina's eyes. Here. Together. The family—whole.

"Thank you, darling."

"Why are you thanking me?" she asked.

"Because you gave me hope," he said. "I missed you."

"I missed you too," she said. It was the first time she admitted it. She missed him, and now he was back. Valentina was back. The best of him returned to his eyes. But hope was too much to believe in. Perhaps she could believe in him.

Chapter 40

The gas lamps of San Telmo flickered in the night like fireflies, and Sofia felt as if the fireflies followed her and Gaston around like halos. The echo of her shoes clacked down the cobblestone streets and off the walls of the neighborhood as she walked. She and Gaston, arm in arm. The air cool. Street lights bright. Her and Gaston. Mrs. Gaston Morales. Gaston and Sofia Morales. The name still excited her. His touch excited her; even after months, her name still new and good enough to drink over and over again. She leaned her head on Gaston's shoulder, the warmth of his coat against her cheek. The sounds of the Buenos Aires night erupted around them. Laughter and music. He didn't need the ranch. He had Sofia. They would start a family; he would stay in the city that she knew he loved.

A night on the arm of Gaston, in her black dress he had picked out, the one that showed her legs and made men want and women jealous, more than when she was a girl and the other girls wanted to share her bicycle or her dolls, and looked with longing at Sofia in case she would share, which sometimes she did— if her mother made her, or her father suggested. Or in school, after Gaston had disappeared and the other boys started to notice the way she walked, her hip swish, her hair to her shoulders, brown and full, and the boys wanted her. And the girls wanted her, in a way, but all she wanted was Gaston. She had him. In her black dress that made people want her, he told her, like all the times before.

The autumn nights could get cold; she squeezed his arm. Laughter bounced down the street, lighter than air and faster than a breath. Gaston watched Sofia and smiled. She wanted to dance. He let go of her arm and grabbed her hand. He swayed with her to the sound of guitars from the cafes surrounding them. No one watched. She wanted them to—for the city to watch her dance, watch Gaston dance, close together, warm, light, loving—to make the city jealous that the people that walked by weren't Sofia and Gaston, to make the city happy that a couple like Sofia and Gaston could exist. He pulled her closer to him and stopped.

"I know where we can go," he whispered. The heat of his breath on her ear. He turned and ran down the street. Sofia followed, drunk on the night, drunk on Gaston. How he touched her. The shock of his fingers on her skin, his eyes—a deep space to lust in, drifting away from the world she knew to the world she wanted to be in—his world, his eyes. The sound of her heels fell behind her. She clasped her shawl.

"You'll love it," he said.

His coat moved with his body. He grabbed her hand, pulled her forward.

"I better."

They turned the corner and stopped at a small door. A curtain covered the window.

"You want to go in?" he asked.

"What are you getting us into?"

"Let's find out."

Gaston rang the bell. Sofia waited for the door to open or the curtain to be pulled away. She heard a click. Gaston entered.

"Where are we going?"

Gaston didn't respond. He turned to Sofia, put his hand out. They had never been here before, but he must have, so sure of the place. They could have continued to dance in the street where everyone would see them, where people would walk by and smile, whisper to one another about the happy couple: Aren't they lovely? Look at them! Why don't we ever do that? A crowd would form, applaud, cheer, drag instruments from nowhere and start a dance party in the street; instead, she took Gaston's hand and followed him up the stairs. At the top of the second floor was another door. Gaston knocked. Paused. Knocked and knocked. A miniature window swung open. Dark brown eyes stared long and deep. From Gaston to Sofia. Back to Gaston. The door opened, Gaston pulled Sofia in.

"Someplace fun," he said.

"We'll see about that," Sofia said. They entered a dark room. The thump of a beat. A drowned melody. Gaston put his hands on her shoulders, lifted her shawl. She wanted her cheek in his hand, to let it linger, the abyss of their bed on their wedding night, where Gaston held her face in his hands. Each line of his palm told her a story of what their life would be like, their life together—their future, how perfect it would be. Whenever he pressed his hand to her face, she wanted to stay there, stay folded and frozen together, stared at by passers-by full of envy for eternity because Sofia and Gaston's love was perfect, evident by her cheek in his hand. But she shrugged off her shawl. Gaston pulled off his hat and coat. He took Sofia's hand again and walked from the dark room. The beat grew louder, and the melody began to breathe, harsher and louder until it was alive and worth feeling.

The room was wide. Long. Dim. Bodies floated around the dance floor. Free of form and gravity. The bar was hidden in a corner, close to the door. People came to dance.

"I would love a drink," she said.

"Of course, darling."

She found a seat at a table off to the side of the room. He returned with a glass of Malbec. Sofia sipped her wine. Rich, dark.

"Did we come to sit?" Gaston said.

"I'm not sure what we came for," she said. She hadn't had a chance to check her hair since they had stopped. Powder her nose. Fix her stockings.

"We came to dance."

"You should have said something." Sofia squeezed his hand. Gaston stood. Sofia followed.

He looked into her eyes. She reached up and pulled at his tie, the tie that matched his eyes. His eyes that she floated in, her brown eyes bigger, her body smaller; she felt smaller next to him, held by him, and in his eyes: smaller, where the room surrounded her endlessly, but alone in his eyes, in his arms, floating in the room but tethered to the world because he held her. Sofia pulled Gaston closer. She could almost taste him—and she wanted to.

She led Gaston to the dance floor. They squeezed between the couples that filled the square. She forced herself and Gaston into the center. She wanted to feel enclosed. Limit their movements. Every motion deliberate. Push themselves closer together. Forever together. And the music started. Another reason to touch. Another reason to be held. By him. Sofia could feel the throb of the drum. The strum of the guitar. The pulse of the bass. Notes filled her. Touched her thighs. Mimicked her heart. Tapped her fingertips. Gaston's hands soft around her back as if they were molded for her body. His fingertips caressed her hip and ran up the side of her torso. She reached for the ceiling. His fingertips followed her arm, up, and up, and up. She coiled her arm around his like a snake and guided his hand to her face. The kiss she wanted. Her lips made of strawberries and wine. Gaston hungry—for her lips. For her. She wanted...to take him. Wrap around him. Melt together, a puddle on the dance floor made of sweat and heat and strawberry lips and the smell of grass. His fingers reached her cheek. But they didn't stay for long. He pulled her close. To be one. Closer. Eyes almost touching.

The embrace is more important than the steps, her mother had told her. This moment—forever: when the music started, she wrapped herself in him, inhaled the smell of fresh grass that always rose from his skin. Stay in his warm breath. Touch his lips with her fingers, dip the tips into his mouth. His fingers on her lips. Her tongue. His lips. Their feet lifted and kicked. She lunged back. Dipped her head. Her leg stretched. Gaston leaned over her. His hand rested on her back. Lifted her into him. Her leg wrapped around his waist. His hand on her thigh. Secure. Forceful. He dragged her back. The floor was theirs, created for them. Owned by them. The world theirs—all the world, created by God for man, but not every man; the whole world created and all the lives that had been lived before this moment in order for this moment to exist, for Sofia and Gaston to exist together, how the universe had evolved to make now possible, to make the guitar hum, the bass deep, the drum beat, the floor echo, her thighs wet, his body strong, from Eden to Buenos Aires, and all the lives in between—for Gaston and Sofia, all of history theirs. The music was theirs. The night theirs. Her movement. Her body. He held her so tight. So close. His hands, how they held her. How their bodies moved together. Embrace. Step. Embrace—The embrace. And the music pulsed through them. And they glided together. And they intertwined. And the music pulsed. And they glided together. And they intertwined. Pulsed. Glided. Intertwined. Pulsed. Glided. Intertwined. And the music stopped. The door pounded. The lights flashed.

"What is it?" Sofia said.

Gaston looked around. People grabbed their coats, left their drinks. The doors flew open and police swarmed in, blowing whistles, reaching for dancers. The musicians scattered first. Gaston grabbed Sofia's hand. His skin was soft but his grip was firm. His look flashed from elated to serious. The room became a blur. They rushed to the back door in the herd of panicked people. Sofia and Gaston never stopped embracing. Their feet echoed in the stone stairway, out into the tobacco-scented streets, until they entered into the notes of the cafes once more, with the whistles and screams of the milonga long behind them. The music never had to stop, Sofia believed. No one could stop them.

They glided together, intertwined, and pulsed down San Telmo, where Sofia could wrap herself around Gaston in the middle of nothing; where they could slide into each other to the sound of their heartbeats; where they could be alone together.

Chapter 41

The box weighed heavy on Peter's legs, about to collapse his bones. It had gotten heavier—no more added in, but harder to carry, harder to open, harder to rest on his legs and watch the rain in the sky turn to mist and hope that the mist would turn to starlight.

He didn't want to look over the box, to read the stamps he had read one million, three hundred and forty-three thousand, five hundred and sixty-three times. The stamps that read with love, the stamps pasted from love, sent to love, written for love when he had no love to speak of but had attempted to imitate the love he knew. He wanted to remember the love beyond the box—beyond the watches—of the times he could have remembered but no longer had the strength to. The box: received with love from ghosts that followed him, ghosts he no longer wanted.

Bury the box, he had thought before, the final piece of the fucked-up puzzle, where the water gets absorbed and sucked back into the sky so he can rid his mouth of the saltwater flavor and replace it with dirt. All he had to do was put the box in the ground; bury the memories, the smell of cigarettes and rum. Papier-mâché wrists. Bathtub sailboat. He wouldn't bury to forget, but to remember—with fondness instead of anger.

Bury the box of his memories in the park, where it could set roots in the soil and grow, like a tree, his tree, which would sprout small at first. Each year the tree would thicken and strengthen, red as a sunset, because it would block out the sky of the apartments that surrounded it and replace the fog with the dark red of the sun that never showed in this city, mature, taller than the sky where the birds have vertigo, too afraid to perch because the leaves, once sprouted, didn't change colors, they changed lives; memories of his life budded from the branches so when autumn came he could sit at the base of the tree and let his memories fall around him.

He wanted to round up the memory-leaves into a pile and dive into them. He could throw his memories around and watch them float back to the grass and shrivel into the earth. They would return in the spring, the thoughts of his father and his mother and his bear settled into one spot; he would never have enough time, no matter how many watches his mother bought him because he had never had enough time with her.

If he could open the door to the trunk of the tree and step through it, into it, to where his memories no longer were past but present, and he could live in those days before his mouth became salty and his thoughts cracked. The days when he could sit in the tub and hold his breath for ninety-three seconds until his lungs would give their lives for a breath of air, fresh or moldy, and Claus would congratulate Peter on a new record, and his mother would call him for dinner and forget the forks, see how much spaghetti they could eat with their hands before it fell all over the floor. To the place his father used to be at a time when Peter could remember his face and not the musty smell of him. Peter would close the tree trunk door behind him and allow himself to fall into the life he couldn't escape wanting.

Light mist dripped from the fog onto Peter and the plants as he sat in the park, the city lights dark from the storm and all the birds blown away by the wind. In a corner under the shadow of the church steeples sat a garden, new, planted in the shape of a heart where mint and basil sprouted from the earth, pumpkin or radish vines, maybe carrots sticking out of the soil, a tomato plant tall and sturdy; drops of water dripped onto the fruit—or vegetable—dripping from the tree where the soil had drowned. The box was heavy on his legs. The tomatoes red and familiar. Tough, like Sofia, the woman who grew them, able to be blown off a roof and settle elsewhere, anywhere, a new life, a new existence, as if they had been there their whole lives, plump, and ready to turn if not picked soon.

"Were you going to say goodbye?" Carly said.

He hadn't expected to hear from her, not since the rain had washed her away. Her voice was soft but fringed with aggravation. He told her he would be here, in a way, hoped she would show up, understand the message and come to the tree where he could add her to his hopes of right-nows and not-lost possibilities.

"I already did." He had climbed to the top of the hill where Carly's building sat lanky over the city. Her windows that looked out to the bay stood dark, filled with the yellow reflection of the streetlights. The city was quiet, the wind almost gone, but a sporadic breeze reminded the city of the storm that had been and wasn't ready to leave. Peter wanted to ring the bell, even if Carly wasn't inside, with the hope he could be sucked into Carly's apartment, back to when he wore her robe in front of the fire, safe from the rain and the water falling outside, the smell of brownies around him, with Carly's hand in his. Carly's self-portrait on the wall, the only self-portrait he wanted to remember. He reached into his pocket and pulled out Space-dust that glowed in the San Francisco darkness. He spread it over his fingers and palms, pressed his hands to the building near the intercom, a place Carly might never see but couldn't miss it—if she wanted to find it—an apology. A sign from Peter that said he would remember her future like he remembered the pasts that they might have had together. His handprint glowed on the building. The gears in his watch slowed. The lights of the building and the street exploded into brightness, the world still around him; he could see into the windows of Carly's apartment where he once was and where his hands floated through, as if Peter finally found a forever he could keep, or a goodbye he didn't want to forget.

"You should have called. You wouldn't have called?"

Peter couldn't get over how, if he put his hand in her hair, it would get lost in the night. She stopped with enough distance between them to watch their breaths fill the gap. The space between them where he once saw himself in his breath, watched himself run over and over and never get anywhere, he now saw only her, in front of him, a mirror image in their breaths, waiting for him to run to her.

"I would have sent a postcard."

"You lie."

She smiled. He wanted the world to stop, to keep that smile forever, the most light he'd seen since he moved to San Francisco, and it was pressed so neatly between her lips that it seemed effortless, but it was the hardest smile he had ever tried to see, to make, to recreate in his thoughts, a smile that even a watch couldn't capture.

"I hoped you would be here," Carly said. "That I'd get to see you one more time. I wanted to tell you…."

"I hoped you would find me here."

"I'm still pissed at you," she said. "I'm still so upset…."

"I know," Peter said.

"I wanted to—needed to say goodbye." She pushed her hair behind her ear. "I saw these handprints on my building. They glowed in the dark—" She couldn't hide her smile. "I heard parts of the city had blown away, umbrellas, chairs, gardens. It's hard to say—"

"I'm sorry," he said. "I wanted to tell you so many—"

"It was hard to watch you go."

"You can't do that. I didn't want to fix—"

"I know. I just wanted you—" he said.

"I know," she said. "Tell me you'll miss me."

"You know I will."

"No one has ever told me before."

She filled the gap between them where their breath had been. She sat beside him, wrapped her arm through his and placed her head on his shoulder. Deep breaths. Almost like a wolf. The smell of her sweet. Cherries. Cinnamon. A scent that could carry out to sea and guide a lost ship home. Guide a lost boy home. Breathe. Breathe her in. And his lungs filled with her.

"Tell me you'll miss me," she said.

He grabbed her hand, wrapped his fingers through hers. A touch he wanted more of, where good enough wasn't enough, not anymore. As if she gripped his hand tight enough to pull him out of the water that had chased him most of his life.

"I'm glad you came back."

"I didn't think you could make it without me."

"I will miss you," he said.

The mist slowed, Carly's breath stilled, the drip of the tree stalled. He dipped his shoulder from Carly's cheek and stood between the drops and tried to play with them, touch them, draw a happy face in the air with them. Her cheek was soft on his shoulder, but he wanted to see her face, to remember her face the way it was now at the moment she heard the words she wanted to hear and the words that he wanted to say. And she smiled. Soft. Bright. Like a sunflower. A sunflower he would never forget. Not now. Not anymore. Shining through the night. He rested her head on his shoulder again. Intertwined his fingers through hers. Took off his watch and placed it in the box. He felt her breath. Heard her sigh.

The box felt lighter.

He looked at the garden, removed from the roof but stronger than one place, than one moment, survived by replanting itself within the shadow of the church, beneath the hazy light of Coit Tower, just like Sofia. No matter how far Peter went, she was a memory he truly wanted to share.

"What's in the box?"

"A tree," he said.

In the center of the new heart grew the rose bush, with blossoms full and white. Peter dug his hands into the soil and lifted. He placed the box underneath the bush and buried it, ready for the roots to take hold and the roses to smell sweet.

Chapter 42

The sky looked more like a colander than the wet blanket that had covered the city since Sofia moved to San Francisco. She had a bag in her hand, in the dim hall, and was about to go to the market, her garden another untouchable memory, beneath the gray light of Coit Tower.

Gaston had agreed to dinner at the apartment. He promised to fix the leaky faucet Peter had never repaired. Gaston was happy for a home-cooked meal, happier for a home-cooked meal from Sofia, more ecstatic over Sofia's empanadas, which he hadn't tasted in far too long, which he was quick to tell Sofia how he had never found another empanada close to hers. All were too soft, or overcooked, or too dry, or too wet, or too messy, or not messy enough. She had looked into his eyes, his green eyes, his green eyes that she missed so much, his green eyes she had worried about seeing again, or never seeing again, and she said, "I know."

She made the dough the night before and let it set. She had made empanadas for so long she could feel when they were right and wrong, and today they would be perfect. She knew it. She felt it. Recipes were a part of her, they couldn't decay, and every time she sautéed the meat, set and packed the dough, allowed the apartment to fill with butter and sweetness, her mouth would water and the hairs on her arms would stand. At first, it was for Gaston. Then it was for Valentina. Then because of where they weren't and where she was—alone in a box. But then for Peter, who opened the cupboard she closed herself in, brought her out and let her breathe in more than her garden. She could almost see him drooling now, across the hall, ready to break down the door at the thought of empanadas, when the smell from the oven seeped through the apartment and knocked on his door and called him over.

Sofia wanted to promise him leftovers. She stopped and raised her hand. But there wouldn't be an answer. He was gone. The garden was gone. Part of Sofia felt stuffed back inside the box she had tried so hard to crawl out of with the garden's help. With Peter's help. But Gaston was here now, and she was more glad of it than she thought she'd be. The glow she had missed when Valentina disappeared, the glow Sofia felt die in herself but tried to bring back when she latched onto Valentina's ghost, or memory, whatever spirit she thought could bring back the spark in her life, in Gaston's life, in their life together, the flame that fell into the ocean, that came with the uncertainty and the vulnerability they both felt but refused to acknowledge until it was too late. He was here now. He offered to help replant the garden. To rebuild a small piece of the San Francisco life that blew away.

Sofia grabbed the bag and let the handles dig into her skin. Peter never said goodbye. Sofia didn't expect him to. That was a lie. She expected him to, even though he probably never said goodbye to anyone else. But she didn't believe she was anyone else. Maybe to Peter, she was another polished conversation, another half-truth to cover the lie. She couldn't believe that. Sofia gripped the bag tighter. Her skin pinched.

The draft grew strong as she left the building. Her body felt heavy today. So did the bag. But the thought of Gaston made the walk easier. Made the draft warmer.

A tree shivered. Sofia listened to the trickle of the leaves. The ranch used to smell like today, when the spring rain would dry, and the smell of the grass would almost lift Sofia off her feet and into the warm sun where she could watch Gaston try to break stallions or direct the gauchos to where the cattle would need herding.

She walked into the market.

It has been a long time, Sofia thought. Valentina would not be a child anymore. She would be grown with a child of her own who would also no longer be a child. Children grow. I wouldn't have been able to stop her; I wouldn't have wanted to.

Sofia bought vegetables and meat to stuff the dough with. It was strange to not walk through the cobwebs to get to the garden, to not have the garden at all. She couldn't wait until Gaston helped plant a new one, where she would watch the tomatoes ripen and force Gaston to eat a vegetable. She should buy carrots. She would make Gaston eat some. God knows he probably hadn't eaten a carrot since he...since she...in a long time. The bag was almost full, and the food was ready to be broken down and cooked up, devoured by her and Gaston. Some wine, some more wine, dim light and music, always music. The day was almost gone. She walked through the park.

My grandchild, where would she be now? Would she have made her way to America, to here? Would I have? Would Valentina have come with, married an American man with radical views that matched her own in a country where radical views were acceptable? For too long, Sofia wasn't sure if she was lost or not. But she knew where she was now, in San Francisco, where a gentle breeze blew small and caressed her face, and night took over.

"Not being lost doesn't mean you know where you are," Valentina, again on the back of the breeze.

"Or where you should be," Sofia said.

"It's okay to rest," Valentina said.

"Tired is tired," Sofia said.

"Rest."

The apartments and restaurants that surrounded Washington Square Park glowed with candlelight through the windows, and for a moment, or for now, Sofia felt like the city remembered Valentina in the darkness—in candlelight, maybe all over the world.

The smell of roses, the breeze almost brought Sofia to them, bag and all in the shadow of the steeples, in the quiet of the bells, the heart garden in the park. The roses at the center. They were different. Somehow. Not lost. Not broken. They looked bigger. No longer a bush of white roses, of petals and leaves, of soil and thorns. It looked like a tree. With a slim trunk. Where the stems of the roses were branches, and the petals, the leaves that blossomed from the bark and branched out full of flowers. A tree. A rose tree. With a hint of passion fruit caught in the breeze. With an outline of a door drawn into the base.

Sofia wanted to reach in and open the outline, see what the rose tree could hold, with no fear of the thorns that were no longer there. The breeze guided her closer to the tree, and she reached her hand through the leaves, through the petals, and let them brush against her skin—soft and sweet. She opened the door and found a postcard of San Francisco. Giant hills bordered by Victorian homes and trolley cars. She scanned the painting house by house, street by street, car by car. She scanned the colors and found an image hidden in the streetcar—a woman's face, her smile, and Sofia knew who this woman was, hidden in San Francisco, painted into Sofia's life by the woman's son. And over the stamp writ large: WITH LOVE.

Sofia turned the postcard over. No other words. No address, no return. She knew there would be a return, that Peter would return. Sofia went back to her apartment, ready to cook. She lit candles and put the postcard on the table with her locket. She looked at the smile on the card—the smile in the photograph next to it—Valentina, Sofia. Gaston would be here soon. Sofia put the vegetables on the counter and took a breath. The world remembered Valentina tonight through candlelight, maybe, for Sofia and for Gaston—tonight, and for the first time in a long time, Sofia felt comfort—ready to rest.

Chapter 43

Peter unzipped his tent, and the snow fell through the flaps and landed at his feet. No wind, not anymore, and Peter was happy with the crunch in his ears when he stepped into the snow, ducked his head and left the tent. He squinted at the ground that flashed too white. In the distance, the gray of the mountain broke the white sheet, towered into the sky, and topped itself with more snow, the only semblance of a cloud in a heaven that had been hidden by clouds yesterday. The sky had collected its nimbostratus like marbles and thrown them across the world, let them break and bleed the rain and the snow until the world soaked or drowned. But today, the mountaintop was the last of the clouds, placed at the top of the world with a clear view of the sun.

It was the first time Peter had seen the sun since he landed in Nepal. It was the first time Peter had seen the sun since his mother sailed away with his teddy bear and left him standing on the shore with a broken watch and a tendency to run. The sun was on him now, and he wanted to let the heat burn into his skin because whoever said that there was too much of a good thing never had a bad thing last too long.

The top of the world or the bottom of heaven, it didn't matter; Peter was happy to be here. He listened to the silence, wanted to see where it started, where it ended. He never thought about where sounds begin and end, but this must be the place. He closed his eyes and felt the air thin around him. It felt strange to breathe in the thinness, to breathe in the silence. The air was cold.

The snow wrapped around his ankles. He had forgotten how snow felt. The cold of it. The crisp of it. The strength of it. Peter bent over and picked up a handful of snow. It crunched as he packed it into a tight ball. His gloves kept his hands warm. His boots kept his feet dry. He had packed light: one pair of snow pants, three pairs of socks, five t-shirts, one sweater, one jacket, the hiking boots on his feet, the pack on his back, a Nalgene bottle, a poncho that covered his head and backpack, a water-resistant sleeping bag, the beanie on his head, no SWATCH watches strapped to his wrist, no tin box stuffed into his pack, but he had added the faded photo of him and Sofia at the redwoods. The photo didn't feel heavy at all.

Peter bit into the snowball he had made.

"There is snow in your tent," Raju said.

"There's snow everywhere," Peter said.

Raju handed Peter a thermos. Peter opened it, the smell of coffee tipped out, a bit bitter, a bit sweet, and the scent dripped over the thermos and onto the snow. Peter wanted to fall in and drink the mountaintop.

"You eat snow?" Raju said.

"It's clean."

Peter met Raju in Pokhara sometime after Peter landed. The marbles had been scattered across the sky, and the city was soaked, as was Peter. Raju agreed to take Peter as high as he wanted to go. Raju, "King of the world." We go high until the world stops. That was all Peter needed to hear.

"Coffee," Raju said. "It is…bad. Very bad." He scrunched his face and stuck his tongue out. Peter brought the bag with him.

"A taste of home," Peter said. He smiled at the taste of the words on his tongue.

"My home taste better," Raju said. Raju had brought Peter in from the cold rain in Pokhara and offered dudh chiya. The amount of sugar Raju mixed into the tea made Peter's teeth crack. Best tea. Nepali do it right. Black tea. Powdered milk. Three kilos of sugar? Peter decided they would drink coffee on the trek. His treat. A return of hospitality, and it was. Peter had brought the bag as a gift. Coffee wasn't common in Nepal. But after he drank the dudh chiya, the offer of coffee was more for him than an act of kindness; otherwise, he would drink that tea every day, almost four times a day. Raju didn't much care for coffee. He reminded Peter every time they sat down for a drink.

"We can make dudh chiya," Peter said, "if you'd like."

"Chaina!" Raju said. "I would not think of it."

Peter took another bite of snow. Water ran down his glove and into his sleeve. His skin swelled from the cold. He let it happen again.

"Today we go?" Raju pointed to the sun. "Where world ends. I never go before."

On top of the world instead of under it, Peter thought. He smiled. The snow in his hand was gone. He took another sip from the thermos and placed it back in the snow, took another handful of the powder and began to pack it into a ball.

"A perfect snowcone," said Peter. "Without the cone." Raju shrugged. "Think we can make it all that way?"

Raju shrugged again. He took a sip of his coffee and scrunched his face again. Peter wrapped his arms around his knees, stared into the sky. The clear sky. The sun. The clear sun. Almost touched it. Why settle for almost when he could touch it? When Raju could lead him to it? To reach up to the sun and hug it, thank it for coming back. Thank it for pushing the marbles away.

Peter reached for his thermos. Pulled it from the snow. Took a sip. He was ready for the world again, a world with or without rain, with or without wind, but a world where he knew the sun would be, at the top. At the bottom of heaven. Above the blanket of snow. Over the marble clouds. Peter wanted to remind the sun to come back more often, even if it couldn't take him back to childhood, because he didn't need to turn the world the opposite way anymore.

Peter put his hands on the snow, ready to lift himself from the ground and follow Raju into the sun. Peter pressed his hand into the snow and pushed. The snow caved. Over his hand. His elbows buckled. He fell into the snow. He could smell the coffee on it. The powder clung to him. He pulled his hands from the snow. Stood up. His hands printed into the snow as if he tried to paint the mountain and the snow into forever. But the snow would melt. Peter wasn't sure he needed to press his hands onto the world anymore. He listened to the crack of his clothes when he wiped the dust from his body. Reached for the thermos. Covered with snow. Peeked over the fallen dust. But it wasn't his thermos.

Peter took off his gloves. He reached deeper into the snow. The warmth of the familiar.

Out of the snow, wrapped in Peter's fingers like a gift—a bear. An eye-patch and galaxy pajamas. The fresh powder on his body. A face Peter hadn't seen in too long, a face that had haunted him, now covered in snow. The same. Except for a smile where a scowl used to be.

Peter brushed the snow from Claus.

"We go," Peter said. He pointed to the ground.

"You mean?" Raju pointed back to the sun.

Peter pressed his face to Claus. Thanks for coming back. They both smiled.

It was here at the bottom of heaven, where the sun was whole and the clouds burned away to give hope back to the hopeless, where the snow fell full and comfortable, where the wind was silent, even if only for the moment, it was here, Peter found his bear and Claus found his boy, and the world held its breath—

HISTRIA
BOOKS

Addison & Highsmith

Other fine works of fiction available from Addison & Highsmith Publishers:

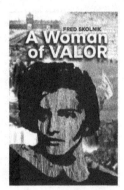

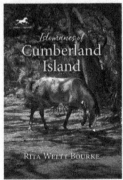
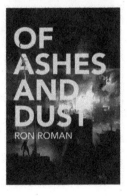

For these and many other great books visit
HistriaBooks.com